A fast-paced, action-packed romantic urban fantasy, **inspired by *The Fast and the Furious*, perfect for** **adult fans of *How to Train Your Dragon*.**

Markus Fredriksen, the First of His Name, more titles to come, always dreamed of breaking a Black Clubtail and becoming a dragon rider. He fails to break any dragon at all, marking the end of his tenure at Dragild Military Academy.

The commandant unexpectedly offers him a broken dragon, but with a caveat: Markus must infiltrate the clan running the Dragon Den, suspected of hijacking semi-trucks carrying precious obsidian.

He jumps at the opportunity to salvage his dreams. He has no idea what he's in for, but the clan leader's daughter is about to become his biggest distraction.

DRAGON DEN

KRISS DEAN

YGGDRASIL PRESS

First Edition

Cover art and design by K. D. Ritchie at Story Wrappers

Map and interior design by Kriss Dean

For those who wish
dragons were real.

AUTHOR'S NOTE

Some themes in this story may be triggering for some readers. If you feel content warnings are spoilers and you don't need them, please skip the next paragraph and jump right in.

This book touches on emotionally difficult topics, including but not limited to hedonistic and misogynistic behavior, toxic masculinity, power imbalance, captivity, forced servitude, animal blood sport, implicit and explicit racism, police brutality, guns and other weapons, bullying, sexual harassment, grief, depression, familial death, on-page death, on-page physical intimacy, drug use, gambling, and underage drinking.

Anyone who believes such content may upset them is encouraged to consider their well-being when choosing whether to continue reading.

Always put yourself first.

xo Kriss

MOUNT RAINIER DRAGONS

Black Clubtail

Blue Daggertooth

Brown Ridgeback

Frosted Whitetalon

Horned Ruby

North American Yellowdart

Orange Ironclaw

Spotted Greenback

Graytail

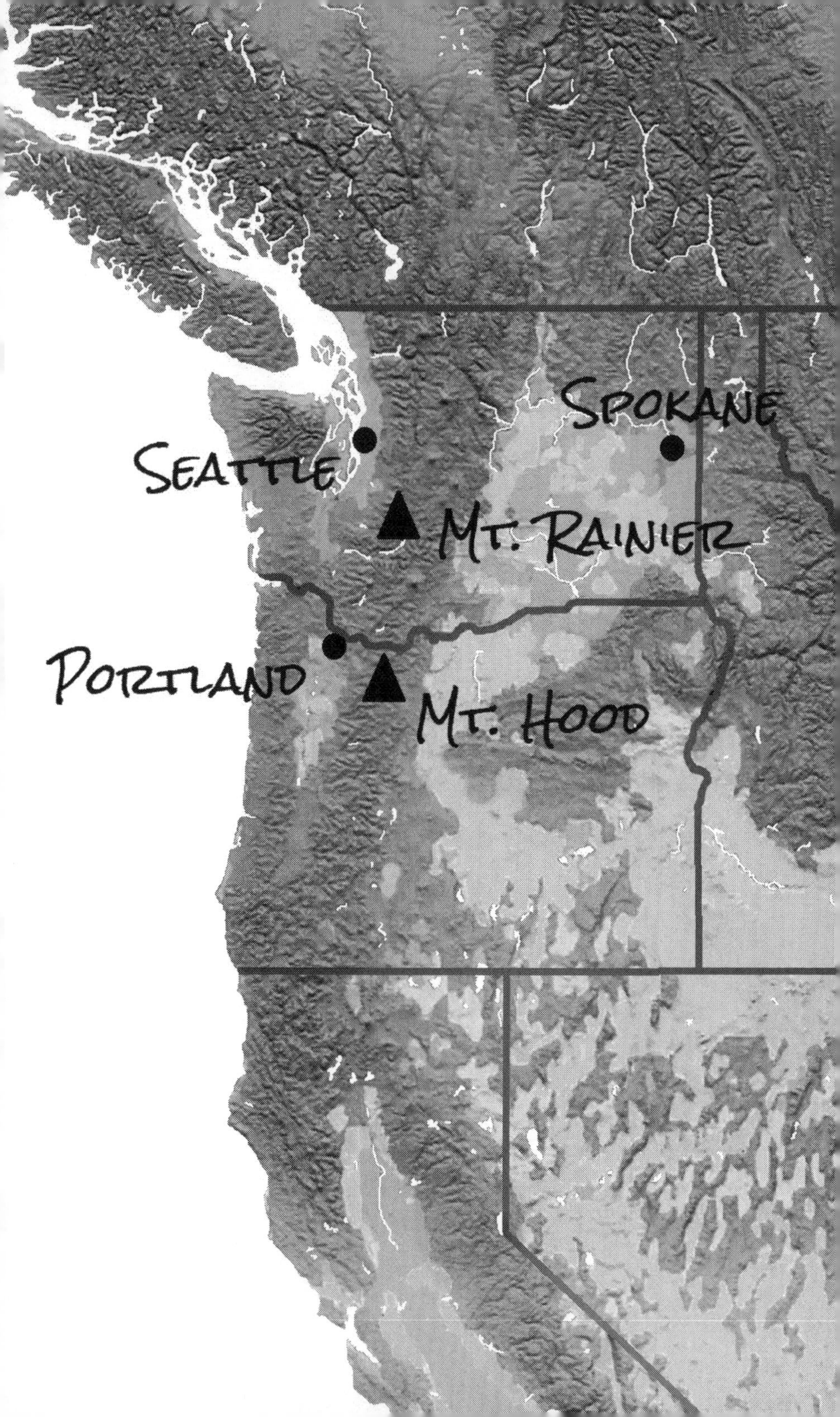
Spokane
Seattle
Mt. Rainier
Portland
Mt. Hood

1

A pillar of fire shattered the darkness.

The driver swerved the semi-truck around the blaze. Clutching the steering wheel with white-knuckled fists, he hightailed it down the central Oregon highway, his heart rate climbing faster than the speedometer. The obsidian cargo wouldn't burn, but his body would.

Gunshots rang out. The windshield shattered and glass rained down, impaling the hula bobblehead. Sulfurous odors overtook the cab. A fresh wall of flames sliced through the sky, and the truck barreled into the inferno.

The dragons clawing their way out of Mount Rainier scrutinize our helicopter's every move. Bright golden eyes, wingspans longer than a bus, sleek bodies built for speed, and flaming breath meant to incinerate. They're deadly, powerful, and about to be broken.

Today, I will become a dragon rider.

Nineteen years ago, my dad's bedtime stories built the foundation of my dreams. Parades and parties kindled my ambitions every time the Goldwings returned from war. Now, my first year at Dragild Military Academy is almost finished, and the fire behind my goals is all-consuming.

I, Markus Fredriksen, the First of His Name, more titles to come, will break a Black Clubtail.

"It's time," Commandant Eirikssen shouts. I can barely hear over the Chinook's tandem rotors. The chopper's too massive to land among the trees.

"Parachute," Amira mouths. She's jumping first, an honor reserved for the class's top student. I throw her a thumbs-up, just like I did at breakfast.

All twenty-three of us students file toward the exit. We're decked out in flight goggles and new black riding leathers that are insulated to keep us warm at high altitudes. It's still chilly up here, despite today being the summer solstice.

My stomach heaves as I jump into the clear orange sky and pretend I'm not falling. Wind rushes past and pulls on my cheeks as I force my eyes to stay open. I yank the parachute's rip cord with shaking hands to stop my freefall, and my body whips into a slow glide. I land safely, just like I practiced. It's a relief when my feet hit the ground.

Katie lands twenty feet away, pulls off her pack, and shoves the parachute into her bag. I do the same. We can repack them properly once we return to Dragild. For now, I just need to get it out of the way.

"I saw a few dragons in that direction." She points north.

"Looked like Greens." Not the dragons I'm looking for. I'm determined to break a Black.

She cuts through the bushes as I start east. A deafening roar shoots adrenaline through my heart, but I take a deep breath and keep walking. Premature death is a reality for dragon riders, and I can't worry about the other students right now.

A Spotted Greenback lifts itself above the tree line, tucks its front legs into its body, and sends the wind raging with its massive wings. The scales on its pale underbelly gleam as it lets out another roar, declaring war on anyone who attempts an approach. We got off easy, considering it could light the forest on fire. Not that a little heat would deter me, but Washington has enough forest fires without help from the dragons.

No more standing around. The summer solstice is the only day of the year when dragons come out to play. They'll climb back into the volcano at sundown, and no human or machine can pass through the magic of the nest while they sleep away the year in hibernation. If I don't return to Dragild by tonight on the back of a dragon, my dreams will burn to ashes. There are no second chances for a Goldwing if you fail your first mission.

I push through the bushes and trees and continue up the rocky side of the mountain, keeping a lookout for my quarry. The Black

Clubtail is a blue-flaming terror with navy-tipped black scales. Its spike-coated tail kills on impact. When it decides you're the target, there's almost no chance of survival. It's too fast to outrun or outfly. Only the fiercest riders attempt to break a Black.

A Horned Ruby launches into the air above the evergreens to my right. Its bright scales contrast sharply against the clear blue sky. Amira Obi, with her bright pink hair and her brilliant mind, clings to its neck. Of course she's one of the first, and of course she went for a Ruby. They're fiercely loyal, whip-smart, and second in power only to a Black.

The Ruby flies higher and higher as it lets out a roar. Amira deftly hangs on, just like we've all practiced. Her legs are wrapped tightly around the dragon's neck, and I can't help but wish her legs were wrapped around me instead. I climb to the top of the closest tree, keeping an eye on her.

She pulls off the dark obsidian collar strapped across her body. It matches the collar on her own neck. I admired them up close this morning; both the collars and her neck. Long and graceful, just like the rest of her. If Amira can get the collar onto the dragon, the Horned Ruby is hers.

Amira hangs on as the Ruby tries to shake her off. She masterfully maneuvers the collar, and just like that, she's done it. She's broken her dragon, and I'm smiling stupidly from the top of a tree.

The Ruby dives straight to the ground. Amira loses her grip while I helplessly hold onto the branches. For a second, she floats.

Then she falls toward the earth, accelerating quickly, as fast as the dragon at least ten feet away from her.

My heart pounds in my ears.

She's the best. How could she fail?

The Ruby suddenly shifts skyward, putting its body below Amira and breaking her fall. Its black collar sparkles as it evens out in the sky, and Amira scrambles on its back. She clings to it as they turn toward Dragild.

I'd be clinging, too.

The tension releases its hold on me, and I climb down from the treetops. No more distractions. You can't be a dragon rider without a dragon.

More dragons have hit the skies with riders by the time I reach the end of the forest. I've passed by an Orange Ironclaw and a Blue Daggertooth. I haven't spotted a Black yet, but I know they're out here. I just need to find one.

With only a couple of hours until sunset, I climb up the rocks.

A Graytail perches at the top of a cliff, basking in the warmth of the sun like the giant lizard it is. Its gray-spotted white body blends in with the stone. They're docile and usually take well to new riders, but they don't garner respect.

At least, not like a Black Clubtail.

The sun continues to sink toward the horizon while I climb up the rocks toward the mountain's peak. Heavy winds stop me in my tracks.

I duck behind a boulder as a Black lands a dragon-length away. This is it.

This is my dragon.

It chases a sheep and bats at the fluffy white snack, sending it into a bleating panic. The sheep must have escaped from one of the local farms. With one swipe, the dragon launches its meal a dozen feet into the air and snaps its mouth, downing the animal in one bite with its snakelike jaws. The lump rolls down its serpentine neck.

It sits and preens with its back to me. It needs a moment to digest. This is my shot.

My obsidian collar is ready. I'm ready.

I'm about to break my dragon.

Releasing a deep breath, I step forward, sliding as a rock gives out beneath me. The dragon's head whips my way. Its gaze catches me, turning my blood cold. It lets out a roar that shakes the earth.

I sprint toward the Black. Its wings flare open, at least sixty feet across. It glares my way and launches itself into the air. I leap to grab its long tail, and my leathers rip as the spikes scratch my side.

The dragon sends a burst of blue flames down to where I was standing a moment ago before it climbs into the orange sky with another roar. Sweat flows from every pore in my body as I cling to its tail like a sloth. It rises higher into the air, curls its tail forward, and swipes at me with its front claws. One of the talons catches on the obsidian collar strapped across my body. It yanks me off its tail and lurches down, my weight hanging from its fisted claw. I dangle over the mountain while the wind rages from its beating wings.

Don't look down, don't look down...

Shit. I looked.

I'm high. I'm so fucking high right now.

Pull it together, Markus.

I grab onto its claw and scramble up its front leg like I'm rope climbing, holding on tight while I barely resist being thrown hundreds of feet to the ground. I need to get to its neck.

The Black shoves its face right next to me as its golden eyes glare with hatred. I jump and grab the Black's long neck, just behind its jaw. Wrapping my legs to secure my body, I clutch it like a koala and thank the gods I never skipped my lunges. Sweat breaks out over my skin from its radiating warmth. With my legs clamped around its neck, I unclasp the obsidian.

The dragon roars, jerks backward, and tries to fling me into oblivion while I cling desperately. Oppressive heat wraps around me as the Black fills the sky with blue flames, setting it ablaze against the orange sunset.

I wrap the collar around its neck, fumbling with the clasp. I've just about got it. Just a snap, so close, almost there...

The dragon jerks and bucks me off.

The wind whips around me.

Why didn't I properly repack the parachute?

I close my eyes.

Sheer terror takes over.

I slam down with a thud.

My heart is still beating?

"Markus, that was ridiculous."

I open my eyes. Amira stares down at me. The wind blows her short pink twists around her face, showing off the black roots that grew in while she was busy training. My hands feel the rough, warm scales of her dragon beneath me.

"Maybe." Probably. Okay, *definitely*. She reminded me twice to properly repack the parachute. But I shouldn't have needed to. After almost a year of training at Dragild, I should have had that.

The sun sinks below the horizon. The Black is flying back to the top of the mountain, and we can't catch up on a Ruby. The obsidian collar is lost.

That's it. No second chances.

I sit up slowly, ignoring the pain in my side. "Why aren't you at the gala?"

Amira narrows her eyes at me. "You almost died. Why aren't you saying thank you?"

"You should be celebrating. I didn't need a babysitter."

Amira glares at me as the dragon chuffs. I guess the two of them have a point. I shouldn't even be alive right now.

I sigh, relieved not to be a flattened pancake. "Thanks for ensuring I didn't become a bloody sack of broken bones splattered on the rocks of the dragon nest."

"That's better." Amira turns around and grabs the pommel of her new saddle, and the tension in her shoulders drops. "You're welcome."

Her Ruby's wingspan is at least fifty feet, which means it's also fifty feet from nose to tail. Amira picked a good ride. Most dragons can only carry one rider, but this one can definitely carry two.

The wind picks up as we fly toward Dragild. I carefully move forward and settle in behind her, tucked between the Ruby's shoulder blades. With my arms securely wrapped around Amira's waist, I let my body sag against her and enjoy it while I can. She's all muscles; all strength; the best view in the gym every morning.

What now? Dad died last year, so it's not like I can get on a bus back to his apartment in Portland.

Fuck. He'd be so disappointed.

My body is as heavy as a dragon. I'm cold and numb, despite my leathers and the Ruby's warmth.

We ride back in silence.

The wide defensive walls of the school greet us, but I'm no longer welcome. Now that I failed my mission, Dragild isn't my home anymore.

The hundred-and-fifty-year-old stone fortress, partially carved into Eagle Peak, houses all the students and professors. The school's two Chinooks rest on top of it. A path leads from the door to the entrance of a cave that's been blasted into the mountain for the dragons. The cobblestone courtyard is empty, but every window is lit up. The gala will run all night. All the booze, sex, and fun a fresh new dragon rider could want...

Amira guides her Ruby down, and it perches softly at the entrance of the dragon cave. The dark gray stone walls are covered in stylized dragons that were carved back in the 1850s. The cave runs deep into the mountain, and bioluminescent orbs light the way with an eerie blue glow.

She unstraps herself and slides down the Ruby's leg, and I follow, landing hard on the ground. We walk into the depths of the cave, and the Ruby happily saunters behind us.

"What did you name it?" I ask.

"Her, not it." Amira pets her dragon's nose, and the Ruby nuzzles her shoulder in return. "I told her a few of my favorite animals, and she picked Tiger. She was miffed she can't go by the name of a god, but..." Amira shrugs.

Hints of red flow through the matching fire-obsidian collars, and a geometric square pattern she designed is carved into the surface. The thicker the collars, the stronger the bond, and yet Amira made her collars thin. They're stunning against Tiger's ruby scales and Amira's dark complexion.

We continue into the depths in silence, getting warmer and warmer the further we travel. The slope evens out as we enter the enormous cavern. It's made to house a hundred dragons, though forty to fifty is the average during the bulk of the year. Half a dozen hallways lead to stalls.

The cave is empty of humans. They're all at the gala, surely.

"Come on, Tiger. Let's find you a snack." Amira guides her dragon to a pen of sheared sheep. They scramble, bleating loudly. Tiger stretches her serpentine neck and snaps two of them up in quick succession.

"Amira, why aren't you at the gala?"

"Why does it matter?" She moves toward a hallway as Tiger and I follow.

"I saw you break Tiger. You were one of the first to—"

"*The* first. I was *the* first." She turns into the first stall and pushes the giant iron door open. Prime real estate.

The bioluminescent orbs cast a soft blue glow across the vast cavern. Tiger wanders into the stall and nudges Amira affectionately. Amira pulls the ruby-colored saddle off and sets it on the wall mount by the door. Tiger snuggles up in the corner, folds her wings, and curls her long tail around her body.

"But you went back out." I want to know. I *need* to know.

Because I would have gone back for you, too.

Tiger's golden eyes narrow at me before she closes them.

Amira locks Tiger in and stands in front of me, crossing her arms. "You should stop by the infirmary and get some bandages."

She isn't wrong. The spikes of the Black's tail really scratched up my side. It still stings, but the riding leathers saved me from worse. So did Amira.

I rest my hand on her elbow. "Okay. Thank you."

She doesn't pull away as she looks up at me, her amber eyes hiding a million thoughts. "Goodnight, Markus."

Considering there's no way the girl at the top of the class wants a dragonless screwup, I understand exactly why she walks away. I watch her go, probably for the last time. It's a shit situation, but I can still enjoy the view. Her riding leathers hug all the curves of her five-foot-nine frame, and they're... unquestionably great curves.

Taking Amira's advice, I drag myself in the opposite direction, down a long, dark hallway. I pass Professor Schloss's classroom. Empty, of course. When I reach the end of the hall, I push open the door to the infirmary.

A quarter of the cavern is meant for humans. The cots are empty, and one is missing the white sheets. White dragon-scaled armor rests on the bed rail. A movable X-ray machine designed for dragons takes over a corner. The white cabinets and counters are spotless.

A Graytail is curled up on the floor in the corner. Its gold eyes glare at our new dragonologist, Kristoffer, dressed in blue scrubs.

Commandant Eirikssen stands nearby, his arms crossed. The gun holstered on his waist serves as a warning. Navy-tipped black scales compose his dragon armor, making him fire-resistant and bulletproof. Tattoos climb his neck up to his shaved head. His sharp chin and strong jawline are also shaved clean. Considering hair is flammable, it's not uncommon to kill the risk. I considered shaving my shaggy hair, but no need now.

I don't see a rider, but they're a worthless rider if they're at the gala while their dragon is in the infirmary. Not a surprise, since they ride a Graytail.

Kristoffer sighs. "He still won't let me near him. His right wing is torn, and if we don't stitch it up, it won't heal. He'll be grounded."

Its rider is such an ass.

"And the rider?" the commandant asks.

The dragonologist shakes his head, and reality hits me like a semi-truck. The Graytail's white scales are tinted blue from the bioluminescent orbs, but scarlet blood coats its back. Their rider is dead.

Shit. I'm the ass.

I step back and hit a metal wheelie cart, knocking it over. The steel tools on top scatter to the floor with a clang.

"Markus." Commandant Eirikssen's piercing gaze churns my stomach. It's the same gaze I get every time he catches me doing something stupid. "What are you doing here?"

"I need a few bandages," I say.

The dragonologist studies my side. "Clubtail spikes?"

I nod, my mouth dry.

The commandant's eyebrows rise over his icy blue eyes, his gaze still locked on me. "You broke a Black?"

Straightening, I keep my expression stoic. "Not exactly. It... flew off."

The commandant crosses his arms. "So you failed."

My gaze lowers to the floor. I'm not going to break the silence. I know I don't belong at Dragild anymore, and it's time to pack my bags. What is there to say?

The Graytail snarls, curling further into the corner.

"The following is confidential." The commandant keeps his voice low. I nod, not that I trust myself. "A rogue dragon rider is attacking trucks and stealing obsidian."

I swallow, staying quiet. The collars forge the connection between dragon and rider, but obsidian also boosts a dragon's power. Exponentially.

"Last night's sting operation failed." His tone is sharp. "We have a hunch the thievery stems from the clans in the city."

"Why tell me?"

The Graytail snaps its jaws at Kristoffer every time the dragonologist moves, but it doesn't light him on fire.

"You're short a dragon, and I'm short an undercover operative." The commandant's tone betrays his frustration. "The clan leader's son is a third-year student here, and they'd never suspect you, considering your... reputation." His eyes narrow. "This is your only chance, Markus. Do you want to remain a Goldwing?"

"Yes." No hesitation. It's not a Black, but I'm not being discharged.

"Then take care of your dragon. If anyone asks where you've been, tell them your dragon was injured during its breaking. I expect you to be in my office at sunrise tomorrow for a debrief."

Commandant Eirikssen reminds Kristoffer to file reports and quickly leaves us behind. It's not like he'd stick around anyway, but they're surely missing him at the gala.

"We need to get this poor guy stitched up." Kristoffer walks toward the empty cot and picks up the dragon-scaled armor. It's the dead rider's. "Here, put this on. Let's see if his own scent will help calm him down."

I take a deep breath before slipping it on over my tattered shirt. It's too big for me, but I'll be the only first-year with a... I can't wear this. Everyone will know I didn't break my own dragon. Dragon-scaled armor takes a year to construct, and the scent of the dragon remains. A dragon won't allow a rider to mount if they're wearing another dragon's scent.

"This, too." Kristoffer picks up an obsidian collar. He hands it to me before turning toward the dragon. He shakes his head and sighs. "This poor guy has had a rough day."

I pull off the collar I forged, tossing it on the bed. Now that the other half is lost, they'll melt it down and turn the obsidian into knives.

As I snap the new collar around my neck, my body fills with overwhelming sadness and shame. I'm being shoved under an unbearable weight from the connection. Two bodies, one very heavy mind.

Kristoffer gestures for me to move forward. The Graytail doesn't move as its gold eyes scrutinize me.

After another deep breath, I slowly walk toward it. "It seems exhausted."

It lifts its head and blows a hot breath my way, stopping me in my tracks.

"He. I'm a he."

My eyes widen with shock as his voice fills my head. "Sorry."

The Graytail lays his head down and glares at me. I continue walking forward and slowly sit on the ground in front of him. His body is the width of the cot, so he's thinner than Amira's Ruby. He closes his eyes and stretches his wing. It's at least twenty feet long and ripped through halfway down. The membrane isn't bleeding anymore, but it can't be comfortable.

Kristoffer quickly crosses to the wing, pushing his blue hair away from his forehead. "Keep breathing slowly. It'll keep him calm. I'm going to put some stitches in the wing, and then we'll put on the skin glue. The membrane should repair itself within a couple of weeks, and his wing will be good as new."

As the dragonologist takes care of the wing, the Graytail and I simply exist.

"Do you know his name?"

"I'm not sure." Kristoffer continues stitching, his green eyes focused. "I didn't have time to check the records. His rider was... in pretty bad shape."

The Graytail opens his golden eyes, but they remain narrowed as he studies me.

"Loki."

His previous rider was a guy. Okay, then. At least we won't have to change his name. "Hi, Loki. I'm Markus." He blinks at me. Right, then. I shift my weight, rocking back. "Do you... um, did you see the hijacker?"

"They were too far away. We couldn't figure out who..." He closes his eyes, and we continue breathing in silence.

It's extremely warm in front of him, but I don't want to move. Kristoffer finishes the stitches and grabs a blue hose and a stepladder. He washes the blood from Loki's back, scrubbing carefully to avoid damaging his scales.

Once Loki is cleaned up, he tucks his wing against himself. I start to move, and his golden eyes pierce mine. I stop instantly as tension grips my entire body, now flooded with adrenaline. He shoots a puff of warm air my way and closes his eyes again.

"We should check your wounds as well." Kristoffer offers his hand and helps me stand. I take the armor and the scraps of my shirt off before sitting on a cot. The blood is partially clotted, but it still stings as he washes my side. "They don't look too bad. I suppose it adds credibility to the story."

"Do you know what happened?"

"Not really." Kristoffer glances at Loki. "His rider lost a lot of blood from bullet wounds. Died here in the infirmary. With the torn wing, they couldn't fly fast enough..."

I nod, not sure what to say. I watch Loki's chest rise and fall. His breathing is slow and even. He's definitely fast asleep. Maybe he's dreaming about sheep.

Relief washes over me, knowing I'll be sleeping in my own bed tonight. A Graytail is far from a Black, but I have a dragon. I'm still a Goldwing.

Kristoffer finishes wrapping bandages around me. "Head up to bed, Markus. We'll let your dragon sleep here, and you can move him into one of the stalls first thing tomorrow. It's been a long day for all of us."

The cavern is silent, aside from the snores of sleeping dragons. I ascend from the cave, stepping into the courtyard. The cool night sends a chill through me. The scraps of my shirt weren't salvageable, even for the walk back. They'd raise a lot more questions than walking shirtless around here, although I prefer showing off my muscles by wearing tight leathers.

The fortress is still lit up, and the gala has grown louder over the last few hours. I slip in through the side door. The smell of the feast hits me, and my stomach growls. The noise echoes through the stone halls. I take the back stairway up to the dorms. I just need to change, and then I'll head to the afterparty.

"Markus!" Katie calls out from behind me. "There you are." Her low-cut dress reminds me of exactly how much fun she is, but I'm not feeling it tonight. She wraps her arms around my neck. She's handsy even when she's not drinking, but now? This four-foot-eleven brunette is a bundle of... well, alcohol.

"How's your dragon?" she asks.

"We got a little beat up." I return her hug, hoping she'll let go after. She doesn't. "Did you get the Green?"

"Nope. A North American Yellowdart! And Bear is *perfect*," she sings. Perfect for her since Yellows are known for their high energy. "You've been gone all day. Come play."

I laugh as she strokes my chest. I keep her freezing hands away from my bandages. "How about when you're sober?"

She pouts as she leans in. "Come on, Markus."

"Lead the way." I'll get her safely to her room down the women's hallway. A shirt and food will come after.

With a strong grip, she pulls me along through the stone-walled hallways. She pushes open her door, and we slip inside. Katie kisses my neck as she flips on the light, knocking her hands against the bandages. The pain shoots down my side.

"Sure, gorgeous." I pull her toward the bed. Fuck this boner—not literally. "Can I trust you to stay here?"

"Are you staying too?" She crashes into her metal desk, and a lamp falls from it. The bulb shatters on the floor as she giggles. That will leave a bruise on her side. Oh, Katie. If only I was in the mood, and she wasn't quite so drunk. She won't remember this in the morning.

I pick her up and set her on her bed, grab a cup of water, and have her drink it with some painkillers. Once she's settled, I clean up the shattered glass. "Let me grab... something sweet, okay? Stay here." Not technically a lie. Maybe. There's probably still dessert left, and I'm not offering to bring it back.

She nods and I slip out of her room. As the door snicks behind me, I breathe a sigh of relief.

"Markus."

This night. I'm so over it. I should have used the secret passage. I turn to face Amira.

"Saying your goodbyes?" She crosses her arms, and her expression is as cold as the stone wall she leans against. She's obviously pissed. Her backless black dress caresses those exquisite curves and leaves little to the imagination. Black and brown tattoos snake down her arms, and some of them fade perfectly into her dark skin. I want to trace every inch of them.

Focus, Markus.

"Not exactly."

Her eyes narrow. "Moving into Katie's room?"

"I'm staying. I'm a dragon rider."

"What are you talking about?" She looks at my collar, and her eyes widen the moment she realizes it isn't the one I forged.

There's no one else in the hall, but I lean in closer. "Keep it to yourself, but a Graytail was short a rider. If I finish a mission for the commandant, the dragon is mine."

"Seriously?" she hisses. "You were—"

"Given another shot. I'm not throwing it away."

She glares at me. "Does Katie know?"

"There's nothing—"

"Uh-huh, sure." She rolls her eyes. "That's why you're sneaking out of her room shirtless."

"Amira, I—"

"Not interested. Keep it to yourself." She turns toward her door, and I can see every last vertebra of her spine. That dress, it's wrapped around her curves exactly the way I want to be. The way I've wanted to be every day for the last goddamn year.

I touch her arm, and she stops. "Amira." I pull her back and nudge her against the door of her dorm room, loosely caging her with my arms. She doesn't reach for the handle, even though she could easily open the door and slam it in my face.

She dedicated her entire year to training, putting in extra hours at the weight room and the obstacle courses, following the recommended protein macros perfectly every single day in the cafeteria, and studying theory and technique until she fell asleep on her textbook. But now she has her dragon, and maybe now she wants more. Maybe with me.

"I was just dropping Katie off in her room." I lean in close, enjoying the hint of vanilla from her lotion. "Feeling jealous?"

"No." Her breath hitches as her lips part.

"Are you sure?" I smirk, keeping my voice low. "I promise my attention is all yours."

She frowns and crosses her arms again. "With your blond hair and blue eyes, you get away with anything. Things are just handed to you. This just in, Markus: some of us have to fight every day to prove we belong here, and it's not easy."

Ouch. She's not wrong, considering I just got handed a dragon, sort of. But ouch.

"Back the fuck up!" Tobias yells.

Fuck. He came out of nowhere.

His black hair is cropped close, and his jaw is covered by a dark five-o'clock shadow. Tobias is *built*, with broad shoulders, bulging biceps, a solid eight-pack, and lean muscles earned over two years of riding. He's protected by ruby-colored armor from the scales of his Ruby dragon. No one messes with Tobias or his gang. At least they're all third-years, so they'll graduate in five weeks.

"Tobias, chill." Amira glares at him as she pushes my arms away. I step back as she stalks into her room, right next to Katie's. Unfortunately for me, Amira's heard... well, Katie definitely had a good time last month.

"Don't touch her." Tobias elbows my side, and pain shoots through me. His amber eyes burn into me. He follows Amira into her room, a bottle of champagne and two glasses in his hand. The door slams behind him.

My appetite's gone, and I'm too exhausted to care.

Back in my room, I toss what's left of my leathers into the laundry and slide under my covers. My feet hang off the end of the twin-sized bed. At least it's a good size for deterring sleepovers.

Gods, today was nonsense. I'm so bloody done.

But I'm a dragon rider.

I wake up well before sunrise and hurry down to the dragon cave. As I enter the infirmary, Loki raises his head. Kristoffer snores away on one of the cots.

"Good morning," I whisper. "Feeling better?"

Loki blows a puff of hot air at me and lays his head back down. He lost his rider yesterday and couldn't fly back to the nest after their bond broke. Now he's stuck with me, and I'm not exactly much of a consolation.

I let out a sigh and keep my voice low. "Well, Loki, do you want to move to one of the stalls?"

Loki turns toward the wall.

I guess not.

I quietly pull the dragon-scaled armor over my shirt. "Come on, bud. We can get you some sheep on the way."

He perks up at the word *sheep*, so clearly he's hungry. He seems to rise about twenty feet tall, all serpentine neck, his shoulder blades about two feet above my head. It makes sense since his broken wing stretched about twenty feet. Dragons are very proportional.

Kristoffer stirs. Loki and I watch him, but he doesn't wake.

"Come on," I whisper.

Loki follows me out the infirmary door. We head straight to the pen of sheep.

"All yours, bud." I gesture to the sheep. "Hungry?"

Loki observes them, but he doesn't move.

He lowers his head and stares at the ground.

I'm not sure what to do. I gaze up at Loki, but he doesn't meet my eyes. The rest of the dragons still seem to be asleep since the cavern is quiet.

"Do you want to go back to sleep?" I know I do.

Loki's entire body heaves, but he follows me as we walk down a hallway toward the empty stalls. I open a stall door, and he wanders in.

I follow behind. "May I see your wing?"

He lays down on the ground and keeps his wings curled tightly against his body.

"Please?" I'm begging, and it's pretty embarrassing. The whole thing, really. I failed to break a dragon, and I have no idea how to help Loki. Thank the gods everyone will be sleeping in after last night's gala.

Loki stretches out his wing, and I take in the glue and the stitches. Kristoffer did a good job repairing it. It all seems to be in good alignment, and it should heal relatively well.

"You'll be okay." I stroke his wing a few times, and he purrs contentedly. He can't help it; that's a dragon's sweet spot. "They'll bring breakfast around soon."

As he closes his golden eyes, I wonder where his last stall was. If he flew his rider here immediately, then Loki probably had another stall somewhere in the cave. I guess I should have checked with Kristoffer last night. Then again, it wouldn't look good to use it, since the neighbors might know...

Never mind.

I hustle out of the cave. The sun touches the horizon as I race across the courtyard to the main building. Two armed guards wave me on, and I enter Commandant Eirikssen's office panting. Maps of the regions cover the stone walls. Antique guns hang from hooks and rest on metal shelves. The black leather furniture with metal trim matches the rest of the fortress. It does a better job resisting the occasional dragon fire.

The commandant scrutinizes me from behind his desk. "Markus." His tone is detached, like always. His frown betrays his disappointment. At least I'm used to it.

I sit in the chair across from him. "Commandant Eirikssen."

"How's the dragon?"

"We got him patched up and washed off. He should be flying in a couple of weeks."

"He's a tough guy." The commandant clasps his hands together on the glass desktop. "His previous rider was so close to identifying the culprits. We aren't sure which clan is responsible, but both the Ejos and the Jonjungs would benefit from selling obsidian on the black market."

"You mentioned one of the clan leader's sons is a third-year?"

"Tobias Obi. Use him to infiltrate the inner circle of the Ejo clan."

Shit. Amira's older brother. This is just my luck.

2

Bioluminescent orbs light my way through the secret passage with a soft blue glow, offering a discreet route across the fortress to the hallway outside my room. Necessary, because I'm wearing dragon-scaled armor from a dragon I didn't break.

My stomach growls ferociously. That's what I get for skipping dinner last night. The rest of the students will be doing their daily workout or eating breakfast. I should be, too. Yet here I am, slinking back from Commandant Eirikssen's office.

He's lost his mind. There's no way Tobias will let me into his inner circle. Hell, he won't even let me into his atmosphere. His ruby-scaled armor is like a giant stop sign. The commandant's mission is a flaming dumpster fire that will end with me getting kicked out of Dragild, dragonless again.

As soon as I'm through my door, I strip off the armor and tuck it in my closet. I haven't earned it, but the scent seemed to comfort Loki. Maybe I could wear a loose shirt on top... I'll have to grab a few from the supply. We're allowed to wear anything, as long as it's black.

The smell of coffee hits me as I enter the food hall. Painted silver and gold dragons fly across the cathedral ceiling, complementing the steel tables and benches. Katie waves as she meanders by, clutching a cup of coffee like her life depends on it.

After grabbing bacon, eggs, hash browns, and an avocado from the line, I scan the room for my target. Tobias and his crew laugh around a table at the end of a row, and there are plenty of open seats around them. Aside from Amira, no one else is stupid enough to get close to those four.

This is a bad idea, but I don't have a better one.

I stomp down my nerves and sit a few spots from Carina, Tobias's girlfriend. Her bright red hair is pulled back in a ponytail, leaving her freckled cheeks on display. Black riding leathers hug her body, as does her green dragon-scaled armor, but there's no way I'm checking her out. I don't have a death wish.

Her hazel eyes glare at me.

Tobias and Jonas glare at me.

Shit. Like I didn't see that coming.

"Tobias." I hope they didn't hear my gulp. I nod in deference before taking a bite of my eggs.

His eyebrows rise as he studies me. He's still sporting yesterday's five-o'clock shadow against his dark skin, and there are bags under his eyes. Guess he was too tired to shave this morning.

"Let's go." He stands and offers his hand to Carina. Jonas and Theo follow them out of the food hall. As they walk off, I hear a whisper of the word *Graytail*.

How did they hear about my dragon already?

Forget it. My plan was shit anyway. It doesn't matter what I try. Tobias wants nothing to do with me, and he definitely wants me to stay away from Amira. He's the reason we've all stayed away from Amira.

Amira...

I polish off my plate quickly, curbing the growls. The other students are already on their way to class, and I'm going to be late for the first day of Dragon Physiology if I don't move.

The seat next to Amira is wide open when I enter the classroom. She's sitting in the front row, the only place she feels comfortable ever since a whiny first-year accused her of cheating. How anyone could cheat on a time-trial obstacle course with all five professors and the commandant watching is beyond me. None of us gave the story any credibility. Even the professors wrote it off, but the commandant was forced to follow up. We were all glad when the kid was kicked out a week later.

Diagrams of dragons cover the walls, and a huge dragon skeleton hangs from the ceiling. Steel tables and leather chairs face an ancient blackboard that probably hasn't been used in decades. Holo-projectors are way more efficient.

As I pull out the chair next to Amira, she nearly jumps out of her seat. I'm not sure if she's surprised by me being on time or me sitting in the front row.

Maybe both.

My palms sweat as I take my books out of my bag. "Thanks for catching me yesterday, Obi."

Her scowl softens. "Don't make a habit of it. I've got better things to do than save your sorry ass."

"I won't." I grin and lean toward her. "You were on fire last night, by the way. Your dress was lit. Not that the leathers aren't."

"You always say that."

"And you never ask me to stop." Got her there.

She studies her notebook, but she has the barest hint of a smile on her full lips. She adjusts her silk headband, the colorful African print complementing her bright pink hair. "How's your side?"

"Thank the gods for painkillers."

Professor Kropp struts into the room. His round glasses need to be sent back to twenty years ago, where they came from. "Congratulations, new dragon riders."

A cheer from the remaining eighteen students of our class echoes throughout the room. Five more dead of the twenty-five that started last year. Dragild trained us to ride, strengthened our bodies and minds, and gave us the tools we need to succeed, but dragons are wild. Even after we break them, there's always a risk of death.

"A special congratulations to Miss Obi, the first to return—and with a Ruby!" Professor Kropp smiles proudly at Amira as a few students titter around the room. Amira ignores them, but she's wearing her fake smile. It's the same one she wore when those racist prospective students were touring campus last week, heckling her while she was trying to study in the courtyard. I hope they all fail their entrance exams.

Professor Kropp starts up the holo-projector and begins our first classroom lecture. It's strange not being outside on the field after spending most of our first year doing heavy physical training and flight simulations. Making our collars, too. But we have dragons now, so it's lectures in the mornings and flight practice in the afternoons.

"What are you doing after class?" I whisper to Amira.

"Library," she whispers back.

"Want to study together?"

"Mr. Fredriksen," Professor Kropp says, his tone sharp. "Would you like to teach the lesson today?"

"No." My cheeks heat. I'm already on thin ice with the commandant. He doesn't need another reason to kick me out.

"Right, then." Professor Kropp turns back to the projector.

Amira suppresses a laugh as she faces the front.

"As I was saying before I was interrupted"—he glares at me for a moment—"when the collars are forged from the same slab of fire obsidian and then magnetized together, it's the *microcrystals* of *magnetite* that keep you connected." He shows a dragon brain on the holo-projector. "The collars cause a current to flow through the neurons in your and your dragon's brain. This alters brain activity and connects you, putting you both on the same brain wavelength. I'm assuming most of you woke up feeling a little different today."

Yes, actually. I hadn't thought about it, but I feel exhausted and emotionally drained. Also, a bit hungry for... sheep? Loki must be awake. A few others nod around the room. I run my hand across my collar, forged by someone else's hands. It's cool to the touch and lighter than the one I made.

Nerve paths light up as the holo-brain rotates. "These are the paths altered by the obsidian collars. The heavier the collar, the stronger the neural connection." I glance at Amira's thin collar. The design really does look perfect on her. "The magnetite of the fire obsidian also catalyzes the production of amino acids and increases blood oxygen levels, making the dragons more powerful."

"Study together after class?" I whisper to Amira as Professor Kropp drones on.

She doesn't look my way, but she nods once.

I'm calling this progress.

S tylized carvings of dragons cover the wooden doors of the library, reminiscent of the walls of the cave. I've never noticed them, probably since I've never actually been here before.

Amira adjusts her bag on her shoulders as I open the door for her. "After you."

"Thanks." She smiles softly, clutching her pink water bottle. Sixteen rows of giant metal bookshelves, each a dragon-length long, cross the center of the silent room. Huge floor-to-ceiling windows let in bright sunlight that bounces off the white walls, and a dozen round steel tables line the perimeter of the room. A couple of students are scattered around the tables. A grandmotherly librarian in a black dress waves to Amira from behind the circulation desk before eyeing me warily.

We wander to the back corner and find Theo at a table, his tablet in front of him. Makes sense since he's smart enough to skate by without cracking a book. "You're in luck today, Amira Obi," he says. "You want to know why?"

"Does it have anything to do with that giant Tupperware sitting in front of you?" She eyes it hungrily.

"It does." Theo pushes it toward her. "My mom sent you spanakopita."

"Yes! She's the best." Amira settles into the leather chair next to him. I sit next to her as she grabs the container. "I'll text her a thank-you tonight."

She cracks the lid, and a delicious pastry smell fills our corner. She happily tucks it into her bag with no offer to share.

"Meanwhile, I didn't get anything." Theo crosses his arms, but he's her closest friend here, so his pouting is definitely fake. "I swear, my mom likes you more than me."

Amira chuckles. "Don't be jealous, Theofylaktos. All we talk about is you. She's probably trying to butter me up so I keep reporting back on your above-ground status. Apparently, you're too busy to even text her."

"Well, you were the one off the radar yesterday. I swear she called me a dozen times to ask how your breaking went. I heard you were the first one back, but then I couldn't find you anywhere."

I swallow. Where is Amira's secret-keeping line when it comes to Theo?

"I was busy getting Tiger settled and fitted with her saddle, mastermind," Amira says sarcastically, glancing my way. "Then I wanted to take her out for a flight."

Her line is drawn firmly in a safe space. The tension in my shoulders drops.

"You sound like your brother." Theo grins, letting out a throaty laugh. "Jonas and I looked for you at the gala."

Wait, Jonas was looking for her? He can stay the fuck away.

She shrugs off Theo's comment.

"How'd breaking go for you, Markus?" he asks.

"Oh. Well, not great. We flew into a tree." That's probably believable. I glance at Amira, who's keeping a decent poker face. "Kristoffer stitched and glued Loki's wing, and then he bandaged my side, so kind of a long night."

"Damn!" His eyes widen. "His echolocation should have... well, Loki's a solid name. Which species?"

"A Graytail."

"Docile, adaptable, low key. Hopefully, he won't hit any more trees after he gets some flight practice in."

I shrug, playing it cool. "I'm sure it was a one-time thing." Since it never actually happened.

Amira grins as she opens her notebook. Five of its pages are covered with notes written in tiny script just from today.

Theo's phone alarm vibrates obnoxiously against the table, but he silences it quickly. "Class time." He starts packing his bag. "Schlossy told us we're grounded if we're late this week since we're setting an 'example' for the second-years."

Professor Schloss gets the third-years all day, every day, for evasive military flight in the morning and weapon training in the afternoon. He even trains his favorites after-hours in special skills.

"Heading to the Den later?" Amira asks.

"Yep, tonight and every night until graduation." Theo finishes packing his bag and zips it up. "July 31st can't get here soon enough." He's out the door moments later.

Alone at last.

The spine of my physiology book cracks as I open it for the first time. "So why weren't you at the gala last night?"

"I stopped by after we got back." Her tone is neutral.

Still evasive. "Did you actually just fly back out for a joy ride?"

"This again?"

She definitely doesn't want to answer.

"Yes, this again." I really want to know.

She sighs with her entire body and rests her elbows on the table. "I was worried about you when you still weren't back."

"Thank you." I lightly squeeze her hand. I knew she cared.

"Now can we finally get to studying?" She glares at me before turning back to her notebook.

"Sure, Obi."

She smiles to herself. Then she ignores me for the next hour, focused instead on her notes, occasionally referencing her textbook and responding to her group chat with her friends from all around the world, none of them local. Her phone vibrates like crazy after she sends them a photo of Tiger.

My stomach rumbles, but I already ate the protein bar from my backpack. I've probably turned five pages by now...

"I'm ready for lunch. Are you hungry?"

She checks her watch and closes her notebook. "I have to change for afternoon flight and get Tiger saddled."

"Do you want me to grab you something from the food hall? Loki probably won't be flying for another three weeks, so I don't need to be anywhere."

"Sure. Thank you." She zips her bag, now stuffed with books and spanakopita, and settles it on her back.

She heads for the dorm while I go straight for the buffet. I load up a to-go container with chicken and stir-fried veggies to eat out at the field, and I grab a handful of protein bars for Amira, shoving them in my backpack.

The cloudless blue sky leaves me with a clear view of Mount Rainier. Crossing the courtyard, I hike the winding path down Eagle Peak to the airfield, a grassy plain surrounded by evergreens. The path is rocky, awkward, and poorly maintained. Not a surprise, considering everyone usually flies down on their dragon.

I hit the base of the path, put down my bag, and settle on a patch of grass near the trees. The space would make an awesome soccer pitch.

Tiger lands nearby, her ruby scales glinting in the sunlight. Amira slides off her back and eyes the food in my hands. She sits next to me, slightly out of breath, while Tiger lies down in the grass. "Thanks for grabbing lunch."

I pull out the pile of protein bars and offer them to her. "I wasn't sure which flavors you liked, but I figured it would be fast and easy."

She looks at the pile and glances at the to-go container, biting her lip. Another dragon lands on the pitch.

I shove the bars back in my bag and hand her the chicken stir-fry. "Here, Obi. Eat up."

Amira eagerly takes the carton. "You're my favorite person today."

"Just today?"

Her eyes light up. "I don't hand out the honor to just anyone, you know. You have to earn it. Quit being greedy."

Says the woman eating my lunch.

I chuckle and unwrap a protein bar.

Katie lands nearby on her Yellow. "Hey, Markus."

Amira stiffens while Tiger shuffles a bit in the grass behind her. I shift closer to her, our knees touching, before greeting Katie with a wave.

Katie climbs down from Bear's back. "No lunch today? I didn't see you in the food hall."

"I was in the library."

She raises her eyebrows. "I didn't realize you knew where it was."

"He didn't," Amira says, giggling beside me.

"Calling me out, Obi?" I nudge her ribs playfully, and she smiles before continuing to eat.

Katie laughs and sits in the grass as a few more dragons land on the field. "Where's your dragon?"

"He's up in his stall. He got injured during breaking, so we're grounded. Ripped wing. Glue and stitches for him, and bandages for me."

Katie frowns. "Bandages?"

I guess she doesn't remember knocking into them last night. It's for the best.

Professor Hauk lands on the field. He gestures for everyone to mount up and gather around. "Students!" His voice is hoarse, probably from spending all morning with the second-years. Those lucky bastards are finally done with classroom theory.

Katie rises immediately and mounts Bear. Amira finishes the last bite of chicken. I take the empty container from her and tuck it into my bag.

"Thanks for lunch. Are you sticking around?" Amira asks, climbing onto Tiger's back.

"For a bit."

She waves as Tiger rises, and they join the lineup. Professor Hauk gives plenty of instructions on the basics before the entire class takes flight, a rainbow of dragons in the cloudless sky.

No Blacks this year. We've got two Rubies, three Oranges, four Yellows, a Green, a Blue, four Browns, and two Whites. And my Graytail makes eighteen.

Amira and Tiger are far better fliers than the other students bumbling through the air. They're definitely on the same wavelength. Amira's a natural, and her hard work from this year shows.

It's a bummer, just sitting in the grass while everyone else is flying. Screw it, I don't need to be here.

Back in the dragon cave, I enter my dragon's stall. "Hey, Loki."

He opens his golden eyes but otherwise remains still. From the looks of it, he hasn't moved since this morning.

"Did you eat breakfast?" I ask.

No response. No movement. Not even a blink.

"How are you feeling?"

A wave of sadness crashes over me, forced through our bond. He closes his eyes, staying silent.

"So... not great. Got it."

I wrangle him a fresh meal from the pen and bring it back to his stall. "You won't heal if you don't eat."

Loki watches it, but he doesn't move. I set my backpack on the floor and slide down the wall, leaning against it. Loki closes his eyes again. The heaviness in my chest goes away once his chest rises and falls evenly. He'll heal faster if he sleeps more, anyway.

The sheep bleats in the corner while I pull out my physiology textbook and check the table of contents. Unfortunately, there's no chapter on navigating dragon feelings. Poor planning on the publisher's part.

I close the book with a sigh and pull out my history textbook instead. The spine cracks, alerting the sheep, but Loki sleeps through it all.

His chest rises, and falls, and rises, and falls... His wings twitch, and his talons scratch the floor... His tail flails across the stall and he lets out a cry, rolling onto his side. I carefully rise to get a better look. His eyes are still closed, but he is most definitely not dreaming about sheep.

Should I wake him? Will I become a dragon snack if I do?

He needs sleep to heal. Maybe Kristoffer can give me something to stop the nightmares.

I throw my book into my bag and creep out of the stall, closing the door softly behind me and locking it with the key. It's a short walk down to the infirmary, but Kristoffer is unfortunately missing. I'll have to come back later.

The door to Professor Schloss's classroom is wide open as I walk past, back the way I came. Second- and third-years fill up the classroom. At the end of the shooting range, Tobias holds a military rifle, and Jonas stands by. Apparently, Professor Schloss thought target practice would be the perfect activity for the second-years' first day with their new schedules.

I lean against the doorframe and take in the dim stone cavern, keeping a low profile.

The brightly lit paper targets at the opposite end of the range have humans printed on them, and holes litter the white space around the silhouette of Tobias's. The bright red bullseye over the heart remains fully intact.

"Are you going to actually hit the target?" Jonas asks, putting his hands in his pockets. The blue-frosted tips of his blond hair are askew, so he probably needs a better hair gel. They're both wearing sonic defenders to protect their ears from the sound of the gunshots. "Maybe if you aim for the background, you'll finally hit the black."

"Fuck off," Tobias says, shooting the gun. Another hole appears in the white space.

Jonas laughs, the tone low. "Come on, T, after a year? It's not even moving. I could hit that with my eyes closed."

"Then go for it, big shot." Tobias hands him the gun.

Jonas fires off five rounds in quick succession, his eyes closed and his smile smug. I look for the holes in the—

Shit. There's one hole in the center of the bullseye. My mouth goes bone dry. Is that level of precision normal? That can't be human.

Tobias takes the gun back. "Show-off."

"May I help you?" Carina asks from behind me.

Bloody hell, I totally didn't jump out of my skin just now. Hopefully, she didn't hear that squeak. "Nope."

Carina's perfectly shaped eyebrows rise, showing off her fancy eye makeup. "Okay then." She enters the classroom and closes the door behind her.

I'm staying far away from the gang after that show.

Amira's definitely the safer option for infiltrating the Den.

A nd thus, the dragons rose from the volcano's lava." Professor Fortid's long white beard contrasts sharply with his black riding leathers. "Don't forget your papers on the origin of dragons are due next week."

The entire class rises. We're all ready to get out of here after another dry history class.

I turn to Amira like I have every day over the last two weeks. "Heading to the library?"

Her eyebrows rise. "Obviously."

"Me too." I shove my books into my bag and sling it over my

shoulder. I've spent more time in the library over the last couple of weeks than I have in my entire nineteen years of life, and my grades currently reflect it.

"Actually, I want to check on Tiger." Her dazzling amber eyes light up, full of playful mischief. "I'll see you—"

"You know, Loki could use a visit, too." I already checked on him twice today, but she doesn't need to know that.

Amira bites back a laugh. She's too smart not to realize exactly what's going on. "After you, then."

Crossing the courtyard, Amira tells me all about a new genetic study done on Black Clubtails and Frosted Whitetalons. The details are over my head, but I love her enthusiasm.

We enter the cave, and she purses her lips. "How's Loki doing? Are you joining for afternoon flight?"

"No, but we'll definitely be ready to capture the flag next week."

She smirks. "You better hope you're on my team, then. Tiger and I intend to win."

"Your team is going down if I'm not on it, Obi."

"Not a chance, Fredriksen." Amira laughs. It's light and musical, and it feels like a win. I've been working hard for those laughs.

Tiger remains curled up in her favorite corner as we enter her stall, exactly where we left her yesterday. I imagine she moved at some point over the last sixteen hours, considering the keepers bring sheep to the stalls each morning. The sheep farms around here have an insane output to keep up with the demand. Feeding up to a hundred dragons every day is no picnic, although it's usually less than fifty after the third-years graduate.

Amira places her bag next to the door, and I toss mine next to it. Tiger perks up. Her ruby scales shimmer under the bioluminescent orbs. She stretches out her front legs, arching her back. With a pep in her step, she prances to Amira and nuzzles her, knocking her backward.

Laughing, Amira quickly regains her balance. "Want to fly?"

Tiger dances in a quick circle. That's a solid yes.

Amira glances at me as she strokes Tiger's snout. "Want to come along?"

"Sounds awesome." Excitement pulses through my veins.

"Did you want to check on Loki before we go?"

Amira hasn't met him yet since he's almost always sleeping. I don't feel anything through our bond. "He's probably still asleep, but I checked on him first thing this morning."

She nods, just barely. There's a hint of a smile. We exit the cave, and Tiger basks in the sunshine.

A group of dragons flies quickly toward us. A Ruby, a Green, a Blue, and a Brown... Tobias's gang. I've managed to avoid him, but apparently my luck has run out. Really hoping I'm not torched by his dragon.

"Mia! There you are." Tobias guides his Ruby to the ground and lands next to us as the other three continue to circle. "Come to the Den with us. You're done with class, right?"

Amira nods. "Yep, until afternoon flight in a few hours."

And we're using the time to fly with Tiger, so fly away, Tobias. You visit the Den every night anyway.

"Dad wants to meet Tiger," he says. "Come on."

Damn, I can't compete. She was so disappointed when her dad canceled their family dinner last week because he wasn't feeling well.

Amira's eyes sparkle with excitement. She turns toward me. "Can we fly later?"

Her question reminds Tobias I'm here. He glares daggers at me. If looks could kill... This isn't the right time to push for an invitation. Especially not when I'd have to hitch a ride.

I give Amira what I hope is a charming grin. "Of course. I'm not going anywhere."

"Come on, Mia." Tobias continues to glare my way. I swear the gang only has one expression, and it's not welcoming. He mouths *'get lost,'* sending a chill down my spine. Considering I'll be kicked out and lose Loki, staying away isn't an option.

But also... I don't want to.

She nods and climbs onto Tiger's back. Once she's safely strapped into her saddle, she waves, and they all take off.

A few minutes later, I'm back in Loki's stall with a bleating sheep I dragged from the pens. "I brought you a snack since you skipped breakfast."

He doesn't move as the sheep wanders anxiously around the

stall. He never does, even after two weeks of this. He eats them after I leave, though. They're always gone by my next visit.

I sit against the wall ten feet away, still thrown by his sadness washing over our bond. "I don't know what to do, Loki."

He watches me for a moment before closing his eyes.

I close mine, too, and lean my head against the stone. "When I started at Dragild, I thought there was no chance I'd fail. I would make my dad proud by breaking the biggest, baddest dragon of my class." I sigh. "Now, here we are."

I'm hit with a puff of warm air. I open my eyes. Loki's sour expression says more than words could.

"I'm sorry, Loki." I shake my head. "I just meant I didn't break one at all. It's... disappointing. Embarrassing. I don't belong here. And if we don't infiltrate Tobias's inner circle..."

Loki lays his head down again. He continues to watch me as the sheared sheep romps around the stall. It seems to realize he isn't interested.

"I'm sorry about your last rider."

He closes his eyes. *"He was the best."*

My body jolts with his first words to me in two weeks, but I quickly regain my composure. "Want to tell me about him?"

Loki opens his eyes again and raises his head. *"We liked to race across the state to Spokane, and I got to fly as fast as I wanted. He'd always get a beer from one of the breweries. He wanted to try them all."*

I lean back against the wall. "We could make that flight, if you want to. Once your wing is healed."

Loki watches me for a moment. He stands and snaps the sheep up with his powerful jaws, swallowing it whole. It didn't even have a second to let out a final bleat. Damn.

He walks toward me and lays down again, resting his head near my knees.

Definitely progress.

3

Amid the fiery chaos, the bullet ripped the dragon's wing straight down the middle. Pain overtook her body as she fell from the sky, landing hard on the cement of the central Oregon highway.

A semi-truck blasted down the road directly at her, but she couldn't move. Couldn't evade. Her heart pounded as she rolled, her belly facing the truck, in a last-ditch effort to protect her rider.

The truck crashed into her.

Her world went black.

Loki's had three weeks to heal, and we're finally ready to fly. Students roam the courtyard as I step outside. There are probably thirty out here, so over half of Dragild's students have come outside to enjoy the sunshine. It's the perfect day to capture the flag.

All five professors and the commandant are congregating around a picnic table in the corner.

"Markus." The commandant scrutinizes me, eyes narrowed. "Join me."

I follow the commandant to his office. He's probably pissed I've been avoiding him. Will I ever meet his idea of a strong dragon rider?

Student profiles cover his desk in preparation for the graduation ceremony in two and a half weeks. The third-years will receive their diplomas and their officers' stations, and I'll officially be a second-year.

He sits, but this time he leans forward. "How's your dragon healing?"

I straighten. After everything that went wrong, something finally went right. "Really well. Our first flight is today."

The commandant nods. "And the mission?"

Not well, but I can't say that. Tobias wants nothing to do with me. "Loki was the primary focus, but I've been working on Amira Obi."

His frown deepens as he leans back. "Tobias graduates in three weeks. You have until then to infiltrate and find the information, or Loki's being moved to a rider who lost their dragon in another attack last night."

Loki and I are finally getting somewhere. Amira is coming around, but it's taking time—time I don't have. I swallow and take a deep breath. I can't fail. "Understood."

He dismisses me with a wave of his hand, and I hustle outside.

More students have filtered out into the yard. A football flies at me, and I dive to catch it. I toss it back to the group, and they continue tackling each other over the ball. They should try soccer instead.

Amira is tucked into the shade underneath a tree in the corner with a book in her lap. Her fresh box braids are tied back. She's gorgeous, as always.

I cross the courtyard and sit on the ground next to her. "What are you reading?"

She glances at me before focusing on her book. "*The Dragon Nest.* Did you know there have been forty-two failed military missions to infiltrate Rainier?"

"I did not. Tell me about them."

She glances at me again, her eyes lit with excitement. "The latest attempt used military androids originally designed for spacecraft repair, but they were covered in dragon scales. Check this out." She flips through the pages, moves closer to me, and holds the book out. In the photo, android limbs litter the field. The scattered metal body parts are rather morbid, but her wide grin is infectious. "They hit the force field and short-circuited, and half of them just exploded."

"Geez. At least humans just hit the wall and bounce off it."

She laughs. "The magic of the nest is awesome."

"Any other attempts of note?"

"Not really. Helicopters, planes, rockets. They all crashed.

That's old news, though." She waves her hand dismissively. "Oh, once they tried digging their way in. But they were... well, the equipment burned up, and half the region had to evacuate as the lava flowed to the surface."

My eyebrows rise, and I blink my expression back to neutral. "I can see why the mission failed. I guess they'll have to catch a dragon like..."

Not like the rest of us. I shouldn't have gone for a Black.

I lean against the tree. "During the solstice, why didn't you go for a Black?"

She closes her book and sets it on the ground before turning toward me. "My dad rides a Black. Mom did, too." Her eyes glaze over, just for a moment. "Dad's biggest disappointment is my brother riding a Ruby, not that he'd say it." She bites her lip. "I didn't want to make it worse for Tobias. But if I rode anything less than a Ruby... Well, I'd never hear the end of it. Tobes would lord it over me."

"Tobes?" I chuckle, picturing the six-foot-six mass of muscle. "How did he get that nickname?"

"When he was a toddler, he couldn't say Amira." She shrugs, seemingly nonplussed. "Mia just stuck. But it wasn't fair that he got to use a shortened name when I didn't."

"So he became Tobes."

"Only one person can call me that, and it isn't *you*," Tobias hisses.

Fuck. He came out of nowhere.

Amira rolls her eyes. "Hello to you, too, big brother. I can't wait until you graduate."

"Like you won't call me every day," he teases.

"Hey, babe." Carina sits next to Amira and gives her a side hug as Theo and Jonas kick a soccer ball back and forth a dragon-length away from us. The gang's all here.

Jonas glances at Amira. I nonchalantly scoot closer to her. She's busy pulling out her phone to show Carina something, probably more photos from her group chat. Jonas watches us, his icy blue eyes highlighted by his blue armor. He still needs a better hair gel.

Tobias grins. "Ready to win today?" Judging by the sharp gleam in his eye, he definitely is. "It's gonna be three years straight. Don't let me down, Mia."

"I would never." Amira tucks her phone and book into her bag and turns toward me. "Is Loki excited?"

"Yep. We both are."

She smiles, revealing two perfect dimples.

Tobias offers his hand to Carina and helps her up. "Come on, then."

We meander down the cave, caught in the mass of over fifty students migrating from the courtyard. The excited chatter echoes throughout the cave. Amira grabs my hand and pulls me along, catching me off guard. We turn into the first hall.

"Markus, Amira," Katie calls out from behind us.

I squeeze Amira's hand tighter when she starts to let go, and her smile makes my stomach flip.

"Ready to win?" Katie is practically bouncing with excitement as her bright blue eyes catch mine. Her brown hair is braided into a crown, showing off her violet streaks. "I heard this year's division is the first half of the alphabet versus the second half."

Amira laughs. "Well, Fredriksen, you don't stand a chance."

"I don't know about that," Katie says with a smirk. "He has hope, thanks to me and Bear."

I let go of Amira's hand and cross my arms. "Just keep trash-talking. I'll be the one on the white dragon waving the flag."

"Yeah, the white flag of surrender." Amira cracks up, and Katie joins in. Damn, these two. They're double trouble.

"See you out there." Katie heads off toward her dragon's stall.

Amira opens the iron stall door. Tiger happily bounces over, nudging Amira with her nose.

"You're clearly game for today." Amira gives her a few pets and walks to the saddle.

"Give me a second to grab Loki." I jog to the end of the row and enter his stall.

He immediately rises. *"Let's fly."*

I strap his white leather saddle between his shoulder blades, and we race back as the stomps of dragons echo loudly in the cave.

I don't think I've smiled this wide in my life. "Amira, meet Loki."

"Hi, Loki." Amira waves.

He nudges her hand happily and snuggles his snout against her, almost knocking her flat on her ass. I'm pretty sure he loves her already. She laughs and rubs his cheeks affectionately. I unclench my jaw, mouth totally dry. Damnit, I feel jealous of a dragon.

"I'd be jealous of me, too. I'm quite lovable."

I roll my eyes, but I don't fight the smile. Loki's bright golden eyes betray his amusement. My dragon. I have a dragon, and we're about to fly together for the first time.

As we exit the cave, Loki nudges me. *"Come on."*

At least half the students are already out. Dragons take to the cloudless sky in a rainbow of colors and circle above.

I climb onto Loki's back and settle in between his shoulder blades, buckling the safety straps of the saddle. "It's fifty minutes and seventy miles to Seattle. Are you sure you're ready?"

Loki blows a puff of hot air at me. *"Twenty-five minutes when you're fast."*

"Okay then." That answers that.

"Are you ready?" He stretches out his wings. The scar cuts across the membrane, but it has healed well. Kristoffer declared him completely safe to fly, so I shouldn't worry.

I shove down the butterflies in my stomach, put on my flight goggles, and grip the pommel. "Rea—"

Loki takes off like a shot, and it's all I can do to hang on. Adrenaline courses through me. The wind rushes past us as we rise toward the flight of dragons. As we approach, Loki banks left, gliding smoothly through the air and away from the group. I hold on tight as his wings beat harder, taking us even higher above the flight.

Below us, the Cascade Range sprawls outward. Clumps of evergreens dot the rocky landscape. Steam clouds rise from the top of Mount Rainier. We look about level with the mountaintop, so we're fourteen thousand feet above sea level.

Holy shit, we're high.

My head feels light from the elevation, but I've never felt so alive. So free. Part of it comes from Loki. Two minds, one wavelength.

We remain high above the flight of dragons. Riding leathers keep out most of the cold, and Loki's body radiates like a space heater, keeping me warm. He speeds and slows, speeds and slows, and happily circles the sky. His joy takes over our bond.

Bear's bright yellow scales are hard to miss within the flight. Amira and Tiger circle with Tobias and Derkomai, his Ruby. Most of the riders have launched, but a few stragglers are still getting settled near the entrance of the cave.

After ten minutes, a Black takes to the sky. Commandant Eirikssen is in flight.

"Time to head down, Loki. Hurry up. We don't want to get in trouble."

Loki dives down without warning, and my heart races. Good thing I was holding on tightly. He banks toward the outer edge of the circle and races to catch up to Amira.

"I swear you like her more than me."

"No comment."

"I don't blame you. She's pretty great." I chuckle and pat his neck, letting the tension go.

The commandant hovers in the middle of the circling dragons, his gun holstered at his waist. "Students," he says through the walkie-talkie earpiece. His bald head gleams in the sunlight. I hope he wore sunscreen. He gives a quick rundown of the rules, but we all know them. We've been waiting for this all year. "Your team captains have the flags. Last names through K, follow Harper. The rest, follow Malcolm." The two third-year captains wave their banners with enthusiasm and fly in opposite directions. "Move out!"

The third-years on our team fly out front with Harper. Loki and I settle into formation close behind her as our team takes off.

"Where should we hide the flag?" she calls out. Her cheeks are flushed, and her energy is contagious.

"It needs to be good." Carina frowns from the back of her Green. "Tobias and I have a bet going, and I have no intention of losing."

Anywhere within city limits is fair game, so we have a ton of options.

"What about the same spot as last year? They'll never see it coming." Theo pushes his shaggy black hair out of his face, but the wind blows it back as he clutches the pommel atop his Brown Ridgeback. Browns have special saddles, but it's still a bumpy ride.

"You're brilliant." Harper smiles wide and raises her arms, hands curled into fists, from atop her White. "Victory will be ours!"

"Tobias is going down." Carina's smile is wicked. "Both during the game and later tonight."

Harper cackles, the purple bun on top of her half-shaved head bobbing. "Babe, you're delicious. He wins either way."

"What's good for the goose is good for the gander."

My body feels light for the first time in three weeks as Loki happily flies along. Katie flies nearby, chattering away, her usual bubbly self. I can't hear half of what she's saying over the wind, but I smile and nod.

The mountain range rushes below us as we fly toward Seattle. As we approach, the city sweeps out in a sea of metal and glass surrounded by water and mountains.

The Space Needle stands out against the skyline. It's a UFO on a tripod. Rising six hundred feet, it offers an amazing view of today's challenge. Even though I can't see them yet, noses will be pressed against the windows as onlookers watch us approach. Dad's and mine used to be pressed against the glass from sunrise through the end of the event. The observation deck was always full.

This exercise is five percent strategy, five percent teamwork, and ninety percent exposure for Dragild. The school's coffers will fill right up with donations over the next week.

"Get in formation," Harper calls out. "It's time for our flyby." We tighten our formation and follow her lead.

Columbia Center punches the sky, as black as our riding leathers. At over nine hundred feet tall, it stands far above the other buildings. The upper floors of its seventy-six stories house an observatory and a lounge, while the lower floors contain office space for hundreds. We fly to the base and spiral around the building toward the sky, circling and preening while people rush to the windows.

As we reach the top, I give Loki a few pets at the base of his neck. "Having fun?"

"Best day of the year." He dives down, and we join the end of the line, working our way up Columbia Center a second time.

Harper leads the group to Rainier Square Tower. We tail the group in the same upward spiral. Halfway up the building, a child in a dragon-print dress presses her tiny hands against the glass, looking out at us from her apartment. She waves shyly as her mother smiles next to her. Loki flies toward her and puts his nose against the glass. Her eyes grow wide as she jumps backward and laughs. Loki shakes with laughter beneath me, and we rush to catch up to the group.

The waterfront is crowded with people as the Great Wheel spins near the seawall. The smaller dragons weave in and out of the Ferris wheel's metal spokes, much to the delight of those riding in the glass cages. Loki spins and dives through the spokes with tucked wings while I cling to him and send a mental thank-you to whoever designed the saddle.

"Remember to aim up," Harper tells us through our earpieces. I guess it doesn't matter if the other team intercepts that message, since our group will be hard to miss.

We line up over Elliott Bay, and our twenty-five dragons light the sky on fire. It's hot. Really hot. The scene looks amazing, though. It was always my favorite display, and now I'm a part of it.

Cheers erupt from the shore as Loki basks in the admiration. *Can we go back over land now? I can't swim like the water dragons.*

"That's because they're fish and you're avian, minus the feathers." I pat his neck and fail to send calm vibes through the bond. We're really fucking high right now.

"Fall in, Goldwings!" Harper shouts. "We're going to split up. All the Rubies plus you three, head to the Emerald. Make it look like we're hiding the flag there. Chase everyone off and be ruthless as fuck." Seven dragons fly off. "You all minus the white dragons, head to the Doppler building and lure in the other team. When they realize it's a distraction, abandon the post and find their flag." Another seven fly off. Harper evaluates the rest of the group. "Whites and Graytail, stick with me. We're heading to F5 Tower."

Frosted Whitetalons are well-known for their intelligence, and Loki's mostly white. Do we get a special mission?

"The rest of you, before you start the hunt, put on a show at Fourth and Madison. The rooftop garden is always full of onlookers with deep pockets, and Chief Paveith will be there. He's kicking off his west coast tour."

This is why Harper will definitely end up with a top position after graduation. Maybe she'll even be tapped to join the chief's Top Squad.

"Good luck," Katie calls before she and Bear take off with the group.

Loki chuffs. *"I don't need luck."*

"Good to know." I give him a pat, still amused.

"To the Tower, my Whites," Harper shouts, throwing her pointer finger out with a laugh. The four of us fly over quickly and land on the white roof. Our dragons blend in perfectly.

"Tuck in that gray tail, Fredriksen."

Well, almost perfectly.

Harper hides the flag carefully within the machinery. The air-conditioning units whirr as the wind blows around us. The city sprawls out below, and the black glass of Columbia Center glitters across the street.

Loki curls up and tucks his tail beneath his belly. I lean against him, and he stretches out a wing to cover me. And now, we wait.

"What do you think, bud?"

"I've always chased the other team's flag. I've never protected ours before. It's kind of boring."

Laughter bursts out of me. "Well, let's hope it stays that way. How's your wing?"

He blows hot air at me. *"You worry too much. It's perfect, like the rest of me."* He yawns. *"Wake me up when something happens."*

Harper has plenty of commentary on the ethics of war, current politics—including Chief Paveith's bid for office—and a sequel to a racing movie coming out next week. I don't know why she wants to watch it. The first was so boring. It really needed more dragons. Her chatter eats up the next three hours as Loki contentedly naps in the sunshine. I can't figure out how she hasn't lost her voice yet, considering I can hear her perfectly from the other side of the roof.

"Blue approaching." She points north. "No one move. We don't want to give away our location if they don't already know it." Blue dragons make the best hunters.

I nudge Loki, and he wakes immediately. *"What? Where are they?"*

"North, coming at us. Hang tight."

A spot of yellow appears at the top of Columbia Center. Katie climbs onto Bear's back as the Blue redirects toward them and picks up speed.

The Blue rises quickly toward the roof, bright against the black glass. Bear dives down and meets the Blue halfway.

Jerking left but dodging right, the Blue attempts to throw them off. Katie and Bear don't fall for the trick and stay the course. Bear and the Blue collide.

She loses her grip and slides down Bear's body.

She didn't strap in.

Her scream turns my blood to ice. Katie claws at Bear, but she can't get a hold. She keeps slipping.

Screw the flag.

I jump on Loki's back, and we take off like a missile.

My heart pounds in my ears. Loki and I race toward her falling body.

She scrambles frantically, grasping at the air.

We fly harder, terror pulsing.

There's nothing for her to grab.

Loki's nose is only a few feet away, but she can't reach it.

Katie hits the street with a heavy thud. The collar around her neck shatters. Her limbs sprawl at unnatural angles. Blood pools around her. All within an instant.

Bear lets out a ferocious roar, now unbroken. He shoots a wave of fire toward the street, and onlookers take cover and rush into buildings.

Loki lands on the ground. I quickly slide off his back. My stomach heaves as I take in Katie's broken body, and suddenly my breakfast is on the street, and my world is covered in shadows. I take a deep breath, and another, and another.

"I'm sorry I wasn't fast enough." Loki stands over me, and his wings are stretched to cover me. Sirens call out in the distance.

"No, Loki," I whisper. I lean against his leg as an overwhelming sadness washes over me. "It wasn't our fault."

Loki tucks his wings into his body.

Bear lets out another roar. His bright yellow body shrinks as he quickly flies toward his nest, where nature intended him to be.

The wind picks up around us, and a Ruby enters my field of vision.

"Markus!" Amira shouts. Her eyes are wide as she slides off Tiger and runs toward me. She hugs me, wrapping me in her calming vanilla scent. "We should get off the ground. The police will be here any minute."

I lean on Loki for support and place my hands on the small of her back, tugging her closer. "Katie was my friend. I don't want to just leave her body here."

Tobias lands his Ruby next to us and jumps to the ground immediately. "Mia, get back on your dragon."

"Tobes, we—"

"Police shoot first and ask second!"

Amira lets go of me, sprinting back to Tiger, and they launch immediately. Jonas follows her closely on his Blue as the volume of the sirens continues to rise.

Tobias's expression morphs into a sneer of pure hatred while he mounts his Ruby. I gulp as he takes to the sky.

The rain tapping against my dorm window is a welcome relief after the stress of yesterday. Flight class is canceled for safety and visibility concerns, although I could have used the distraction from my thoughts.

Katie's death was a stupid accident. It wasn't my fault. It wasn't Loki's fault, especially not with how hard he flew. Premature death is a reality for dragon riders.

At least the game was over quickly. When half the team rushed toward the commotion, it was pretty obvious our flag was on the roof next door. Tobias captured the flag and lorded it over us all evening. Meanwhile, Amira was nowhere to be found.

I sigh and shove the covers back before crawling out of bed. Moping won't get me into Tobias's inner circle.

Harper jogs up to me in the hallway on my way to breakfast. Her skin has a hint of sunburn from sitting on the roof yesterday. "Hey, sorry about Katie. Yesterday sucked."

Yeah, it genuinely did. I take a deep breath. "Thanks. Counting down to graduation yet?"

"Absolutely. Eighteen days, six hours, and twenty-three minutes."

How helpful that she knows exactly how long I have to get my shit together.

As we enter the food hall, the excited chatter overpowers the rain pounding on the roof. Apparently, everyone is ready for a day off. It smells like fresh coffee. Not surprising, since last night's party ran late.

Harper grabs a coffee as I join the end of the breakfast line. I arm myself with one of every pastry, determined to find Amira, before I load up a plate with eggs and smoked salmon for myself.

Amira's sitting alone with a book. I beeline for her table and sit across from her. "Congrats on the win."

"Thanks." Amira finishes the last bite of her fruit. She doesn't look at me.

"Still hungry?" I slide my tray her way, and she picks up the plate of salmon and eggs. I pull the tray back and take a bite of a pastry. I should have known. "No partying last night?"

"I wasn't in the mood." She turns the page.

It feels like we're starting over. Like the last three weeks never happened.

"Obi," I say softly. "Do you want to talk about yesterday?"

Her gaze meets mine. "Tobias was right about you. Us."

"What do you mean?"

Amira sighs, slumping her shoulders. "I'm a Black woman in America. Mistakes aren't an option. And even when I play within the lines society drew, sometimes that's still not enough to guarantee my safety. It's not something you can relate to."

My cheeks burn. She's right. Her safety hadn't crossed my mind.

I swallow and take a deep breath. "I really did appreciate you coming down, and I'm sorry I didn't fly back up with you immediately. I should have. I wasn't thinking."

She bites her lip.

Jonas walks up to our table. His fists are clenched at his sides. "What are you doing here?"

"Chill, Jonas," Amira says.

"It's fine, Obi." I tamp down a pang of jealousy and stand up. "I'll see you later."

"Later?" Jonas glares.

Amira doesn't appreciate overprotective assholes, and sticking around won't win any points. I walk away.

Jonas's steps pound behind me as I approach the end of the table. He grabs me from behind and shoves me against the stainless steel. My hip hits hard. That's going to bruise. Breakfast beverages slosh out of mugs and glasses onto the tabletop.

Fuck this.

My fist curls. I turn and throw a sharp punch at his cheek, and he snaps back.

Jonas bends forward, running my way. His shoulder smashes into my stomach as he pushes me into the wall, knocking the air out of me.

A crowd forms around us. I can't back down. I can't look weak.

My heart races. I wrap my arm around Jonas's neck and push him down, throwing another punch.

"Tobias, stop them!" Amira shouts. I can barely hear her over the pounding in my ears.

Jonas gets a hold of me and slams me onto the soaked tabletop. A moment later, he's three feet away and Tobias is standing over me.

I stand slowly, lifting my arms in surrender. "He got in my face."

"Well, now I'm in your face." Tobias holds an arm in front of

Jonas. Jonas makes a move toward me, and Tobias snaps. "Relax, Jonas! You're embarrassing yourself."

Theo grabs Jonas's arm and pulls him quickly out of the food hall as Carina follows behind. Amira's already gone.

The vein pulses on Tobias's neck. "Stay away from her."

I cross my arms. "He started it. This is bullshit."

"What's bullshit is you thinking any part of you is worthy of my sister." He turns and leaves, and the crowd disperses.

Back in my room, I throw my sopping-wet clothes into the laundry basket. Somehow, I have a cut along my arm. It looks like my stomach might be bruised, and I know my hip is going to turn purple.

I'm not getting anywhere near Amira or the inner circle of the Den until I earn Tobias's respect. I should have seen it weeks ago. The commandant obviously saw it.

Well, fuck.

4

Loki stands ready at the mouth of the dragon cave. I'm standing next to him, questioning my sanity.

After napping in my room all day and taking some painkillers, I made my way to Loki's stall and woke him up. When I told him the plan, he also questioned my sanity.

An airplane's lights blink in the distance among the stars. The sky over volcanic Mount Rainier glows red and orange against the cool night. Soft moonlight brightens the snowy mountaintops and Loki's white scales.

We shouldn't be going anywhere, considering there are only two hours left until curfew. But no one actually monitors it...

Loki's gray tail flicks as he paws at the ground with a front leg. *"Are you sure?"*

"Yep." I double-check that the straps on his saddle are secure, climb up, and buckle myself in safely. I won't go out like Katie. Shoving away the nerves, I pull down my flight goggles. "Let's go."

We need to find Tobias, and I need to earn his respect. Otherwise, I'll be saying goodbye to Loki and Dragild.

Loki's muscles tighten below me. He spreads his wings and takes a running start. We launch into the sky and aim south. The wind whips around us, and my stomach churns as the ground falls away.

"Any other dragons nearby?"

"Not right now." His echolocation would pick them up.

He beats his wings, speeding along above the mountain range. Loki's radiating body heat fights against the icy chill of the high altitude, but I'd really like a hot chocolate right about now. At least it's summer.

A hundred miles later, Portland's light pollution erases the stars from the sky. The city's bright, jagged skyline beckons us forward. Its towering skyscrapers don't have the scope or the height of Seattle's, but thanks to the clans, they're far more menacing.

Welcome back to the city I grew up in.

Loki drops our altitude and slows his momentum. *"It's not too late to turn around."*

I give his neck a few good scratches. "We have to find Tobias."

He settles into a glide over the Willamette River, keeping a steady pace south. The Park Avenue West Tower glows against the sky to our right. That's the destination.

We aim for Battleship Oregon Memorial Park and land near the foremast. The white cylinder rises from a platform of red bricks and is lit up in the darkness. It's dented and covered in scorch marks, but it's all that's left of the scrapped battleship. The rest was melted down after... maybe the last war? There were a lot of them, thanks to dragon power. Amira would know.

I jump from Loki's back onto the soft grass, happy my feet are finally on the ground. "Solid flying, bud," I whisper, even though there's no one around to hear us. "Let's take a walk."

"We can still go home."

If we turn around, my dream of being a dragon rider would be over. "I'll be discharged, and you'll be bounced to a new rider."

Loki sighs. He doesn't offer any other response, but he also doesn't protest.

I must be growing on him.

Not all the streets can accommodate his wingspan to allow for flight, but he's less than the width of a car when he tucks in his wings. We walk toward the parkway and turn down Southwest Morrison Street. My stomach rumbles as the delicious smell of Chinese food drifts out from Dragonwell Bistro, though it's already closed for the night. We pass dark shops and empty streets.

A cat screeches, a trash can falls, and Loki's golden eyes light up. *"I didn't know you could jump that high."*

Just gonna ignore that.

The Park Avenue West Tower rises thirty floors into the sky on our left. The sharp lines of the glass and metal were designed to deter visitors.

I wipe my sweaty palms on my jacket. "How do we get in?"

"The garage door along Park. We were only here once, but we didn't find anything." Loki's head drops. His last rider must be on his mind.

"Next time, we'll go to Spokane. Promise." I doubt that's much consolation.

We cross the empty street and approach the two-story garage door. I knock twice, the sound hollow. A light on a camera above the door blinks.

A hatch in the door slides open, creating a tiny window at my eye level. Dark eyes assess us.

"Password?" The tone is gruff.

I gulp and glance at Loki.

"Pussywillow."

"Pussywillow," I say.

The window bangs shut, but nothing else happens. I swallow, breaking the silence. Has the password changed?

Footsteps pad softly behind the door before it creeps open with a groan. An empty, dimly lit garage greets us. It's about twenty feet to the ceiling, tall enough that Loki doesn't have to duck his head after we enter. The door slams down the moment we pass through.

"Head on down." The bouncer gestures toward the far wall. I'm six-foot-three to his maybe-five-ten, but he could take me down fast.

Okay. We can do this. Tobias has to be here. I take a deep breath, and off we go.

We descend the circular car ramp, and the bare cement entombs us. I keep my breathing steady, and Loki keeps his wings tucked.

Totally normal to wander down with a dragon, I guess. It's a dragon-sized ramp.

Three levels down, I'm sweating, and not from the exertion. This is Tobias's home turf, and we're intruding on it.

I wouldn't be going through this if I had applied to the Kilauea Academy. Not that I'd have been accepted, considering they only accept the top five applicants each year. Hawaii doesn't have enough resources to support as many Goldwings.

Or I shouldn't have gone for a Black. That would probably have been the better solution.

"Is this really where we're supposed to go?" I whisper.

"Only two more floors."

At the base of the ramp, bright yellow lines cross the cement, denoting parking for cars that... well, they certainly aren't here. It's completely empty and completely silent.

"It's through a secret door across the lot."

"Thanks," I whisper. "Is it too late to turn around?"

Loki blinks at me. *"Yes. They have cameras everywhere. They'll probably send someone out soon if we don't move."*

Shit. "Okay, on we go."

As we cross the lot, there are no signs of motion. No signs of a secret door. No signs of any life in this godforsaken tomb. My heartbeat pounds in my ears.

I trace my hand along a small plaque mounted on the soot-covered concrete wall. "'Let it burn.' That's all you, bud."

Loki blows a small stream of fire on the wall that blasts heat and reeks of sulfur. Gears grind as the entire wall lowers slowly, revealing darkness.

"Well, that was anticlimactic," I whisper.

I take a step forward and light bursts forth, brighter than the sun.

"Oh!" I catch my balance, thanks to Loki. My eyes struggle to adjust.

Loki chuffs and nudges me. *Go on. It'll be fun.*

"Okay then." I gulp as I take another step forward. "Let's do it."

Tobias will be here. He has to be.

We enter the chamber and are greeted by a harsh chorus of roars and growls. A shot of ice hits my veins when the concrete wall rises behind us, eliminating the possibility of escape.

"Welcome to the Dragon Den," says a crotchety old guard seated at the top of another ramp.

"Thanks." I approach a half-wall behind him and dare to look down.

The balcony juts out at least four stories above the bottom of the ginormous cavern. The center of the pit is lit up, but shadows shroud the edges of the room. Dragons in a variety of colors are tucked into corners and on ledges cut into the concrete walls. Half of them are asleep. Lazy things.

A half dozen steel tables—hosting card games—circle a steel bar in the middle like a scene from outer space. They look dollhouse-size compared to the room, and they're all surrounded by people dressed in dark clothes.

One of the tables hosts a trio of dragons. They throw dice, snap at each other, take bites out of sheep shish-ka-bobs... *Just kidding. Focus, Markus.*

The lights turn off behind us as Loki and I walk down the long ramp toward the base, passing beneath an Orange. The air smells like sulfur thanks to all the dragons.

"Watch it!" A rider with a mohawk glares at me. No idea how his hair stays up during his flights.

"Sorry." I move to the side and let him pass.

Loki and I scope out the room, but there's no sign of Tobias.

"There are a couple of Rubies along the walls," I whisper. "Stay alert. Perch where you can keep an eye on things."

Loki nods, lifts off the ground, and settles silently onto a ledge near the ceiling. I comb back my hair, now ruffled from the wind of Loki's takeoff.

"I don't see Derkomai."

Damn. Maybe he isn't here yet... but Theo said they'd be here every night until graduation.

I strut to the bar and lean against the polished steel top. The green-haired bartender is busy serving other patrons, creating the perfect opportunity for me to scope out the joint. I'm cool, calm, and collected. An A-plus secret agent.

One of those DJ remixes plays at a low volume from speakers

mounted to the bar. Some guy crooning about luck be a lady. I hope lady luck isn't holding back like Amira tonight, or I'm screwed—and not in a good way.

At least three people occupy each of the six surrounding tables, but waiters and onlookers all dressed in black meander around the area. I spot a couple of second-year Dragild students, although they aren't friends with Tobias. The rest of the patrons are older. Each table has a different game going. I cleaned up at blackjack in high school; that's the table I need to find while I wait for Tobias to show.

Roars echo through the pit. I steady myself with a barstool. Wasn't expecting that.

"What are you drinking?" The bartender quickly wipes the bar in front of me. Tattoos snake up her arms.

"I'll take a hot chocolate. Thanks." I'm only nineteen, and I don't know if they ID. I definitely don't want to give her my ID while I'm on a mission. Too big a risk. She grabs a mug and uses chocolate sauce. Perfection. I pay for it with cash. No trail left behind. My secret agent skills continue to be top-notch. "Where's the Blackjack table?"

She points me toward a table surrounded by four patrons. The dealer's hands fly as he passes out the starting cards for the round. I settle in at the end of the table and watch, keeping an eye out for Tobias. Once the round is over, I put all my cash on the table. "Deal me in."

He replaces the bills with chips, and I place my bet in a rush of adrenaline. The dealer begins flipping the cards and laying them in front of us. Queen, eight, three, eight, and a ten in front of me. Solid start. Queen, four, six, three—damn, that makes an eleven for them—and a four in front of me. Fourteen for my hand, and plenty of face cards left.

I take a sip of hot chocolate and look around the room. Still no Tobias. I'll give it one more hand after this round before I follow the sound of the roars.

Our dealer flips their first card over. "Dealer shows a three. Your play."

The first player stays, of course. They're sitting pretty with two queens at twenty. The second player taps for a hit. King of spades—a straight bust. They're out. The dealer turns to the third, who doubles down. Solid strategy at nine. So does the fourth. No surprise, since he's at eleven. I gesture to stay. The fourteen in my hand is fifty-fifty for a bust and with my luck as of late...

The dealer flips a queen, putting the house at thirteen. He draws a ten and busts. Maybe my luck is turning around.

I win the next three rounds. My game is on fire. The table is blazing. I'm—

"Markus."

Shit.

Loki's panicked voice fills my head. *"Theo's behind you."*

Thanks, Loki, I got that.

If Theo is here, Tobias must be here, too. Somewhere.

I settle into my seat. Definitely did *not* almost knock it over with a startled jump. "Theo."

"What are you doing?" His brown armor gleams over his riding leathers. He rakes his hand through his black hair, the same way he does when he's annoyed at something on his tablet in the library.

"Playing blackjack. Join in." I gesture to the empty seat on my left.

He gives me a strange look before he pulls some chips out of his pocket and sits next to me. The dealer spreads the first round of cards, turning up an ace in front of me. Perfection. I have a great shot at landing a tenner.

"Do you come here often?" I ask. *And is Tobias here?*

"Yes, which is how I know you don't." Theo scrutinizes me as the dealer flips over an eight in front of him and a queen in front of himself.

"Loki's wing finally healed, you know? We just haven't had a chance. And it's not like there are that many places big enough for a dragon to hang out."

Theo spots Loki on the ledge. His expression darkens for a moment and then softens, taking in all the cuteness. It looks like Loki is napping. My expression softens, too. He's had a rough month.

The dealer places a nine in front of me. Solid twenty. That's a stay. Luck is my best friend tonight. He flips an eight in front of Theo and circles back to the first player.

"He flew well yesterday, at least from what I saw. It probably helped that there weren't any trees in the city."

"For sure." I gesture to stay, thanks to this fabulous twenty in hand, and the dealer moves on to Theo. "You have a little..." I point to a black spot on his face.

"Oh, thanks." Theo rubs it off and wipes his hand on his pants before he pulls out more chips from his pocket. "Split." The dealer divides the eights and flips a king and a seven. That makes eighteen and fifteen.

I nod as the dealer flips a nine. With his nineteen, everyone else at the table just busted. He doubles the chips in front of me.

"Damn." Theo sighs as the dealer picks up his chips.

"Statistically, that was the right way to play."

"Yeah, the odds were in my favor." He lets out a chuckle. "But in the end, the house always wins."

"Another round?"

Roars echo through the cave as Theo shakes his head.

The dealer cashes me out, and I happily tuck the two grand in my pocket. Dragild pays for most of our expenses, so I'll put it in the bank with what's left of the money from Dad's life insurance. He'd be proud of that choice.

"I prefer games not left to chance," Theo says.

"Which ones?" I look around the room while we rise from the table and head toward the wall.

"None of..." He bites his lip.

"The dragon fights." Loki's voice is strained.

Those can't be sanctioned. The Goldwings would never allow it. *Though here we are in the Dragon Den, and with how expensive it is to break and maintain a dragon, almost all riders start out as Goldwings...*

"You mean the dragon fights?" I keep my voice low.

Theo frowns. "No. I bet Jonas would challenge you after your fight this morning, though. Lucky for you, he didn't come tonight." He hesitates. "Tobias..."

"Wants me to stay away from Amira. She's at school." I shrug, hoping he takes the bait. "Clearly, I'm staying away."

He sighs and keeps his voice low. "I like betting on the races."

Those definitely aren't sanctioned.

"That sounds fun." Loki's tone is borderline chipper. A complete one-eighty.

Tobias lives for speed. He has to be there.

"I definitely want in." I keep my expression neutral.

He bites his lip again. "You didn't hear it from me." I nod, just once. "They start from the roof, but only on the nights we know Goldwing patrol is low. There's usually a big crowd."

Loki flies down from the ledge, and I climb onto his back while Theo mounts Baldur, his Brown. We head back the way we came and go straight to the roof.

Not a single star is visible as we land on top of the Park Avenue West Tower. The rooftop is lit brighter than day. Three dragons tower over two dozen people crowded around a makeshift dance floor. No Tobias, though. Dance club music blasts from a set of speakers near the elevators. None of the partying crowd wear flying leathers, so they must be here for a good time. Their skimpy clothing and red plastic cups support my theory.

Theo slides off Baldur and they wander toward the center. I climb down from Loki's back.

"Who do we have here?" A pretty brunette in a pink top and white skirt smiles at Loki. He positively preens as she circles him. "A Graytail? And it looks like his wing took a hit." She laughs, light but cold in tone. "Probably a loser."

Loki sinks his head and narrows his eyes. *"Loser? I could snap your head off or burn you to—"*

"This is Loki." I place my hand on his nose. He's not a Black, but...

She ignores me and wanders back to the group. She dances along the way, stopping in front of another rider.

"You should have told her off." Loki chuffs.

"Sorry, bud," I whisper. "Don't worry. We'll show them."

I tuck my hands in my pockets, and we watch the festivities from the edge. Tobias will be here. I'm sure of it.

The elevator dings, the doors slide open, and more people join the crowd.

One of the men in flying leathers walks over to us. His smile feels welcoming. "Who are you running tonight?"

"This is Loki. I'm Markus." I hold out my hand, hoping it's not too sweaty.

He shakes it and pulls me in, slapping me on the back. "Typical white boy name."

"Norwegian, actually."

He chuckles. "Well, 'Mar-kuss,' it definitely matches your white dragon."

"I'm a Graytail." Loki glares at him.

Same feelings, Loki. His pronunciation is atrocious.

"Who are you running?" I ask.

He points to the opposite side of the roof. "See the Orange over there? That's mine." His dragon straightens and flaps its wings. "We aren't racing tonight, though."

Good, since Oranges are known for their agility. "Why not?"

"We're aiming for the Dragon Wars. You heard about them?"

"Oh, yeah." *Nope. Totally haven't.*

"Gotta rest up." He glances at Loki. "What's up with his wing?"

"What does it matter to him? He's not even racing."

I hook my thumbs through my pockets and try to look chill. "Small accident. Healed now, though. Good as new."

Another man in leathers joins us. A sweatband is wrapped around his head. "This Graytail yours?" The question doesn't feel particularly welcoming.

I nod and adopt his tone. "Obviously. I'm standing right next to him."

Both Loki and I straighten.

"That's funny." He laughs, but the sound is hollow. "It doesn't matter how you stand, it matters how you *race*. You better learn that before we take off tonight."

"Sweatband Man is a prick."

The pair wander off, apparently done with the conversation.

"Fuck them. We've got this," I whisper to Loki. We need to have this. This is our shot to win over Tobias. "How's your wing?"

"It's perfect. You worry too much. Stop it." Loki blows warm air at me. *"When do we get to race?"*

"Here they come!" Sweatband Man points up, and half the group turns toward the sky.

A Ruby with two collars circles the rooftop and lands slowly in the center of the dancers, sending them scrambling with laughter. Tobias climbs down from Derkomai while Goose and Carina land nearby. Goose's green scales and Carina's green dragon-scaled armor glitter under the floodlights. Tobias shakes hands and greets people like a king. Carina glares at the woman in the pink shirt when she approaches Tobias. The woman quickly wanders to the other side of the roof. Loki and I stay back, keeping our distance.

"Theo." Tobias greets him with a half handshake, half high-five, followed by a one-armed-hug-slash-shoulder-bump. "One race, two grand buy-in, winner takes all. You hold the cash."

So much for saving my winnings...

What am I saying? We'll win it back, and then some.

Sweatband Man scowls. "Why does he get to hold the cash?"

"He's too slow to run away with the money." Tobias smirks, looking too tired to deal with this shit.

"Ha, ha." Theo rolls his eyes. "Hilarious. Way to be a dick, T."

Loki chuffs. *"He really is."*

I step forward, sweat coating my palms. "Loki and I want in."

Tobias turns my way, raises his eyebrows, and crosses his arms. "What are you doing here?"

Theo shrinks back and disappears into the party. I'm on my own, but at least Jonas isn't here to argue.

I cross my fingers behind my back. "I'm just here to race. We have the buy-in."

He frowns, and his eyes narrow. "Get out of here."

"Really. And if I win, you can have your two grand buy-in back." I straighten. "I'd rather have your respect."

His eyes light up as he laughs. "Respect. What's that even worth?"

"For some people, it's worth a lot."

Tobias looks at Loki. A shadow of a doubt crosses his face, just for a moment. *That's right, cower in fear at your impending loss to my terrifying dragon.*

He blinks a few times. "A small Graytail who can't even evade trees, up against my Ruby? You don't stand a chance."

"Then you have no reason to turn my offer down."

He looks at me like I'm nothing more than dirt.

"You're in. Let's go." Tobias strides to his dragon with a cocky grin.

Sweatband Man crosses his arms. "We should all get—"

Tobias whips his head around and glares at him.

"We'll definitely beat Sweatband Man. His Brown looks overfed."

Loki cocks his head. *"Happy, though. You should bring me an extra sheep in the morning. My happiness is a top priority."*

I suppress a laugh and whisper, "If we win, I'll bring you two." Not that we'll tell Kristoffer. He monitors all the dragons and their calorie intakes. Loki's one-sheep-per-day diet is based on his weight and muscle mass, designed to keep him in optimum training form.

Sweatband Man shrinks back and walks over to his Brown.

Tobias waits patiently for Theo to cross the roof and then hands him a wad of cash. "Confirm the Goldwing patrols are out of range. We cut it too close last time."

Fortunately, the music drowns out my gulp.

The Goldwings are at the top of the food chain when it comes to rank. People expect our dragons to fly around the city, and we're allowed to fly anywhere, even in restricted airspace. As students of the military academy, we're allowed all the same perks—at least, when we're sent on missions. But racing? Totally illegal. Anyone supporting it gets fined, and participants risk being stripped of their dragon.

But if I don't infiltrate Tobias's inner circle before the third-years graduate, I'll lose Loki, anyway.

Theo approaches me as he pulls out his phone and looks through his apps. He keeps his voice low. "Markus, you know Tobias lives for racing, right?"

I hand over the cash. Damn, that hurts. But we'll win it back. "I don't think—"

"Yeah, I got that." He chuckles at his own joke.

Sweatband Man hands him the buy-in.

"We're gonna win." Loki nudges me. *"I'm faster than Derkomai, even if he doesn't know it."*

My head feels light, but I take a deep breath and blink the feeling off. "We'll win. You can bet on it." I climb onto Loki's back and buckle myself into the saddle.

"The second the dragons take off, you know I'll be betting on..." Theo clears his throat. "Well, I'm probably going to clean up tonight. Make sure you avoid the trees." His expression remains neutral.

I can't tell if he thinks we will win or we will fail miserably, but I doubt he's betting on me.

"We're about to knock the spots off the other dragons. They won't even see what's coming for them." Loki stretches his wings, sending out a breeze that ruffles some of the dancing partygoers. I bet they're enjoying the brief respite from the summer heat.

Tobias settles onto his dragon and buckles up. "We race out to Government Island and back. The first dragon over the island signals with fire. Make sure you fly under the radar."

"Got it." We're going to win. I hope. I put on my flight goggles.

Theo looks up from his phone. "We should be solid in six minutes based on their path. Line up."

I push aside my nerves. "How do you know?"

"Tracking." He taps his fancy phone. Tobias glares at him, and he turns his attention back to the glowing screen. I haven't heard of apps that track military movements. Another thing that's probably not legal.

Loki shuffles and paws against the roof. *"Five minutes now."* He looks down the row, sizing up our competitors: Tobias on Derkomai, Sweatband Man on a Brown, a woman on a Blue, and a man on a Green. *"They've got nothing on me."*

All five racing dragons are perched at the edge of the roof, eager to take flight and hungry for a win. The party is in full swing behind us, and the energy level keeps rising. Music pumps through the speakers. I have no idea how they haven't been caught. This rooftop is loud and bright, and we're basically a beacon at the top of the city.

Theo leans against the half-wall at the edge of the roof, safely between me and Tobias. His eyes are glued to the screen.

With a drink in her hand, Carina wanders over. I'm not surprised she isn't racing Goose tonight. Greens are brutal on the attack, but they don't have the stamina for long distances. With the flight distance to and from Dragild, and against Tobias's Ruby...

"Good luck, babe," she tells Tobias.

"Don't need it." Tobias glances at me, his eyes expressionless. "Signal the start."

Loki chuffs. *"Luck won't help Derkomai."*

I bite back my laugh as the Brown roars at the Blue. The Blue lets out a puff of fire and snaps back.

Carina blows Tobias a kiss and stands next to Theo. "Two minutes left."

Loki stretches his serpentine neck and flicks his gray tail. *"Are you nervous?"*

"Nope," I whisper back.

"Really? Because you're shaking."

I guess I am. I take a deep breath and settle into the saddle, getting comfortable between his shoulder blades. Just my future at Dragild on the line. No big deal.

"One minute," Theo calls out.

"It's okay to be nervous. Just don't let Tobias see. It's bad for my image."

I give Loki a pat before gripping the pommel.

Theo nudges Carina, and she holds up both hands. She gives Tobias a sly smile, and he winks in return. I face forward, focused on Loki. Focused on the race. We have one chance to win.

"Three, two, one, *go!*" Carina drops her arms and all five of our dragons take off into the sky. Deafening cheers erupt behind us, but they're quickly drowned out by the whips of the wings as we speed away.

My entire body feels light. My excitement, palpable. My energy, off the charts.

It's coming from Loki. From our bond.

He pushes his way through the group. My jaw clenches as Derkomai and the Brown squeeze us out.

"Fly up!" I nudge Loki and he lifts, putting us out of the crash zone. It costs us precious seconds, and Tobias pulls further ahead. I grip the pommel of the saddle hard and hang on tight.

The steel bridge casts a bright light across the dark Willamette River as Loki and I race toward it, keeping below the radar. Cars zoom along the interstate, but we're zooming faster. We're tied with the Brown for last place. Not the ideal spot, but with about twenty miles there and back, it's anyone's race.

Sweatband Man grins from his dragon's back, and the Brown jerks toward Loki's wing.

"Look out!" I shout.

Loki dives left while I cling to the pommel, and we dodge the other dragon. *"Not today."* He speeds up, flicking his gray tail at their snout. The Brown lets out a roar, and Loki chuffs.

And just like that, we're in fourth.

"Smooth moves!" I pat his neck.

Neighborhoods are dimly lit below us, with a couple of house lights on here and there. A few cars drive along, but for the most part, the streets are empty.

We're definitely below the radar, flying close to the dark shadows of the terrain that keep us camouflaged. We'd be plastered against a tree trunk by now without Loki's echolocation.

The Blue in front of us flies at a steady pace. Loki and I dive and speed up underneath them, skimming treetops and rustling the leaves. They're a shadow against the moonlight until we pass them and drift back up.

I glance at the rider, who frantically scrambles to push their dragon harder as we rise in front of them.

We're officially third. Derkomai and a Green are still in front of us, but we aren't even halfway through the race yet. We have plenty of time to overtake them.

Loki flaps harder as we approach the Columbia River. The sky fills with dragon fire, just for a moment. The first dragon hit the halfway point.

My stomach drops, but I shove the nerves down.

"We're less than a mile behind to the halfway point, and they still have to get back to the Tower." I lean forward. "We can still beat them."

He pushes his body to move faster, and it sends my stomach lurching. The pace is only slightly terrifying. Please, all that is good in the world, don't let me fall off. Thank goodness our saddles are made for high speeds.

"Don't get lost," Tobias shouts as he passes by us in the opposite direction, the Green at Derkomai's tail. "Or do!"

Fuck. Him.

Government Island's shoreline is directly below us. Only ten miles left. Loki makes a sharp turn, and we're officially halfway through. He speeds up on the turn, so no complaints from the peanut gallery.

The Green struggles to keep Derkomai's pace. This one flew too hard, too fast, too early.

We catch up quickly, only a dragon-length below them, close to the treetops. They drop from the sky directly toward us.

"Watch out!" I shout.

Loki jolts back to evade, but they get a direct hit on his wing with their back legs. Loki tucks it in as he roars, knocked out of the air.

I grip the pommel hard as we tumble downward. The ground rushes toward us, and all I can do is cling.

Loki throws out his wings and glides above the highway, straightening us out. White, red, and blue lights crawl across the bridge below us.

"Good save, Loki. Six miles left."

His chest heaves. He climbs into the sky and picks up speed, the fastest he's flown tonight. There's a metaphorical fire with every stroke of his wings. The level of power. The strength behind it. I can feel it through our bond, through our movement, through his body. A good kind of high.

We stick close to the treetops and pass stealthily underneath the Green and their rider this time. We clear their path and rise into the air in front of them, maintaining our momentum.

Derkomai and Tobias keep a quick pace, but Loki is quicker. We're gaining on them.

"This is it. Last few miles."

We surge forward, precious dragon-lengths closer to Tobias.

The air whips around us. I press into Loki's body, doing everything I can to cut our wind resistance.

We are so close Loki could snap Derkomai's tail with his jaws.

Loki flaps harder as we rush through the sky. The precious inches are ours.

Neck on neck, we finally match the Ruby. We're moving. We're flying, literally and figuratively. We're tied for first.

The Steel Bridge shines brightly below us. Only a mile of the race left.

"Go, Derkomai!" Tobias's harsh cheer drives his dragon harder.

"Come on, Loki."

Loki's muscles tense as his nose pulls in front. He pushes harder, and we inch ahead. We're going at full speed, and we're winning. It's inches, but we're winning.

The Park Avenue West Tower is within easy range, still lit up. Onlookers watch from the edge of the roof.

"You can do it." I cling tight as Loki's energy and enthusiasm flare through our connection.

Tobias's Ruby lets out a mighty roar, and they regain the inches we stole.

Loki lurches as he gives the flight his all.

We stay neck and neck with Tobias and Derkomai, rapidly approaching the tower.

"Three sheep in the morning!" My hands grip the pommel like my life depends on it. We just need another couple of feet.

There's no hope for Tobias.

The inches are ours. The win is within our grasp.

"This race is mine!" Loki pushes for the finish line.

Derkomai takes off like a shot with a burst of energy, crossing over the rooftop before us. He lets out a roar.

The partygoers cheer, drowning out the music.

Well, fuck.

We just lost.

5

Loki touches down on the roof of the Park Avenue West Tower and tucks in his wings. He huffs and paws at the roof. We're back to where we started. The volume of the party grows louder as scantily-clad onlookers swirl around Tobias and Derkomai, celebrating his win.

That should have been us. We came in second, but barely. It was a hell of a race. Loki was powerful. Strong. Borderline unstoppable. It was like Derkomai got a second wind at the end.

Tobias dismounts and grabs Carina, lifting her by the waist. She's probably a whole five-foot-zero and less than a hundred pounds soaking wet. She wraps her legs around him and kisses him like no one is watching. She looks happier than him, so she's probably going to score big later tonight.

I wish I could say the same about Amira right now. I wonder what she's up to...

My adrenaline level comes down a notch, and some of the tension drops. I wish I had some painkillers. The bruises all sting, both the literal and the figurative ones. Jonas really turned me into a punching bag in the food hall this morning. At least he's not here to see my defeat—though I'm sure he's going to hear about it the second Tobias returns to Dragild.

The Green lands behind us, completely exhausted.

I unstrap myself from the saddle and jump down. The solid ground is a relief. I turn back to Loki and scratch under his chin. "Good racing, bud."

"Not good enough." Loki shakes his white body.

I let go of my frustration, and Loki's feelings wash over me through our bond. Instead of a racing high, it's sadness and shame. The feelings take me back to the moment I first put on the collar, when the weight of his loss hung around us both. Not as intense, but still heavy.

"Sure, it wasn't quite good enough for the win, but we were right there. And you *just* healed up, bud. We had Capture the Flag yesterday and flew a hundred miles here today, and then you went top speed for twenty miles. You were a *badass*." The tightness in my chest eases, just a little.

The Blue from the race lands behind Loki, startling us both.

Loki's head drops and nudges my shoulder. *"I'm sorry we lost."*

"No way, bud. Don't worry. We'll figure something out."

Loki blinks his golden eyes at me. Yeah, I don't really believe myself either.

I rest my forehead against his scales. They're hard and rough, but they're also a comfort. We're in this together.

"Tobias coming up."

"Thanks," I whisper, turning around.

Tobias stands in front of me with a wad of cash and an obnoxious smirk on his face. Carina's arm is wrapped around his. Her beautiful hazel eyes study me from beneath her furrowed brows. He shoves the cash in his pocket and crosses his arms, forcing Carina to let go.

His dark eyes bore into me. "Well, you lost. Are you done with your nonsense?"

"We were barely a dragon snout behind you." I straighten and take a breath. I can't give in. "It was basically a tie."

Tobias glares at me as the crowd circles us, dancing and cheering him on. "Ask any racer. Any *real* racer. It doesn't matter if it's an inch or a hundred dragon-lengths. Winning is winning."

I know he isn't wrong, but we were *right there*. I can't just let this go. It's our place at Dragild on the line. "Yeah, but—"

"We're so done with your games, Markus. Get out of here, and *stay away from Amira*."

The music stops mid-beat, and the world goes—

Not silent. Shit.

Sirens fill the void, and everyone scrambles.

My eyes widen as adrenaline floods my body. The wails of the sirens get louder. We're getting busted for this. We're getting kicked out of school, and any hope for a military career is dead.

"The cops are mobilizing! Goldwings en route!" Theo shoves his phone into his pocket and rushes to a metal panel near the elevators, opening it so fast it slams against the wall. He jams a blue button down as the partygoers rush toward the open elevator door.

My feet won't move.

A couple of people cry out as they push their way forward, and I really don't blame them. This is a mess.

Tobias grabs Carina's waist and kisses her. "The Den's garage door will be open. Theo, you too. Wait them out."

Her face turns a ghostly white. "But Jonas isn't here."

"Get down there!" Tobias pushes them toward their dragons.

Theo and Carina mount and take off, skipping the buckles. Fools, the pair of them. They've learned nothing from Katie's accident yesterday.

The sirens blare louder. The cops can't reach us on the roof, but the Goldwings can.

"Stop standing around and get on!" Loki smacks me with his gray tail. Sharp pain shoots down my side, thanks to the bruises from this morning's fight. Loki winces. He would've felt that pain, too. *"Sorry."*

"It's Jonas's fault, from earlier." I take a deep breath and pull myself together.

All the other dragons took off already. Loki and Derkomai are the only two left.

The partygoers fight their way into the already-full elevator. Derkomai sticks close to Tobias, who rushes over to the doors.

"Fucking animals, let them down first." He pushes the crowd back from the door. It closes as the remaining people panic. They're drunk and terrified.

We can't just leave them up here to trample each other. We can help manage the crowd. We're sticking with Tobias and cracking his shell, even if it means getting arrested. Maybe I can win him over in the jail cell. At this point, there's nothing to lose.

Tobias's expression is strained, and if I thought he looked tired earlier, it has nothing on this.

"Aren't there stairs?" I ask as I rush to his side.

His eyes narrow, and he smacks the back of my head. "Get out of here."

"Ow!" I didn't deserve that. I rub my hand over the sting and wipe the scowl off my face.

"Yes, there are stairs, but it's thirty floors down and half of these people are shit-faced." The lights above the second elevator flash, and the doors open. "Ladies first. Get moving." Tobias shepherds another group as the sirens get louder. The doors close, and there are only eight people left. "Get out of here, Markus."

I get out of his way and climb onto Loki's back. I strap myself into the saddle and double-check the buckles are secure.

"Ready?" Loki dashes to the edge.

"We aren't leaving Tobias behind. This is our chance to win him over." I scan the ground from our bird's-eye view at the top of the tower. There aren't any lights flashing on the street below, but with how loud the sirens are now, the cop cars will cover the empty street soon. "Theo said the Goldwings are on their way. Are any dragons within range?"

"Not yet." Loki can find them with echolocation, but they'd know he pinged them since they can hear each others' frequency, so we're screwed either way.

The elevator doors slide open and Tobias ushers the last group in. Sirens blare from the ground as the cops park in front of the building, red and blue lights flashing. That settles it, then. We won't be joining Theo and Carina in the garage.

I'm hit by a wave of dread.

Loki jolts. *"Dragon to the north!"*

A large shadow moves through the clear, moonlit sky just past the bridge, and it definitely knows we're here. It's flying directly for us.

"Tobias, dragon alert!"

"Fuck!" Tobias shuts off the roof lights, pitching the entire rooftop into darkness.

My eyes struggle to adjust. I'm glad I'm already strapped in. "Get ready, Loki. How far are they?"

"A mile, tops. They're flying fast." He's jumpy with nerves.

So am I.

Tobias climbs onto Derkomai's back as the elevators close on the last group. "Which way?"

"Go south!" I push down my goggles.

Loki runs across the roof and leaps into the sky, and Derkomai follows. I grip the saddle's pommel as we speed up above Eighth Avenue. The fountain in the center of the empty park is still lit up, but the rest of the park is shrouded by trees. The sirens wail from the ground, and two cars follow our tails.

"This idea was objectively horrible."

"I'm aware, but you can berate me later." I glance behind us, and my stomach drops. The shadow is gaining on us. "Fly southwest."

Loki turns above Salmon Street and cuts across the tops of buildings, increasing our speed. We lose the cops within a few blocks.

I turn back to Tobias and Derkomai. They're barely a dragon-length away. My eyes widen.

"Behind you!" I shout to Tobias. The dragon rider chasing us has gained major ground. The moonlight reflects off their scales, and it's either an Orange or a Yellow, although the dragon isn't close enough to tell. Oranges are extremely agile, and Yellows are extremely energetic. Neither bodes well for us.

Tobias glances back quickly and faces forward, his expression hardened. "Turn down the highway."

We have to evade them. I turn forward and lean close to Loki. We pivot south and duck under the overpasses, blending in awkwardly with the cars driving along the highway. "Keep traffic's pace. We'll hide from their echolocation." I don't see a dragon shadow in the sky, although who knows how long that'll last.

A blue Ferrari convertible to our left honks, and the passenger waves. His hair is a greasy mess. "Sweet ride," he shouts.

That's very true. My entire body feels light, free, and ready to go. Ready to race.

"At least someone appreciates me," Loki says.

"I will appreciate you more when we aren't at risk of being caught and arrested."

"Well, whose fault is that?"

Mine. It's one hundred percent mine.

Red and blue lights flash to our right. A cop car hiding along the side drives onto the highway. The car's max speed is a hundred and fifty-five miles per hour, and we've been cruising along with traffic at seventy-five. Immediately, it's on our tails. They'll report our location to the Goldwings.

"Up!"

We rise, and Tobias and Derkomai follow. And there's the dragon and the Goldwing behind us, chasing at top speed. It's definitely yellow. Very, very yellow. Two more dragons follow from further behind, and all three are gaining on us. Shit.

Another cop car drives down the entrance ramp, and its flashing lights blind me. *And then there were two.* Double shit. Their sirens blare out, interrupting the night.

Loki already flew a hundred miles to Portland at high speed, plus another twenty miles racing at top speed. We've probably gone another twenty miles by now. This race against the police isn't sustainable. And there's no telling how Derkomai is feeling. I don't know how far he's flown today.

I nudge Loki with my heels. "Turn off at the next block. We'll evade the cops."

This still feels like a horrible idea, but I'm pretty sure I've had worse.

Loki turns north toward the dark buildings. They're just as malicious and unwelcoming as they were a couple of hours ago. Tobias and Derkomai keep pace, still a dragon-length behind us.

"Dive between those towers and do some evasive maneuvers," Tobias shouts. "We need to find cover."

I hold tight to the pommel as Loki dives toward the ground. Derkomai sticks with us as we dodge and weave through the streets. The streetlights throw a pale glow over the road as we zoom above the asphalt and stay well below the line of rooftops.

Our plan has a glaring flaw: the other rider may or may not know where we are, but we definitely don't know where they are.

A pharmacy glows brightly at the street corner. We fly past it, avoiding the trees spread along the sidewalk.

I twist back as the wind roars in my ears. "Tobias, parking garage," I shout. I don't know if he hears, but he gives me a thumbs-up.

Loki slows down and lands with a jolt. I press my chest flat against his body. He tucks in his wings and ducks his head as he squeezes into the parking garage, knocking into the yellow bar denoting eleven feet of clearance. Cars and trucks take up the front spaces, but the lights are low and there aren't any people around.

Derkomai crouches to fit as they follow us in. Tobias's leather scrapes against the ceiling, the sound jarring against the quiet.

Holy shit, this is ridiculous. So ridiculous. But we're here, and we're hiding out of sight. The sirens' wails sound distant, broken up by a dragon roar. Hell, my heartbeat is louder at this point. We have a minute to regroup and figure this out.

I take a deep breath, and then another. Exhaustion hits in a wave, and I'm not sure if it's my own body or the bond trying to pull me under.

Loki tucks himself safely against the back wall. I unstrap myself from the saddle and slide down to the ground. "Squeeze in a short nap, bud. You deserve it."

He yawns, curls his tail around him, and closes his eyes. *Let's not do that again.*

I would also like to not do that again. "I don't see any cameras. We've probably got a half hour."

Tobias slides down and hits the ground with a thud. "Get some sleep, D." He strokes his dragon's wing and receives a deep purr in response. His eyes soften as he takes in his dragon's form, curled up and exhausted against the back wall. Tobias towers over everyone at six-foot-five. He could be a lineman for the Seattle Seahawks. But even he looks tiny next to his Ruby.

I lean against the wall between the dragons and slide down

slowly, grateful for the insulated leather against the cold concrete. The wall is the only thing holding me up right now.

"Loki's spent." I already hear his soft, familiar snores. "How's Derkomai?"

"He's flown harder." Tobias sits next to me and leans back with a sigh. "You really are a dumbass."

"Because I didn't leave you to fend for yourself?" I cross my arms when he doesn't respond. "Well, I didn't, and we're here, so deal with it."

He's such a dick.

I focus on Loki's steady breathing. It's soothing after all the crazy.

Flashing red and blue lights zoom past. We're tucked far back, so the cops can't see us unless they slow down. I close my eyes and lean back, releasing the tension from my shoulders.

"You raced like you've done it before. A fucking *Graytail*." Tobias's tone betrays his disbelief. "Were you playing me?"

"No. Loki was just cleared to fly before Capture the Flag. He loves flying fast. It..." I'm not sure how exactly to describe the feelings through our bond. "It was really amazing, feeling his energy. It was like we were unstoppable. Unbreakable. Completely free."

"Racer's high. I live for it." Tobias hums. "You're the last person I would have expected to stay behind." Tobias's tone is open and actually sort of friendly. He's never used it around me—not that he speaks much when I'm around.

This is not the time for me to make some snarky quip. This is the time to be honest. I can still turn this around. I can still earn his respect.

"It looked like you could use a sidekick, with Jonas not there."

He leaves me hanging in silence. Maybe not.

I adjust my body against the wall. "I don't get why you dislike me. I didn't do anything to you."

He rolls his eyes. "I'd have to care about you to dislike you."

Ouch. Shots fired. "Why are you such a jerk?"

"Amira deserves the best, and you already proved you aren't good enough."

"How? You barely know me." I probably sound like a child, but fuck if I care.

"Did you put Amira first during Capture the Flag? Because the police were on their goddamn way to find a Black woman standing next to a dead body. Black riders have been arrested and stripped of their dragons in the past, without cause. What if she lost Tiger and her place at Dragild? Or worse, if she was the next dead body?" His voice is choked up, matching his pained expression. "You did nothing to get her out of the situation. That tells me everything I need to know."

His shots were nothing. This was a bloody grenade. I can't even keep my thoughts straight. During Capture the Flag... My arms were wrapped around her. Surely, she would have been fine tucked against me. Surely, a woman providing comfort and snuggling into my body wouldn't be killed just because she's Black. I get it, she's his baby sister, but...

"She's a dragon rider on a Ruby, and she definitely doesn't need you babying her." I keep my tone even despite the tightening in my chest. "She's the top of our class, and she can bloody well make her own choices."

He looks away, settles back against the wall, and closes his eyes. "She deserves someone who will look out for her."

What the hell? Are you kidding me right now? I can't stop the racism she faces, but I always have my girl's back. Wrapping her wrist after she punched that asshole out in the courtyard, holding her tight after she spent an hour in the commandant's office...

I laugh because I just can't help it. This is so stupid.

He stares at me like I've grown a second head. No, I've just grown a set of balls.

"If she wants me around, I'm staying around. She's probably going to kill both of us after our stunt tonight."

His eyebrows raise. "I'm safe. Family sticks together."

"Well, if she wants me around, I'm sticking with her, too, so deal with it."

He studies me, and I stare right back at him. I won't bend on this.

He leans against the wall and closes his eyes.

Point for Markus. "You know I really like her, right? And Loki *loves* her. Since the *moment* he met her."

Tobias frowns, but it's not as deep as it usually is. "That was never a question."

"*Amira's the best.*" Loki watches me a moment more before closing his eyes again.

Yeah, she definitely is.

"Ｗe shouldn't stick around much longer." My voice stirs the dragons. "How much more time does Derkomai need?"

The dragons have had twenty minutes to nap. Tobias kept his eyes closed the whole time, but his unsteady breathing meant he was faking sleep. Cops only passed by once, their lights flashing through the darkness.

Tobias doesn't move. "Five more minutes."

"*Me too.*" Loki adjusts his body a bit, scooching closer to me.

"Should we go back to the Den?" Is it even safe? Will Carina and Theo still be there?

He chews on the inside of his cheek, the same way Amira does, and his usual confidence is missing. "At this point, we should head back to Dragild. The Den will be on lockdown until it's clear."

"Got it." The roof was crazy. The entire scene plays over and over in my head. "What was the blue button Theo pressed?"

"The panic button. It lets the door guard know we're heading down fast. To be ready." He sighs. "We're gonna have to take a racing hiatus. Lay low and let things cool down. This is the second time in a row we were almost busted."

"No fair. We only got to race once." Loki huffs a sigh.

My dragon is an adrenaline junkie. We're going to talk about this later.

"When did you start racing?" I readjust against the concrete wall and try to get comfortable. I'm eager to get out of here.

"The day I broke Derkomai." He wears a far-off look with a weak smile. "I've spent my entire life trapped by society and politics. But racing?" He looks straight at me. "It was pure freedom. A pure rush. I've been chasing the feeling ever since."

The level of openness throws me. I choke on a response.

"Let's get out of here." Tobias stands up, and that's the end of that.

We guide the dragons out to the street. Loki shakes out his body and stretches with relief, raising his neck and pushing back his shoulders until he towers over me.

It's a hundred miles back, and Loki's still tired. His exhaustion comes through our bond. He's definitely going to sleep well tonight. I will, too.

I climb up, buckle in, and secure my flight goggles. "We'll stay below the rooftops and head north. That will keep us below the radar and out of sight of the other dragons."

We take off, keeping a slower pace as we fly close to the street. Almost every building's window is dark at this point, contrasted by the dim glow of the streetlights. Other than the soft beat of our dragons' wings, the world is silent.

A shadow crosses the moon above us.

I blink a few times. Are my tired eyes playing tricks on me? "Loki, did you see that?"

"See what?"

I twist around. "Tobias, did you see the shadow?" He shakes his head. I must have imagined it.

But what if I didn't?

"Head to the riverfront," Tobias says. He leans forward, focusing on the air in front of him. We turn east toward the river and pick up the pace.

The shadow cuts above us again. It's definitely another dragon.

"I saw it this time." Loki speeds up, flapping harder and faster. *"Their ping just hit us. They know we're here."*

The wind rushes past my ears. We break free of the buildings, finally along the riverfront. Our dragons fly north over the river, keeping close to the seawall. The waves of the Willamette compete softly with the steady beats of our dragons' wings. The moonlight glitters on the water.

Engines rev in the distance, cutting into the quiet.

The top floor of one of Portland's fancy hotels lights the sky to our left. The shadow of the dragon swoops in front of the building, and my stomach lurches. It disappears quickly.

"Speed up!" Tobias shouts.

The metal trusses of the Hawthorne Bridge are lit up, a shining beacon against the night. The bridge rises at least two dragon-lengths above the water, so we clear it easily.

Engines rumble from on top of the bridge behind us. I risk the glance back. White lights race across the deck of the bridge, heading toward the west side. In front of us, purple lights illuminate the concrete piers of the Morrison Bridge. We race above the river toward it. The white lights chase us via the west side, and the roar of the engines gets louder as the lights accelerate north. It's a motorcycle gang.

The shadow dragon reappears against the moonlight above us. It can definitely see us thanks to the light of the bridge.

I twist back. "Tobias, look out!"

He flattens against Derkomai as we zip underneath the bridge.

The shadow dragon swoops down and knocks against Derkomai's body with its front legs.

The Ruby tucks his wings and falls sideways into the water. Tobias is flipped underneath the waves.

Head above water, Derkomai struggles to right himself. He's flailing on his back and getting nowhere.

Why isn't Tobias popping up?

Shit, shit, shit. He's probably trapped in the saddle, and the weight is preventing Derkomai from righting himself.

"Go back!" I shout.

Loki turns around and hovers close to Derkomai. I unbuckle

myself from the saddle and jump into the frigid water. The shock of the cold stuns me.

I take a deep breath and dive below the Ruby's body. Derkomai knocks me away with his flailing wings, not letting me close. I come back up for air and dive again, fighting my way down beneath him.

Tobias pulls against the buckles, but he's struggling to grip them as Derkomai jerks in the water.

He's panicking. They're both panicking, thanks to the bond.

I grab onto the buckles and we both pull hard, releasing them. Tobias pushes away from Derkomai, creating space for me to grab him. I kick my way to the surface, pulling Tobias with me.

My lungs burn as we break through to the air.

Tobias coughs and sputters water, but he's up. We're up.

"Breathe, Tobias."

He's hyperventilating, furiously splashing water as he keeps himself afloat. The weight of the wet clothes pulls both of us down.

"Tobias!"

He looks at me, his eyes wide with panic.

"Breathe. Calm thoughts. Push the calm on Derkomai."

Tobias takes a couple of deep breaths, fighting the panic of his dragon. He closes his eyes, keeps breathing and concentrating, and soon enough he's mostly calm as he treads water. Derkomai slowly rights himself, and the splashing subsides.

I swim toward the shore as they follow. Lapping waves compete with the sound of motors.

Loki flies down and wraps my arms with his toes. He lifts me, keeping his body well above the water. His wings push air down toward me, and my body shivers from the cold. He drops me on the shore next to Battleship Oregon Memorial, and relief washes over me as my feet hit the ground.

My awesome dragon flies back over the water. He scoops Tobias up and drops him next to me with a thud. Tobias's black hair is pressed flat thanks to our impromptu swimming session. His five-o'clock shadow might as well be called scruff at this point. He pants, catching his breath. He coughs a few more times, expelling the last of the water.

Derkomai climbs slowly up the seawall, talons scraping against the metal. He shakes his body and flaps his wings, sending droplets of water and frigid air my way.

I'm sopping wet from my hair to my boots. I'm tired. My dragon is tired. This is nonsense.

We are never coming back to Portland.

Loki lands nearby in the grass.

Motorcycle engines rev as the gang circles us. They all cut to a soft purr and turn off, and the riders shut off their headlights. At least they aren't blinding me anymore.

Seven bikes. Nine bikers. This is definitely a gang.

The bikers wear full leathers, all in black, but their bikes and helmets are a rainbow of colors. Some have tattoos snaking down their wrists and up their necks, peeking out from their leathers. As they pull off their helmets, they reveal a variety of skin tones and hair colors. At least their gang doesn't discriminate.

No collars. None of them are dragon riders.

Their expressions range from pissed to really pissed. Frowns, scowls, glares, flushed skin, clenching fists... This is not looking good for us.

The shadow dragon appears above the buildings and darts down toward us. Blue flames fill the sky and send out a wave of heat. The dragon is a giant Black Clubtail, bigger than the one I failed to break. The blue-tipped scales and two collars glimmer in the light of the memorial. They land in the grass and snap their jaws at us as their rider releases the saddle's buckles.

The motorcyclists all dismount. A couple of them plant their feet wide, while others pull out guns and point them in our direction. A semi-automatic rifle, military issue, points directly at me from three feet away. I gulp. My head feels light, and my heartbeat pounds in my ears. My wet boots squeak as my weight shifts.

Tobias focuses on the dragon rider. His nostrils flare, and the vein in his neck looks like it's about to pop.

"Do you know them?" I whisper to Tobias.

He puffs his chest and straightens, adding another inch to his height. "Markus, meet the Jonjung clan."

6

The Jonjung clan has us surrounded with their colorful bikes, and they don't look friendly.

The Black Clubtail snaps her jaws our way and glares at Derkomai. They're eyeing each other, but the Ruby just got knocked into the water by the snarling Black ten minutes ago, so I'm pretty sure we know who'd win. I take a step back.

"She's in a bad mood." Loki flutters his wings before tucking them back in, visibly uncomfortable. *"Do you think she's hangry? Maybe she needs an extra sheep."*

I don't think a snack is going to fix this.

"Tobias." The dragon rider hops down with a thud and casually struts our way. He's in black leather, like the rest of us. His narrow, angular eyes glint in the light of the memorial. Black hair frames his flat face and high, square cheekbones. His flat nose looks like it's been broken before.

"Ren." Tobias's frown is deeper than any he's aimed my way. "I see Yongwang is in fine form."

"No Jonas tonight?"

"Meet Markus," Tobias says. "He's filling in."

Ren inspects me. "No armor?"

"He's a first-year." Tobias crosses his arms. "What can we do for you?"

"I thought we came to an agreement." Ren crosses his arms, mirroring Tobias. "The east side of the Willamette is ours. You stay on the west side, and everyone is happy."

Tobias tilts his head. "Unless we're flying above it to another destination."

Ren clenches his jaw. "And where exactly were you going?"

"Government Island. Not on the east side. In fact, half a mile north of the east side."

The gang chatters angrily, guns click, and goosebumps cover my body. My wet boots squeak as I shift my weight. One of the bikers steps forward and points a gun directly at Tobias. Ren lifts his hand, and the biker immediately steps back, but his gun is still raised.

"I don't think they agree with the technicality."

No, Loki, I don't think so either. I glance his way, but he doesn't take his eyes off Yongwang. She snaps toward Derkomai.

I'm glad I don't have to say anything. My mouth is bone dry, unlike my clothes.

Ren curls his fists. "The entire goddamn police force was swarming our streets thanks to you and your goddamn race tonight."

Tobias raises his eyebrows and tries to play it cool, but the vein pulses on his neck. "They swarm every night thanks to the shit you've got going on."

This might be news for the commandant. It's definitely news to me.

Based on Ren's deep scowl, he isn't here for the snarky tone. "We had a shipment coming in from the docks." He steps forward and straightens, but his height barely reaches Tobias's nose. "The entire operation was almost busted thanks to your dumb ass."

"Almost." Tobias shrugs, but his expression is as cold as ice. "But it wasn't. Clearly, it's fine."

"Only because the warehouse is right there! It was dumb luck we were able to delay the truck." Ren's voice rises. "Your stunt almost cost us millions."

Truck? Millions? This is definitely news for the commandant, and it might be the information that keeps me at Dragild.

Tobias stares him down, unflinching. "*Almost* still being the operative word. Nothing to justify all this." Tobias waves one hand toward the bikers and stops at the pointed gun. His other hand is closed in a fist at his side.

Loki takes a step back. His nervous energy climbs through our bond.

I ball my fists, but they won't be worth much against the guns. I hope their aim is as bad as Tobias's. If they shoot like Jonas...

"You know what? Fuck it. The cops are still around, and we don't need any more shit tonight." Ren drops his arms and jabs a finger at Tobias's chest. "I'll see you in the Cascades four days from now. Prepare to have your pathetic ass handed to you."

Derkomai snaps his jaws at Yongwang, and she roars in response.

"I don't lose." Tobias's eyes laser-focus on his target, his fists still clenched. "Definitely not to you."

"Yeah?" Ren laughs. "Well, your Ruby's going to need more than a little boost to keep up this time." He turns back to the gang. "Let's go."

Ren mounts Yongwang and takes off. The motorcyclists put their helmets back on, start their engines, and ride off along the river.

When the sound of their motors is replaced by the waves crashing against the seawall, Tobias lets out a deep breath. He loosens his fists, unclenches his jaw, and places his hand on Derkomai's leg.

Loki stomps his feet and shoots a small puff of fire. *We showed them who's boss.*

Sure, Loki. You're utterly terrifying. Especially since Graytails are known for being docile and adaptable. I chuckle. "It was all you, bud."

I glance at the bridge, relieved the deck is still empty. I'd like to avoid a repeat. "What was that all about?"

"Long story." Tobias turns back to Derkomai and mounts quickly. "I'll tell you later. Let's get back to Dragild."

Flapping wings invade the quiet as the Black swoops down out of nowhere.

"He's back!" Loki cries, panicked.

Ren's laugh rings out, and Yongwang shoots blue flames across the river. The heat hits me from at least three dragon-lengths away, and a chill runs down my spine. I wipe my sweaty palms against my pants as Ren and his dragon fly off again, heading east across the river.

"Shit, he's luring the cops. Come on." Tobias takes off.

I mount Loki and buckle into the saddle. We lift off and head north, flying close to Tobias and Derkomai. We aren't taking any more chances.

Loki's pings don't find any other dragons in the darkness, but that doesn't mean they aren't staying below the radar. At this point, the beat of his wings is music to my ears. It will be such a relief to get back.

"Seriously, what was that all about?" I ask Tobias.

"It's a long story."

"Well, we have a hundred miles back to the school, so there's plenty of time to tell it."

"I'll lose my voice shouting it at you, dumbass."

I can't tell if he's rolling his eyes, but I'd be willing to bet on it. "Then give me the highlights," I shout back.

"A lucrative business deal between our clans went up in flames." Tobias faces forward, and that's the end of that.

L oki and Derkomai land at the mouth of Dragild's dragon cave and tuck in their tired wings. Tobias and I release ourselves from the saddles. My leathers are stiff after their full immersion in the water. We're dry thanks to the hour-long flight, but it was definitely cold up there. Even the heat radiating from Loki wasn't enough to keep me warm after the swim in the river.

Loki's body releases the tension he's been holding since we took off. I hop down, thankful to be back on solid ground where no one is trying to kill me.

Well, Amira's somewhere around campus. She's not going to be happy when she hears what happened...

Loki nudges me. *"I'm hungry."*

"Yeah, I bet you are." I place my hand on his nose. "We've flown over two hundred fifty miles today."

Tobias slides down Derkomai's leg, and we head straight for the pen in the center of the cave. The sheep bleat louder than usual and push to the center of the pen, probably because Derkomai keeps shooting puffs of smoke at them. A bunch of them aren't sheared yet, so a new shipment must have come in this afternoon from one of the local farms.

"Quit playing with your food, D." Tobias leans against the pen as Derkomai gobbles down his midnight snack.

As soon as Loki is done, we head to his stall. I pull off the saddle and hang it by the door. His white scales shine with a hint of blue under the bioluminescent orbs, and I check for any damage after the crazy night we had. A couple of scales are loose and fall out easily, so I add them to the stack for my armor before hosing him down. I look over his wings too. The jagged scar through the membrane actually looks pretty cool now that it's fully healed. He's right; I've been worried about it for nothing.

"Enough excitement for your daredevil heart?" I ask.

Loki yawns and curls up in the corner, wrapping his gray tail around his body. *"For now."*

"Good." I chuckle. "Get some sleep. We've got flight practice tomorrow."

He doesn't respond; he's already snoring. I step out into the hall and lock the door behind me.

"Ready?" Tobias growls.

I jump back, and my face heats by a hundred degrees. I figured he went back to the dorms. Nope, Tobias is leaning against the wall with a grin. Wait, worse. His eyes are crinkled. He's silently laughing at me.

Shake it off, Markus.

"Yeah. Loki's already passed out."

He straightens, and we aim for the mouth of the cave. Our slow pace and the steady rhythm of our echoing steps are a relief after this insane day.

"D's out, too," Tobias says. "He'll probably sleep all morning."

"I might do the same. It sounds like a great idea."

He laughs. "Yeah, it does. Maybe I will, too. Class doesn't matter much now that we've got two weeks left, and I'll be in Portland after graduation anyway."

"I thought Goldwing posts were assigned at the ceremony?" With over seven hundred military bases and a dozen dragon-riding schools around the world, he could be sent anywhere.

He shrugs. "My parents were at the Portland Air Base until they retired."

We cross the courtyard and enter the school. The halls are silent except for our footsteps. At the base of the stone stairs leading to the dorms, Tobias turns my way. "Want to join us for a beer? I'm sure everyone is back by now."

My eyes widen. Holy shit, I did the thing. Respect actually earned. I blink off the surprise and school my expression. "Sure. Sounds good."

We climb three flights and enter the third-year lounge. It's twice as large as the first-year common room, even though their class only has two-thirds the number of students. The stone walls and ceiling are white, but they're covered in painted dragon shadows. The furniture is the same black leather and stainless steel we have everywhere else, but there are gray blankets and pillows in a dozen different fabrics and textures all over the place. White lights hang around the edge of the ceiling, and giant potted plants grow from black pots in the corners. No wonder they banned the first and second-years. We'd never leave.

The lounge is vibrant and full of energy. It's a continuation of the party on the roof, except everyone's a dragon rider dressed in black. Empty beer bottles and dime bags litter the tables. Carina dances happily in the center of the room with a trio of third-years. Harper and Malcolm are making out on a couch against the wall. Theo focuses on the tablet in his lap, just like he always does when he studies with me and Amira in the library. Jonas has a beat-up electric guitar in his hands, and he's strumming away, filling the lounge with punk rock. The amp is covered in random stickers from eighties grunge bands.

I shove my hands in my pockets. I'm not supposed to be here, but if Tobias invited me...

Tobias cracks his knuckles, walks directly to Jonas, and places his hand on the neck of the guitar, cutting the music off immediately. Jonas leans away, his posture rigid.

All eyes in the room turn their way.

"Where the fuck were you tonight?" Tobias's tone sends a shudder through me. I'm glad it's not directed my way.

"I was training with Professor Schloss before meeting up with Amira. I came up to the lounge when she went back to her room." Jonas puts his guitar down and straightens, only an inch shorter than Tobias. "You know how she..."

How she *what?* Why was she with him all evening? Why couldn't he have raced with us instead?

Jonas sways a bit, clearly buzzed. "We've raced two years without problems, T. Then we get hit back-to-back like this?"

This is not a conversation I want to miss. I sit on the lounge chair closest to them.

In silence, Tobias glares around the room. A couple of people leave, and the rest pretend to go back to whatever they were doing, but they still send glances toward the pair.

Carina turns on music. Her dancing resumes, although she lost a couple of her dance partners. I'm not about to let her distract me.

Tobias lowers his voice. Between his new volume and the music, I can't hear their conversation, but I do manage to make out *Jon-jung* and *truck*.

"Get back to your own lounge, first-year," Malcolm says from the comfort of the couch across the room. He laughs as Harper rolls her eyes.

I cross my arms.

"He's fine. He's with me." Tobias waves him off and goes back to his conversation with Jonas. It's getting heated, and neither of them is backing down.

Malcolm straightens on the couch. "We made an exception for Amira since she's your sister, but *Markus?*" That got the whole room's attention. Everyone turns his way. "He rides a Graytail like Benny used to. Come on."

Harper narrows her eyes and smacks his arm. She's awesome. I mouth *thanks* her way, and she smiles back. It's a sad smile, though.

"Agreed." Jonas crosses his arms, a frown etched into his face and his posture stiff. "Benny named his dragon after an animal, like the girls. At least Markus went with a god, but he's not worth keeping around either."

Shots fired. What did I ever do to him?

Oh, right. That bruise on his cheek is from my fist this morning. Well, he also got some good hits on me, so he can't be too sour.

Tobias taps his foot. He's losing patience, and I don't imagine he's used to being questioned. Especially not by his right-hand man.

"You guys are assholes." Harper's lips press into a thin white line. "Benny and Stallion *died*, and you still can't stop dragging him."

"Come on, babe." Malcolm shifts back on the couch. His tone is obnoxious. "This is why you shouldn't get attached, especially not to the weak ones. Benny didn't stand a chance."

"Don't make me reconsider my attachment to you," Harper snaps.

"Would y'all just calm down?" Tobias heavily punctuates the end of that sentence. "Markus is staying. End of story."

"Why'd you bring him?" Jonas glances at me.

"Because this fucking first-year on his fucking Graytail saved my ass while you were busy getting shit-faced." Tobias doesn't look my way, but his tone leaves no room for arguments.

And just like that, everyone goes back to their business. Maybe for real this time.

Tobias and Jonas continue their conversation, too low for me to hear.

I lean back in the chair and cross my ankle over my knee. Yep, I'm staying. Take that, Malcolm.

Harper pats Malcolm's leg, rises slowly, and meanders over to me as his gaze follows her. She sits on the arm of my chair, leans close to me, and keeps her voice low. "You don't know what you're messing with."

"I'm fine. Thanks, though."

She cocks her head to the side. "Blink twice if you're being held against your will."

My laughter turns heads. Oops.

She smiles gingerly. "Be careful, Markus. Don't do anything stupid."

Too late for that.

Harper wanders down the hall toward her room, leaving Malcolm behind. He slinks out awkwardly down the opposite hall. They're soon followed by the rest of the third-years, who quietly exit the lounge. Party's over.

Only four of us are left. Jonas picks up his guitar and settles back onto the lounge chair. Carina turns off the music and hugs Tobias from behind. She's tiny next to him, a foot and a half shorter. "I'm glad you're back, baby. You okay?"

"Am I okay?" His eyebrows raise, but he turns around and lifts her up. "I'm fucking exhausted."

She wraps her legs around his waist and rubs his shoulders. "You do look tired. Let's go to my room, and you can give me a massage."

He smirks and walks toward the dorms while Carina clings to him. At the threshold of the hallway, he turns back toward me. "Grab anything from the fridge. Thanks for—"

The door of the lounge flies open, and Amira rushes in. Her expression screams bloody murder. "Where have you been, Tobias? Dad's been blowing up my phone all night."

My body rejoices and recoils at the same time, and it throws my stomach into a lurch.

Tobias carefully sets Carina down and faces Amira.

"I'm fine, Mia. Glad to know you love me enough to worry." Tobias hugs her briefly, a grin on his face. "I'll call him tomorrow. My phone took a dive."

Her exquisite eyes widen as her dark lashes flutter. "How did that happen?"

"Ask Markus. He saved my sorry ass. He doesn't have anything better to do." He chuckles and nods toward me.

Amira turns my way, her expression unreadable. She blinks a few times before turning back to Tobias, but he's wrapped his arm around Carina and they're walking down the hall.

"Goodnight, baby sister."

"Have fun," Carina calls back with a laugh. They close the door behind them.

Looks like I'm being spared. Tension drops from my shoulders.

Jonas slows his strumming, shifting the melody. "Sticking around this time, Amira?"

She bites her lip, glances between us, and takes a deep breath. "Sure."

He smiles and starts a cover of a song that just came out last year. I don't remember the lyrics, but I'm pretty sure one of the lines is *burn for you*. I'd like to burn that stupid guitar right now.

"Want a drink?" I ask, rising from the couch.

She nods and follows me to the kitchenette, a frown on her gorgeous face.

I want to kiss that frown away and make her forget whatever has her worried. Instead, I open the fridge. It's way better stocked than the one in our common room. "What can I grab for you?"

Amira lifts herself onto the granite counter. "Anything cold."

It's a fridge. Everything's cold. That's a trap I'm not about to fall into. I think back to all the gym sessions I've glued myself to her side, our study sessions, the meals I've eaten with her... she always carries a reusable water bottle around. She must have forgotten it, rushing up to scold Tobias.

"So now my brother likes you." Amira crosses her long, leather-wrapped legs. "He doesn't generally like people."

"Well, I'm a generally likable guy." I grab a couple of beers and set them on the counter. Handing her a bottle of water right now would be pretty lame, and she'd be annoyed by the waste of plastic. "I'm pretty great, you know. You like me."

"Sure, Markus." She chuckles. "You're so damn cocky. You and my brother are a perfect match."

I cage her lightly with my arms and lean in close, enjoying the hint of vanilla. "I know you love your brother, so I'm going to take that as a compliment."

She laughs, and it's halfway to a snort. "You do that."

It physically hurts to leave her space, but I push myself away. I dig through the drawers until I find a bottle opener. "Did you have a good night?"

"It was fine. I learned how to shoot a rifle." She takes the bottle from my hand and sips. "What about you?"

Jealousy pricks at me. Jonas has been in her space all evening, up close and personal. His music carries our way.

I sit on the counter next to her. "Well, I can honestly say I've had better."

"What happened?"

"Just a bunch of shenanigans. Usual run-of-the-mill stuff for your brother, I think."

Jonas stops playing. "Coming back out?"

"In a minute." Amira glances toward the doorway. "Do you want anything?"

He grunts something unintelligible and resumes the song. Guess not. I definitely don't feel like sticking around with him, but if Amira is here...

She bites the inside of her cheek. "What actually happened with Tobias tonight?"

"You heard him. I saved your brother's sorry ass." I grin; this is going to drive her crazy. She'll be dying to know, and I'll have her all to myself.

"From what?" She studies me. "There's more to it."

I pull her box braids over her shoulder and lean close. "Maybe, maybe not," I whisper into her ear. "I'll leave my door unlocked, just in case you want to find out."

I finish my beer, hop down from the counter, and go back to my dorm room.

With her, it's always a waiting game.

Fluffing my pillows on my bed, I settle in and prop my dragon warfare book against my thighs. At least it's more interesting than the physiology, history, or ethics books. All three of those are perched on the shelf above the freshly cleaned desk in my now-tidy bedroom.

Hope is a dangerous thing.

Footsteps approach from the hallway. My heart beats faster.

Amira enters my room and quietly pushes the door closed behind her. She leans her shoulder against it, keeping her distance. Her orange nightshirt flutters before settling at her knees. "What really happened with Tobias?"

I let out a breath. Straight to the point. All things considered, I'm pleased she didn't hang around with Jonas instead. I gesture to the end of the bed and set my book on the nightstand, raking my hand through my hair. She doesn't move, but her alluring amber eyes don't break our gaze.

"I'm assuming you knew tonight was a race night?" I ask.

She nods once but says nothing.

"When we got back to the Tower, the police busted up the party. Your brother and I had a fun ride through the city and accidentally took a bath in the river." I rise from the bed and walk over to her, stopping an arm's length away. "In the end, he decided I'm not that bad."

Her gaze wanders along my bare chest down to my gray sweatpants. My abs seem to have distracted her. All the gym time and flight practice were worth it.

She looks up again, and her eyes narrow. "That can't be it."

If Tobias didn't tell her about the gang surrounding us or their delayed shipment... should I tell her? Will I lose his respect if I do? I definitely need to share that tidbit with the commandant, though.

She opens her mouth, closes it again, and shakes her head. "You're a shitty liar."

I blink, not sure how to react to that. "Definitely happened. I was there. You can go ask him if you want." I lean a little closer. "Or you can stay here."

"Your room is a mess," she says.

"If that's what you're thinking about, I'm doing something wrong."

Hints of her vanilla-scented lotion lure me in. Decisively and deliciously Amira. Her baggy nightshirt hides her form, but I memorized it the day we met. Dream about it at night. I've watched all year as her arms and legs gained muscles. As her breasts shrank while her exquisite ass rounded out from all those squats. The physical changes embody her dedication, and it's sexy as fuck.

My cock hardens, desperate to please her. I want to trace her curves, feel her touch, and explore every last inch of her with every last inch of me. Considering sweats don't hide much, she can see the effect she has.

She raises her eyebrows and crosses her arms, looking quite amused as she leans against the door. "You need a shower."

Laughing, I take a step closer, entering her space. I trace my hand along the dragon tattoos on her arms, following the inky path up to her neck. "Want to join me?"

She bites her lip. It's not a no.

Give me the green light, Amira.

My heart beats so fast, I'm convinced it's going to fly out of my chest. As I cup her chin and run my other hand along her spine, she shivers. Electricity sizzles between us.

She swallows, and her lips part. Her fingers find the waistband of my sweatpants, and she pulls me toward her, closing the distance between us. She leans against me, and her nipples harden beneath her thin nightshirt.

I remember to breathe. Not much else comes to mind.

She smirks. I want nothing more than to kiss that smirk off her face. My entire body craves her, and she knows it.

Her captivating amber eyes darken, pulling me deeper into her orbit. She's breathing harder, releasing hints of peppermint. But she isn't moving, and I don't want to rush her.

I run my hand along her spine as I grip the door handle with the other, desperate for something to hold. I resist the urge to take her body against the door, press myself into her, and find sweet relief tasting every inch of her. Her pouty lips, her graceful neck, her sharp collarbone...

Amira bites the inside of her cheek, her expression uncertain. She places her hands on the nape of my neck, and my body tenses. It's maddening, but I don't move. Don't breathe.

"I'm all yours," I whisper.

I am so fucking gone for this girl.

Her mouth crashes against mine. Her soft lips exceed every facet of my imagination. As our tongues meet, she lets out a soft mewl that drives me wild. I want to hear the sounds she makes as her body sings with pleasure. I want to hear her scream my name.

She buries her hands in my hair. I drag mine down her body and grip her thighs. Her legs wrap around my waist as I lift her against the door, putting her at the perfect angle to begin my exploration.

I want to tear off her awful nightshirt, run my fingers along her body, and learn exactly how soft she feels beneath my calloused hands.

A layer of urgency coats her kisses as our tongues collide. To my delight, she doesn't yield to my increased pressure against her lips. She pushes back with needy thrusts, heightening my desire.

I give her swollen lips one last kiss before nudging her cheek and kissing down her neck. Her hands tighten in my hair as she pants, eyes closed, jaw slack. I gently nip and suck as she grinds against me, searching for pressure. Her underwear is soaked through, and her wetness presses against my stomach, all for me.

She whines when I adjust her body against me, but I need her at a better angle. I trace her folds through the panties until she lets out a gasp. My thumb circles slowly against her clit, with only the wet fabric between us. She rewards me with a small, throaty moan that sends my mind reeling.

I set her down on her feet and curl my thumb through the waistband of her underwear, pulling them down with me as I sink to my knees in front of her. She steps out of them, and I toss the pink scrap over my shoulder.

The sweet scent of her hits me. I lean forward and kiss the inside of her knee, working my way up and caressing the backs of her thighs. She shifts her weight with an air of impatience, but I'm not even close to done. I hook her leg over my shoulder and her body shudders while I continue exploring.

"Please," she begs, pushing my desire into overdrive.

"Anything for you, Amira," I whisper. I push a finger into her tight, slick folds. Then a second. My fingers curl inside her until I find the spot that leaves her shaking as her hands dig into my hair. My other hand palms her firm ass.

I run my tongue from her entrance to her clit, and her arousal sends my taste buds screaming with pure bliss. She whimpers while I press my tongue against her and alternate between long, slow licks and short, fast flicks that leave her bucking against my face. I'm starved for her sweetness, and I can't help but lap up every last drop. It's a feast after being lost in a goddamn desert.

Her thighs tighten around me. I drive her forward and offer no pause, no chance of escape from the pleasure. She shakes against me, and I push her harder. My lips gently tug on her clit, and I continue flicking her sensitive nub relentlessly with my tongue while my fingers curl inside her, trying to shove her over the edge into bliss.

Heat rushes down my spine as she comes apart under my mouth, using her own hand to selfishly muffle her cry.

Next time she comes, she'll scream my name.

Her breathing steadies as she comes back down.

With both feet back on the floor, Amira looks at me, her eyes round. She swallows, opens the door, and pivots before closing it behind her, leaving me on my knees staring after her.

What the hell just happened?

With a sigh, I stand up.

I can't think straight. My body is hot. Painful. Gods, it's desperate for release.

I enter the bathroom, throw my sweats in the laundry basket along with Amira's lacy underwear, and step into the shower.

I'm still pulsing with desire. I languish in the memory of her whimpers as she begged for release. Moans as I kissed my way up her body. I imagine her fingernails leaving crescents along my back as I thrust into her, completely branded by her. Her touch becoming desperate as I memorize every inch of her body.

My hand grips my cock, and it only takes a few strokes to find release as the water runs down my body. Quick, dirty, and unsatisfying. I wish it was Amira's hands instead.

My breathing slows and my mind clears slightly. We'll talk this out in the morning.

I hope.

7

Last night, I thought I'd cracked the final piece of Amira's shell. What did I miss that had her running? Did she not enjoy herself? Her desperate moans as she came beneath my tongue... No, that can't be it.

My heart stops the moment I see her in the front row of the class. She's wearing her favorite peasant top and jeans, her black clothes offset by a colorful hair wrap around her box braids.

Pictures of ancient dragons in golden frames stare menacingly from around the history classroom, covering almost every inch of the stone walls. They're terrifying, but it's Amira that has my heart racing.

Do I need to go to the infirmary for arrhythmia?

Can we just *be a rational human here*?

Pushing through the paralysis, I wander over and pull out the leather chair next to her, playing it cool. My favorite early bird has bags under her eyes and a thermos of coffee in place of her usual water bottle. She stares at her open book, but her eyes aren't moving down the page.

"Good morning," I say. "Did you sleep all right?"

She closes the book and nods slowly. "You?"

Her gaze is locked on me. After seeing each other every day for the last year, she can see right through me. There's no hiding anything from her.

Be honest, Markus. One of us has to cross the gap. Show her it can be you.

I swallow. "Well, not really. I was worried about you."

Her expression falls, and my heart pounds in my ears. The beautiful amber eyes that haunted my dreams last night soften. "I wasn't sure—"

"Good morning, class," Professor Fortid says as he enters the room.

"Can we talk after the lecture?" Amira whispers.

"Sure," I whisper back. I twist my chair forward and pull my notebook from my bag.

"I've graded your papers from last week." Professor Fortid passes them out, and the B+ on the top of mine has a dragon doodled next to it. Not the most artistic of renditions, but it's rather charming in a kindergartener-drew-it sort of way. It's better than I could have drawn.

"Thanks for your help, Obi," I whisper to Amira, flashing her the paper.

She grins briefly. "You earned it."

"Some of your papers were..." Professor Fortid turns on the holo-projector. Mount Rainier lights up bright orange, rotating slowly. "Shall we say, quite entertaining? Miss Obi, for the benefit of your more... *creative* classmates, could you please summarize the origin of dragons?"

A couple of students mumble, but Amira forces a smile. I hate it.

"Dragons first appeared during the Triassic period alongside the dinosaurs." Her eyes are missing their usual brightness. "Dragon skeletons were regularly confused with those of the Diplodocus during early archaeology excavations. Dragons living in volcanoes easily survived the meteor that wiped out the dinosaurs and adapted to the dwindling resources by hibernating. Only the smallest and strongest survived since they'd be best suited to the new conditions on Earth, but we don't know the true scope of the population because the magic of the nest protects them." Her tone is dull, lacking its typical enthusiasm.

"Thank you, Miss Obi." Professor Fortid offers her a smile before turning back to the rest of the class. "I hope you all paid attention. Now, moving on to the water dragons in the volcanic trenches of the oceans. Turn your books—" The door opens at the back of the classroom, and Professor Fortid blinks in surprise. "Commandant, what can we do for you?"

"I need Markus." Commandant Eirikssen's tone leaves no room for argument—not that anyone would try.

A couple of my classmates snicker as my cheeks warm. This isn't anything new. I shove my notebook into my bag and swing it over my shoulder. After a quick wave to Amira, I follow the commandant to his office. We pass by the guards at the door, who remain as solemn as they were on my first day of school.

The commandant closes the door and sits behind his spotless desk, gesturing to my usual seat. "I heard about the mess you got into last night."

Shit. I've been so worried about Amira that I forgot to check in with him. "I can explain."

His brows raise as he gestures for me to go on.

"I went to the Den looking for Tobias." I detail the events of the evening. The commandant listens closely, his eyes locked on me. "We ended up cornered by the Jonjung clan. Things got a bit out of hand, but Tobias invited me to the third-year common room after we got back."

"Keep the details to yourself." The commandant clasps his hands atop the desk. "I'm surprised you pulled it off, Markus."

Yeah, I am, too.

A knock on the door stops me from responding.

"Come in." The commandant rises, gesturing for me to do the same. "Chief Paveith. Welcome."

My eyes go so wide that the skin on the bridge of my nose stretches uncomfortably. Chief Paveith is a goddamn *legend*. His armor is very, very black like his dragon, Zeus. He graduated from Dragild thirty-two years ago and was immediately stationed at Fort Bragg, skipping right over lieutenant to captain. After he single-handedly turned the tides in America's favor during the war and served twenty years as a general, he was promoted to chief of the Goldwings. Rumor has it he's gunning for the Oval Office. I don't deserve to stand in his presence.

"Commandant." The chief's beady eyes scan the room quickly before settling on me. "I assume this is Markus."

I swallow and nod once, and that seems to be enough.

The chief drops a giant stack of folders on the desk with a thud and rubs a hand over his shaved head. "Three truck hijacks, two in the last month. Three dead drivers. One dead rider. One dead dragon. Millions of dollars in obsidian from Glass Butte just vanished without a trace. Not even a hint since some of the rocks turned up in Portland two months ago."

My limbs are heavy. We all sit around the commandant's desk.

"There was a media leak this morning." The chief scowls. "The cabinet is on our tails to fix this. We're in the political fire now, thanks to the upcoming election. A truck driver probably sprung the leak, putting two and two together after a third truck didn't return."

The commandant picks up the top folder, flipping through it. "Multiple undercover riders are working to infiltrate the clans, and Markus worked his magic on Tobias Obi, the son of the Ejo clan's leader."

"Right." My head is light. "If he's part of the clan's inner circle, he has to know things. I just need more time to—"

"Time?" the chief yells. "We don't have time!"

I'm absolutely, one hundred percent not going to throw up right now.

"Eirikssen, our reputations are on the line. My campaign is on the line. Get me something I can use." He stands abruptly and exits the office, slamming the door behind him.

And I thought the commandant was scary.

The commandant presses his lips together. "Don't turn your back on Tobias. His dad has half the city of Portland under his thumb."

I take a deep breath. "Last night, when we were surrounded by the Jonjungs, they said something about a delayed shipment. They moved it at the last minute, what with the police swarming."

The commandant buries his forehead in his hand. "Why didn't you lead with that?"

Yeah, I probably should have.

"Well, Markus, see if you can figure out what night it was moved to. If we have something concrete... Let's just say it will look very good for both of us." He leans back in his chair. "Get out of here."

Don't have to tell me twice.

The bright spot of all this is I don't have to go back to class. Today's lecture was sure to be a snooze.

I grab my bag and venture to the courtyard. Tobias, Jonas, and Theo kick around a soccer ball in the grass. I throw my bag on the grass next to Theo's.

"Heads up!" Tobias kicks the ball my way, and I kick it to Jonas. He lobs it right back to me, and I juggle it between my feet and my thighs just to mess with him before passing it to Theo.

"Skills, Markus." Tobias nods approvingly.

"I played varsity in high school." It was fun on and off the field. The girls were always happy to screw the striker.

Jonas glares at me. "We all can juggle the damn ball. We're just too tired to give a shit. We had Military Flight while you sat on your ass in a classroom. Speaking of, why aren't you there now?"

"Called into the commandant's office. Didn't feel like going back."

Tobias tenses, just a bit. "What did you do this time?"

Think fast. "They thought I was cheating now that my grades are respectable."

Jonas crosses his arms. My inner voice screams to ignore him, especially since Amira joined me last night.

But then she left my room without a word. Fuck.

"All that studying with me and Amira is paying off, huh?" Theo smirks the same way he always does when he hears I've gotten into trouble. "Glad to see you're finally pulling your shit together, Markus."

"You've been trolling all of us, man." Tobias laughs. "J, you should have seen this pimp last night. On his fucking *Graytail*. He could have won with a boost, for sure."

It's true. Loki was on fire.

"We need to get you racing with us so I can make some more money off you. Dragon Wars. You're coming with." Tobias turns to Theo. "By the way, Ren will be there. He confirmed last night. We'll need a good boost to keep up. For Carina's Green, too. What can we do in the next two days?"

"Not a whole lot..." Theo kicks the soccer ball my way, initiating a scrimmage. I'll have to ask what he means about boosts later.

The moment Amira walks out the door into the courtyard, my eyes are on her. Her peasant top flutters in the light breeze. She comes directly to me.

The soccer ball hits the side of my head.

My face heats. The group laughs as Amira smiles at me.

Theo pulls his tablet from his bag and sits in the grass, ignoring all of us.

"Way to drop the ball the second a pretty woman walks by," Jonas says.

"You should see him when we're studying in the library," Theo chimes in.

Thanks, Theo. Not helpful.

"You guys can play with balls while I hang out with the smartest person on campus." My eyes don't leave Amira's.

"Wipe that drool off your face," Jonas says.

Tobias groans. "That's my sister, dickheads."

"Hey, Jonas," Amira says sweetly. It sends my stomach into knots, but I keep cool as she watches him. "You mentioned a restaurant while we were studying last night. What was it?"

"The one with the amazing sunset views of Mount Rainier?" He juts his chin out, and his tone is hopeful. Is he the reason she ran out last night?

At this point, my stomach is a punching bag, and I'm a goddamn sucker. I force my hands to stay unclenched at my sides.

"Yeah, that one."

He smiles. "Summit House. A quick flight east."

Amira turns to me. "Markus, you can take me there tomorrow."

Hello, euphoria. My body releases a giant breath and a whole lot of tension. I'm on cloud nine, and I'm bringing her with me.

Jonas stalks off toward the dorms.

"Damn, Mia, that was cold." Tobias's tone betrays his affection for her, and his eyes dance in amusement.

"I learned from the best." She sticks her tongue out at him.

"Don't cause any more trouble. I have enough messes to clean up." He chases after Jonas, leaving us behind.

"I spend enough time cleaning up yours..." she says quietly, watching him go. She grabs my hand. "I hope that was okay?"

She could tell me to jump off a cliff, and I'd do it. "I can't wait. You should ride Loki with me. He loves you."

"Loki loves me?" Her eyebrows raise.

"Since the moment he met you."

"Then sure. That sounds great." Amira places her hands on the nape of my neck. "Could we also talk about last night?"

My heart rate picks up, and butterflies beat up my churning stomach. I wrap my arms around her waist and pull her in, enthralled by the delicious vanilla scent of her lotion. "Yep. Talk to me, Obi. What happened?"

"I'm sorry I ran out. I felt like there was something you weren't telling me, and it threw me off, but you were half-naked, and—Why are you smirking?"

"My abs distracted you. Admit it."

"Gods, Markus. *Focus.*" She looks up at the sky before shaking her head. "Was I right? That there was something else?"

"Yeah." Of course, she knew. I should have known better. "Do you know Ren? From the Jonjung clan?"

"Sometimes my father invites him for dinner, to talk business."

"I met him last night. He was the reason for the bath. His dragon knocked Derkomai into the river. When we made it out, the clan surrounded us."

"You definitely should have told me. I'm really glad you're both okay." She squeezes me in a hug. "That was it. That was your fuck-up freebie. Don't try to hide things from me again, okay?"

"Okay." I rest my chin on top of her head.

Does finding information about the Jonjungs to secure my place at Dragild count as 'hiding' something? I hope it doesn't, or I'm already in violation. I already told her about Loki, even though the commandant told me I'm not supposed to say anything. But she knew I was short a dragon after her rescue mission...

Amira steps back, taking her warmth with her. "Library?"

"Yeah, let's go. Do you want anything to eat?" I slept in after hardly sleeping last night, and I'm pretty sure Amira skipped breakfast since she was anxious this morning.

"Coffee and a banana would be great. Thanks." She turns around. "Theo, you want to come to the library with us?"

He looks up from his tablet. "What?"

"Library?" she huffs. "Want to come?"

"Oh, sure." He puts his tablet in his bag and hands me my backpack.

We wander into the main building. I head to the crowded food hall, grab a tray, and load it up with three coffees, fruit, and a plate of lamb and rice. With my hands full, I go straight to the library. The fancy double doors are propped open. Our grandmotherly librarian waves and smiles from behind the circulation desk. I beeline to Amira's favorite table in the back corner.

"Ooh, that smells delicious." Amira happily takes my plate from the tray. I should have grabbed an extra serving. Clearly, I'm off my game today.

Theo grabs one of the coffees. "Thanks, Markus."

"You're welcome." I settle into the chair across from Amira.

"What are you guys studying?" Theo asks.

"I'll let Amira answer that." I take a bite of fruit.

"We just finished the unit on dragon origins. Today was water dragons." She gives me the highlights from class. "You missed a good lecture, although Professor Fortid failed to cover the illegal overfishing."

"I'm lucky I have a great tutor."

She rolls her eyes, but the barest hint of a smile crosses her full lips.

I turn toward Theo, who's gone back to his tablet. "What could you possibly be studying? You have like two weeks left until graduation."

"Sixteen days." He glances at Amira before meeting my gaze. "Obsidian collars and their effects on dragons."

"That's awesome," I say.

Amira bites her lip. "I'm going to grab more food. Do you want anything?"

"A protein bar?" There's no chance I have to share. "Thanks, Obi."

As she leaves, Theo rotates the tablet toward me to show me the screen. "The magnetite in the collars catalyzes the production of amino acids and increases blood oxygen levels. In theory, more of it can give the dragons a boost." The screen shows a model of a thick collar. "This would be a second collar. But it's still in research and development. The effects are unknown."

"How did you figure this out?"

"Oh." He lowers his voice. "Well, it's housed in the Goldwing servers." He flips to another screen. "I've been building a model prototype on my tablet and running simulations based on the documented effects." He shows me an image of a thick collar. "One of the outstanding questions is interference with the main collar, of course."

Yongwang enters my thoughts. "Ren's dragon had two collars. Does that mean there are prototypes already?"

"Yeah. They're a mixed bag. Some are effective, but others..." He takes his tablet back. "Anyway, I hope my assignment is with the research branch."

"I'll keep my fingers crossed for you. This is wicked smart, Theo."

"Thanks. It calms down my messy brain."

Meanwhile, I know exactly what I'm looking for in Portland tonight.

A re you sure about this?" Loki touches down on the roof of Ren's three-story warehouse overlooking the Columbia River. Trees cast dark shadows across the rooftop—perfect for hiding a dragon. The moonlight outlines Government Island in the distance.

"We just need to find the information for the commandant, and then we're home free. We'll be in and out of the warehouse in no time." I unbuckle the saddle and slide down, catching my balance against Loki's leg. "Don't worry, bud. I don't want a repeat of yesterday either." I pat his nose and creep to the edge of the roof.

At the base of the warehouse, a party rages on outside under the floodlights. The latest club remixes blare out of giant speakers. They're all distracted, so we're safe up here, and the music even masked the sound of Loki's wings as we landed. Our spy skills remain top-notch.

Red plastic cups litter the pavement, and the wind carries them toward the motorcycles lining the seawall. Hopefully, they'll pick those up before the wind blows them into the river. Amira would not be impressed.

Roars ring out from the building next door. That must be their dragon stable. We're staying far away from that, for sure. I don't want to get caught up with Ren's dragon, especially when we're here without backup. I shake out my hands and refocus, scanning the crowd.

Ren is surrounded by beautiful people dancing away. He's way more chill than he was after the race. I recognize a few of the motorcyclists from yesterday. It's warm tonight, and they certainly dressed for the weather. Some of them wear riding leathers, but most are in dresses or skirts and crop tops. The men in the crowd favor jeans and Henleys. Those would attract Amira. I should grab a few...

I silently back away from the edge. "Guess we aren't pretty enough to be invited, huh?"

Loki huffs. *"Speak for yourself."*

Dragons. So sensitive.

I wipe the sweat off my hands. It's not safe to leave Loki out in the open. If someone comes by, they could break his collar and sever our connection. The risk is usually small, but here? At a warehouse owned by a clan with Goldwings and dragons? I'm not letting Loki out of my sight.

We cross the roof to the opposite end of the warehouse. It's quieter, but a guard stands by the only open garage door. He's armed with a military-issue rifle, so we can't just hop down.

I close my eyes and take a deep breath. We need a distraction.

Back in the saddle, I strap in safely. "Set that tree on fire. When the guard runs over to see what's going on, we'll fly through the door."

Loki blinks at me.

And blinks at me.

And blinks at me again. *"This is a dumb idea."*

"Come on, bud. We'll be fine." My mouth is as dry as the asphalt of the Las Vegas Strip.

His body heaves, and he sets the tree aflame.

The guard's feet crunch the gravel as he races toward the burning tree. "What the hell?" He runs around the corner.

Now's our chance.

Loki jumps down the three stories and we rush into the warehouse. It's poorly lit and completely empty. There's nothing in here—just a massive expanse of cement floors and exposed metal beams, with garage doors on all four sides.

"Get the dragons!" the guard shouts at the top of his lungs.

Loki's fear pushes through the bond.

The music cuts out, partygoers scream, engines start up, and metal scrapes as the doors of the dragon stable open. Sirens blare in the distance.

My throat is thick. This really was a dumb idea.

"The fire department is on their way," the guard yells. Gravel crunches outside, getting louder as the guard heads toward us.

"Back door!" I push my urgency through the bond.

Loki runs to the back and uses his nose to press the button. The garage door slides open to reveal our escape into the—

Metal wall?

We face a smaller room with a wide concrete ramp leading down into darkness. Where's the outside?

"The guard is coming," Loki says.

The sirens wail louder.

My heartbeat pounds in my ears. "Let's go. Close the door with your tail, bud."

The garage door slides shut with a low hum behind us, cutting off the commotion. Silence surrounds us, but there's no telling if Ren or his lackeys will come this way.

Down we go.

Into the unknown.

Again.

At the bottom of the ramp, we enter a giant bunker lined by thick cement walls that transition to stone halfway down. A dozen hallways lead off from the main chamber. It's surprisingly dust-free down here, though it smells a bit musty.

Canned lights in the ceiling cast a dim glow on wooden crates as far as we can see. They're all the same size—approximately three-foot cubes. There must be at least a hundred.

I close my mouth, undo the saddle's buckles, and jump off Loki's back. "Look at us! We found the stolen obsidian."

Loki looks around. *"You can tell that just from looking at wooden crates?"*

"Well, they're really well hidden and were obviously brought in late at night on trucks. What else would be in them?"

He blinks at me. *"Literally anything else that fits inside a crate."*

"Well, Debbie Downer, there's only one way to find out."

Metal brackets hold the crates closed. Stepping through the aisles, I scan for something to open the boxes with. A crowbar sits on a shelf.

"Here we go." I shove the crowbar between the lid and the bracket. It doesn't budge. I pry harder, and the air fills with the crack of splintering wood.

"I feel like there's an easier way to do this."

"Probably, but here we are." My heart races as elation takes over my body. I'm staying at Dragild.

One more shove, and the metal bracket flies off and clatters against the wall. Shit, that was loud, but we can't hear anything from above, so hopefully no one heard us. Three more brackets to go, but I make quick work of them. With one final thrust of the crowbar, I've got it open. I push the lid to the side, set it on the floor, and lean over the crate.

That's...

"That doesn't look like obsidian."

Elation, gone.

"Why are there..."—I dig around in the box—"bags?" I hold one up. It's a lavender leather purse with a giant *Y* stamped on the outside. It's empty, but the inside is lined with patterned silk. "Do you think Amira would want one?"

Loki blinks at me for the millionth time today.

"You're right. The color would clash with all her favorite hair wraps." I put it back and dig some more. There are a bunch of different colors in all sorts of shades. The leather is soft and grainy beneath my hands. Definitely the good stuff. A burnt orange purse catches my eye, and I lift it up. "She'll like this one."

"It's abnormally large." Loki sniffs the leather bag and rears back. *"That's—"*

"Markus?" Tobias says from behind me.

Oh, fuck.

8

Tobias walks toward me, rubbing at his brow. His slow footsteps are deafening in the silence of the bunker. He's fully
decked out in leathers and his ruby-scaled armor. "What the hell
are you doing down here?"

I have no good reason to be in an underground cavern owned by
the Jonjung clan in the middle of the night. None.

Technically, as part of the Ejo clan, neither does he.

Jonas follows close behind him, narrowed eyes locked on me.
One bullet from the military-issue rifle he's holding would kill me.

My pulse races and my legs go weak.

Loki paws at the floor behind me. *I told you this was an objectively horrible idea.*

Not helpful, Loki. Not helpful at all.

Tobias waits stoically for an answer.

"Shopping for Amira." I hold up the burnt orange purse. I hope
they didn't hear that gulp.

"Bullshit," Jonas grunts. His nostrils flare. "He comes around,
and the race gets busted? It's not a coincidence."

Tobias crosses his arms, his expression ice-cold. "I'm only going to ask this one more time, Markus. Think very carefully about the next words out of your mouth. What the hell are you doing down here?"

I can't tell him about my mission for the commandant. If I don't come up with something good, I'll be kicked out of Dragild and lose Loki and Amira. That's if Jonas doesn't kill me first.

"The best lies are rooted in the truth."

I shove gratitude through our bond. Thanks, Loki. Actually helpful.

My knuckles are white from gripping the purse's handle. "I was hoping I'd find a second obsidian collar for Loki, to give him a boost during Dragon Wars. I saw Ren's dragon wearing two, so I thought he might have another."

Tobias lifts an eyebrow and cocks his head to the side. "And why did you think he'd have a spare lying around? The obsidian alone is hundreds of thousands of dollars."

"Ren said you'd need more than 'a little boost' to win. With the way he laughed, the tone he used, it seemed like it was worth a shot." I clench my teeth to stop them from chattering.

"Bullshit." Jonas points the gun in my direction. The black hole of the barrel sends a shiver down my spine.

"They aren't buying it."

They're about to kill me. I'm going to die down here, in an old bunker full of stolen cargo.

"You know I can't lose again," I rasp. My throat is thick. "I could barely afford the buy-in for the last race. Loki's fast, but we need all the help we can get to win."

"Excuse you?" Loki's tone is incredulous.

"He's a fucking rat, T!" Jonas's face flushes with rage.

Tobias steps toward me, still wearing his signature cold stare. "Are you a rat?"

I swallow the lump in my throat and shake my head.

Please don't kill me, please don't kill me.

Tobias stares me down, breath smelling like stale beer. He studies the bag in my hands and silently judges my poor choices.

The muscles of his face relax.

I release a breath.

My brain is mush.

"Clean up your mess and come with us." Tobias strides off toward a hall. "Hurry up."

Jonas lowers his gun and follows Tobias. His scowl stays plastered to his face the entire time, aimed my way until he gets to the hall.

Gods, what a mess. I put the top back on the crate, latching it down.

The purse fits perfectly in the saddle bag. Loki tilts his head toward me. *"I don't know if Amira is going to like it."*

"Why?" I whisper.

"It's made from water dragon skin."

I press my lips into a grimace. Amira spent hours raging about the environmental impacts of illegal water dragon fishing and the damage to the population. I'd look stupid putting it back in the crate, though.

"Too late now," I whisper, returning the crowbar to the shelf.

Why are they down here?

We scramble to keep up with the pair, our footsteps echoing. Down the brick-lined hall, through another small bunker, and down a second short hall, we finally stop in front of an ancient, freestanding metal safe. It's a few inches taller than Tobias, whose expression remains stony.

Was I right about the obsidian?

Jonas sets the gun down and steps up to the safe. "It's just an old Cary vault. Shit company, useless security. Easy enough to crack open."

I guess safe-cracking is one of the skills he's learned from Professor Schloss.

He turns the dial to the left four times. Then he starts spinning it back and forth, back and forth, taking his time.

Loki lays down with a yawn. *"How much longer?"*

My skin tingles with excitement when the safe clicks. Jonas pulls the handle and swings the door open.

Guns fill the bottom of the safe, but a dozen obsidian dragon collars neatly line the top shelf. A thin layer of dust coats them. Some are thicker than others, but they all glitter with streaks of deep red.

"Grab one, kiddo." A relaxed smile crosses Tobias's face. "You weren't wrong."

I pull out the thickest one, slowly releasing a deep breath. It's heavy in my hands. Goosebumps coat my arms as I wipe off the dust and trace my fingers along the pattern. It would have taken months to craft. "It's beautiful."

Tobias grabs two collars and hangs them from his shoulder. So they were here for obsidian...

"The pattern's Dancheong. Ren's family is Korean." Tobias's voice is flat. "Make sure you file it off in the shop before Dragon Wars."

Nodding, I tuck the collar into the saddle bag with the purse. I need to tell the commandant about the stash. This is my ticket to staying at Dragild and becoming the dragon rider I was always meant to be.

Loki bolts up and turns his head toward the door. *"Someone's coming."*

Shit. We're sitting ducks holding the obsidian collars. This is definitely as bad as it looks.

"We have to move," I whisper. "Loki hears someone."

Jonas grabs a collar and closes the safe with a small click before picking up his gun.

Tobias carefully opens a large wooden door on the far side of the room. Loki squeezes through first. The rest of us follow into the barren storeroom, and I close the door softly behind me.

My eyes adjust to the darkness, the only light source coming from beneath the door. We're crammed together in this small room with stone walls and no escape route.

Loki lays down in the corner, pulling away from all of us. His body curls, tight and small. I'm not sure if the anxiety is mine or his coming through the bond. Probably both of us. I lean into him, and his body relaxes, just a bit.

"What the hell happened out there?" Ren roars. His voice echoes down the bunker, and footsteps grow louder. "Trees don't spontaneously combust!"

Okay, maybe it wasn't my most brilliant idea.

"Not gonna say I was right." Loki shifts a bit.

"I have no clue," the guard from the door says. His shaky tone betrays his nerves. "Nothing looks disturbed down here."

Their footsteps approach the door.

I hold my breath. Jonas raises his gun.

"I got ahold of the truck driver and pushed the shipment to tomorrow, now that the cops and fire department are swarming," Ren says, exasperated. "Gods, this is nonsense. Tobias has to be behind this shit."

Tobias shrugs, but his fists clench at his sides.

"No wonder Ren pushed Tobias and Derkomai into the river," Loki says.

Definitely sounds like bad blood.

"Ren," a new voice calls out, bright and energetic. A single set of footsteps mixes with the sound of something dragging against the floor. "We found this guy creeping."

The dragging sound is his body.

I slam my eyes closed, straining to hear some sign of life.

"Where was he?" Ren asks.

"Just outside the south door."

A sharp thud is followed by silence. Ice flows through my arms.

Loki's warmth radiates even hotter than normal, but I don't bother wiping the sweat from my brow. I don't want to move. Sure, I have a dragon, but if Ren brought Yongwang...

The safe door creaks open.

My throat catches, but I can't swallow.

"Where the hell did four collars go?" Ren bellows.

A groan comes from their captive. I squeeze my eyes shut even harder.

"You!" Ren roars. "Where did you hide them?"

My heartbeat pounds in my ears.

Tobias and Jonas don't move. None of us even breathe.

"I don't know what you're talking about," he whimpers. "I didn't touch anything."

I don't recognize the voice, although it sounds young.

"You're creeping around and four collars go missing?" Ren asks. "And I'm supposed to think it's a coincidence?"

"Awful timing on their part." Loki's heart beats as fast as mine.

"I don't know," the voice cries.

The smack of skin echoes through the door.

My stomach lurches. This is partly my fault.

"Fucking tell me!" Ren screams.

"I don't know!"

He can't know. The collars are in here, barely a dragon-length away.

Metal clicks. "One last chance."

"I don't know," the voice cries out. "I didn't—"

A gunshot ends the conversation.

The safe door slams shut. I don't breathe.

"Clean this up," Ren says. "He didn't get far. The collars are here somewhere, probably behind the bushes where you found him."

Footsteps quickly pass outside the door.

The tension in my shoulders drops slightly. At least I got the information for the commandant. We just need to stay quiet.

Gods. I really need to start making better decisions.

Other than shaking out my limbs every time they fell asleep, I haven't moved for an hour. I almost vomited at the scraping sound of the dead body being dragged out, but I held it in. Thank goodness, or we'd probably be dead right now.

Tobias stands and brushes the dust off the back of his pants. "The coast should be clear," he murmurs. "Let's go."

"Finally." Loki stretches his neck.

I crack open the door, and my gaze immediately follows the blood-stained cement, a jagged reddish path along the floor.

Fuck, that could have been us.

Deep breath.

I step out of the storeroom and shake out my body. It's so good to move around and get out of the sauna. Not that it's Loki's fault he radiated hotter than ever from all the stress...

"How are we getting out?" I ask.

Tobias studies me. "You broke in with no idea how to get yourself out?"

I hesitate to answer. "Um... yeah."

He laughs and readjusts the collars on his shoulder. "Come on, dumbass. The tunnels are this way."

Loki ducks his head as we follow Tobias and Jonas. We enter another bunker, this one full of barrels of soju, a Korean alcohol. Amira had a bottle last month.

At the end of the room, Tobias pushes on the wall, swinging it outward to reveal a dark hallway. It smells mustier, but it's just as silent. He pulls out his phone and turns on the flashlight. Must be new since his phone got a bath yesterday.

The hewn stone walls are the same mundane shade of gray as the dragon cave on campus, but they lack the dragon carvings.

I step through the entry. "How did you find out these were down here?"

"Portland's Shanghai Tunnels are a legend." Tobias closes the door behind me and Loki. We take off down the path, footsteps echoing over the barren rock. "Most people hear about the tunnels on the west side, and there are even tours taking people down. There are just as many tunnels on the east side, but they're way better hidden."

"I used to live here. How did I not know that?"

Jonas shrugs. "Were you sneaking illegal goods?"

Tobias snorts a laugh.

"We most definitely are now," Loki says.

"What does that have to do with anything?" I ask.

"That's what they were used for back in the 1850s," Tobias says. "They connected the waterfront to underground brothels, opium dens, gambling houses... Even abducted people were tucked down here. We have some tunnels below the Den."

We slow down near a hallway branching off. Tobias opens a large metal door, revealing Derkomai and Poseidon asleep in the room. Their scales shimmer from the flashlight.

"Okay, D. Nap's over." Tobias tucks the pair of collars into his saddle bag.

Derkomai blinks off his sleepy expression, already wearing both his collars. One has a geometric design similar to Amira's. The other is smooth.

Jonas clasps the collar he grabbed around Poseidon's neck. The Blue blinks a bit, shakes out his body, and nudges Jonas.

The dragons duck through the doorway, following their riders in a single file. Loki and I bring up the rear. One short hallway later, we exit the tunnels near the docks. The moonlight reflects on the water, glittering along the waves.

Jonas immediately mounts his dragon. "Let's try this boost," he says to Tobias. "Ready to race?"

"Me too!" Loki's excitement shoots through our bond.

Tobias shakes his head. "We don't need another swarm of cops. Besides, I want to take Markus back to the Den."

Really? Why?

"Come on, T." Jonas glares at me as he finishes buckling his saddle. "Can't we race the Cascades? Send the kid home."

Rude. But if I head back now, I bet Amira will still be awake. *The joke's on you, Jonas.*

Tobias mounts Derkomai. "Jonas, why don't you head back? We can race tomorrow night."

His mouth drops. "Are you kidding me?"

Tobias stares him down, gaze unwavering.

"Fine." Jonas huffs a sigh, drops his shoulders, and flies off into the stars.

"Come on, Markus." Tobias straps himself in, and Derkomai takes off.

I mount Loki, and we chase after him.

"Can we race with them tomorrow night?"

"Nope." I finish clasping the buckles on the saddle and avoid looking down. "We've got a date with Amira. But maybe she'll want to go to Spokane after dinner. How does that sound?"

"Like fun. Approved."

The breeze is refreshing as we zip over to the Park Avenue West Tower. We land in front of the garage door. Tobias knocks and the door immediately opens, revealing the dark-eyed bouncer. The perks of being the son of the Ejo clan's leader, I suppose.

The ramp down is as empty as it was yesterday. Derkomai throws flames at the soot-covered wall, sending it upward, gears grinding. We enter the chamber, and the motion-activated lights blind me again, but at least I'm ready for it. I didn't appreciate almost falling flat on my ass the first time.

"Tobias." The crotchety old guard nods his way as we pass.

The smell of sulfur attacks my nose. Four stories below the balcony, Goldwings swarm around the tables and the bar, just like they did yesterday. Piercing roars echo along the walls of the cavern.

At the base of the ramp, Tobias stops. "Derkomai, head up." As his dragon flies to the upper ledges, he turns to me. "Have Loki follow. They'll be fine up there until we get back."

I don't have much of a choice, considering my mission is to infiltrate their inner circle. "Where are we going?"

Tobias rolls his eyes. "We'd be halfway there if you'd move."

Loki nudges me. *"Don't do anything stupid."*

"Okay, up you go," I say.

Loki flies to the ledge and perches next to Derkomai. He'll be safe up there next to the Ruby. No one would mess with them under the Ejo leader's own roof.

We cut across the cavern to the back and cross through the archway, stepping onto the top level of an elliptical amphitheater reminiscent of the Colosseum. It's entirely hewn from stone. The benches are covered with leather pads. An ornate metal clock hangs from the center of the ceiling, counting down.

Roars stop me in my tracks.

A Ruby versus a Black, both absolutely ginormous, face off in the pit. Their riders stand on raised platforms off to the sides. They stare menacingly at each other while the dragons snap and snarl.

"Welcome to the dragon fights." Tobias walks down the stairs to the second level and keeps going. "Come on."

I hustle to keep up. "Where are—"

"Tobias!" An older man, tall with a mohawk and a clean-shaven face, approaches us. His lip is pierced, and a tattoo of dragon scales climbs his neck. His green armor needs a polish. "Long time, no see. How are you?"

"All good. Two weeks left until graduation, and then I'll be around every day." Tobias greets him warmly with a hug, and then he gestures to me. "This is Markus. Markus, this is Luz."

Luz appraises me. "No armor?"

I shake my head. Isn't it obvious when I'm not wearing any?

Tobias chuckles. "He's a first-year for another two weeks. Just broke his dragon. Apparently, I've started slumming it."

Laughing, Luz pats me on the back, jolting me forward. "Well, kiddo, save those scales. You'll have a coat soon enough." He turns back to Tobias, fortunately done with me. "How's Amira doing?"

Tobias beams. "She just broke a Ruby last month."

"And she's the top of our class," I say.

"That's my girl," Luz says, his voice cracking with pride. "Tell her I said hello. Are you sticking around tonight?" His eyes light up, expression hopeful.

Tobias hesitates. "Just for a round. I'll be back in a couple of days, though. Weekly dinner."

Luz leans in and lowers his voice. "Your dad still shutting himself away upstairs?"

Tobias nods once, his lips pressed thin.

"Well, hang in there. Losing your mom was a devastating blow for all of us." Luz hums, straightening. "Have fun tonight. Tobias, I'll see you in a few weeks."

Tobias settles onto the bench and gestures for me to sit. I guess we're watching the fight.

Luz wanders down to the pit. About two dozen people wait in the stands, chattering and drinking. A few place bets with Luz as he passes by them.

The clock hanging from the ceiling continues its countdown. I wish we had popcorn.

"Do you ever fight with Derkomai?" I ask Tobias.

"No. I live for the races. Got that from our mom. She lived

and breathed for speed." He chuckles. "Amira got the rest of her, including her snark, so good luck."

"Her snark is the best part about her." That, and everything else. What's she up to tonight?

"Only true because she won't race Tiger. She'd kick ass."

The clock tolls, and Luz claps once, drawing everyone's attention. "Riders, welcome! Our reigning champ, Persephone, will be facing off against Hades."

The crowd cheers as the Ruby and the Black growl and gnash their teeth, ready to fight. Their riders eye each other from the platforms at either end of the arena, scowls on their faces.

I lean closer to Tobias, keeping my voice low. "Is this legal?"

His eyebrows rise.

Right. Of course not.

"The only rule is *no fire*." Luz steps aside, safely out of the way. "Best of three rounds wins. You may begin at the bell!"

A bell sounds, and the dragons circle each other, showing off their white fangs. My gaze stays locked on the pair.

Persephone puffs her black-scaled chest and rises on her legs to her full height, flaring her wings in challenge. A gust of wind ruffles my hair.

Hades charges at her, but she growls and thrashes toward him, stretching her mouth wide with fury.

My heart races as she lunges and traps his nose between her jaws. He loops his tail around, but she pulls his head down to the ground and knocks him over with one shove. The bell rings, complemented by claps from the audience.

"Point for Persephone!" Luz cheers.

No surprise, a Black beat a Ruby.

The dragons back up toward their riders, facing off again. Both riders focus their dragons, channeling fighting anger through their bond.

I clench my fists at my sides, but Tobias stays still.

The bell rings, and Hades immediately circles Persephone, wrapping his neck around hers as the sound of his snaps fill the air. He yanks her straight down.

She pulls back, barely slithering out of his grip.

My mouth is dry, but there's no way I'm leaving to get a drink in the middle of this.

Persephone opens her jaws wide and roars as Hades lunges, looping his neck around hers again. He keeps hold this time and knocks her over.

Her rider radiates fury, kicking at the podium, but Hades keeps Persephone down. The bell rings as the crowd cheers.

"Point for Hades! The next point takes the win!"

Persephone snaps at Hades as she takes her place next to her rider, slightly calmer now. The bell rings, and she charges toward Hades with lightning speed.

Hades jumps back, flares his wings with a whoosh, and lifts himself up, but he's too slow. Persephone lifts herself onto her back legs and yanks him right out of the air, knocking him to the ground. The crowd's cheers drown out the bell.

"The win goes to Persephone!" Luz screams, barely audible above the standing ovation.

Tobias remains stoic.

My fists slacken, and the tension in my shoulders drops. Loki and I definitely won't be joining in.

Hades and Persephone rise, wary of each other. Their riders jump off the platforms, cross the pit, and meet in the center to shake hands as the cheers die down. The Ruby's rider scowls.

"Follow me." Tobias waves to Luz and takes off for the opposite end of the amphitheater. I race behind him. Tobias places his hand on a blinking scanner, and the garage door opens a moment later, revealing ten dragon stalls and an elevator. The walls are stone, but the doors are iron. "Family stable."

The door shuts behind us. Tobias beelines for the first stall and carefully opens a small window in the door. Warm air drifts out.

The stone walls inside the stall are painted a textured grayscale, almost like dark storm clouds. They're beautiful but surprising since the rest of the walls throughout the Den are natural stone. A path is worn along the floor near the stall door.

Peeking in, I make out a sleeping Black Clubtail in the corner. They're large, but thin. Incredibly thin. Ribs and bones are outlined by deep shadows. Their muscles have atrophied, and their legs are swollen from disuse. Scales litter the ground, jut out at odd angles, and are missing in patches from their body where they should have regrown. Scars mar their wings.

I swallow, throat choked up. "Your dad's?"

Tobias shakes his head. "No, Mami is down the row."

"Which god is Mami?"

"Mami Wata. She's a Nigerian water goddess, often depicted lifting a snake. My dad was a romantic, and he loved the symbolism behind it." Tobias briefly cocks his head toward the dragon, his gaze affectionate. "This is Black Mamba. He's named after one of the fastest snakes in the entire world."

I study the dragon, just snoring away in the stall. The wings flutter a bit but tuck right back in. "Your mom's."

"Ding ding ding." His shoulders drop as he watches Mamba.

"What happened? To your mom, I mean."

"Amira didn't tell you?" He frowns and runs his hand through his hair.

I shrug, giving him an awkward half-smile. "She doesn't want to talk about it. I don't push."

"Yeah, Mia was sixteen."

Three years ago. Amira is the strongest and sharpest person I know. How much of that stems from losing her mother? "You don't have to tell me. It's fine."

"No..." He closes his eyes, and his fists clench. "An asshole had been tearing her down at work and throwing slurs her way for weeks. My mom called him on his shit, and he challenged her to a dragon fight. She never participated, but she wasn't about to back down after..." He grits his teeth. "That asshole played dirty. His dragon burned my mom alive, at his command. And thanks to dirty politics, he got away with it."

Damn. No wonder Amira doesn't want to talk about it. No one deserves to have their mother stolen, especially not... like that. At least mine just left before I could remember her.

"I'm sorry," I say. It comes out closer to a whisper.

He shrugs. "At least Amira wasn't with us when it happened."

In silence, we watch the dragon's body rise and fall steadily in sleep.

A minute passes, then two.

The dragon's neck is bare. "No collar?" I ask.

"Mamba broke it off the moment my mom died, but the emergency doors closed immediately and trapped him in the arena. It took a dozen people to lure him out of the fighting ring back to his stall. A few of them didn't make it."

This dragon has no human tethering him. Like Bear after Katie's accident, he's returned to a wild state. But unlike Bear, he's trapped below ground and can't fly away.

"Will he get a new rider?"

"I wanted to..." Tobias swallows. "Mamba attacks fast, asks questions *never*, and his strike is lethal. He hasn't let a single person near him since my mom was killed. He's already incinerated three who tried." He points to the side wall. Two collars rest on the ground, one for a human and one for a dragon. "That outline is all that's left of one of them."

My stomach churns. The walls aren't painted black; they're covered in layers of soot from the dragon's fire. The dragon who tried to burn this place to the ground to escape, who's being held against his will.

Like Loki, who was trapped in the infirmary after racing home to save his rider's life.

I clear my throat, but I'm speechless.

Mamba wakes, and his golden eyes pierce mine. He lets out a roar as Tobias slams the window shut. A moment later, a blast of heat radiates outward.

I shove my shaking hands into my pockets.

"So, Markus. Your date is tomorrow?"

Taking a breath, I nod.

He leans close to me. "You break Amira's heart, and I'll throw you in Mamba's stall. Got it?"

My stomach lurches. "Noted," I rasp.

"Good." He straightens and rests his arms at his sides. "If she comes to her senses, you're welcome to race with us."

"Thanks." My tone drips with sarcasm.

He laughs. "Let's head back to Dragild."

The commandant's desk is spotless this morning, so I bet they finished all the military assignments for the third-years. With fifteen days left until graduation, I've beaten my deadline. I've already gotten all the information he asked for. My place at Dragild is secure.

I'm floating on cloud nine.

"How's it going with the mission, Markus?" The commandant leans back and gestures to my usual chair.

I take a seat and detail my findings from the Jonjung clan's warehouse. "The shipment was moved to tonight. Ren told one of his lackeys down in the bunker. He didn't know Loki and I were hiding in the storeroom."

"No issues getting in or out?"

"Nope." He doesn't need to know I had help on the getting-out part. It's not relevant to the mission.

"I'm impressed." His expression doesn't quite say *impressed*. It looks more like *dubious*. Forget it, I'll take his compliment at face value. "And what about Tobias?"

Shit. Does he know I cut part of the story?

"What about him?" I try to keep my tone light, but it comes out with a bit of a squeak.

"You were playing soccer together yesterday. Have you found any evidence that implies the Ejo clan is also involved?"

"I don't think they have anything to do with it." Other than stealing the stolen obsidian from Ren and the Jonjungs, which is probably relevant. But I don't want to share that. I took a collar, too. It looks bad for all of us.

The commandant stares at me. "And how are you sure?"

"A feeling."

He stares at me.

...six Mississippi, seven Mississippi...

He narrows his eyes. "Keep working on Tobias."

"The Jonjungs are definitely behind it. The collars were in the safe, and there were a ton of crates with water dragon leather bags."

The commandant pinches his lips together. "There's no room for error. The chief will be here tomorrow, and he wants a bust."

"He'll have one. The Jonjungs are definitely behind it."

He studies me, glances toward the ceiling, and sighs. "Okay, I'll get in touch with the chief. Good job, Markus." That's the first time he's said that. "I need to get ready for the open house today. Get out of here." Not the first time he's said that.

Don't have to tell me twice. I've got a date to get ready for.

9

The mastermind nodded. "Tonight."

The muscle of the operation continued to clean his long-range rifle. Come hell or high water, he would be ready.

I scrub every inch of myself twice with the mahogany-scented body wash I grabbed from the pharmacy after class. Loki and I flew at top speed to pick up condoms and girly shit after an intense flight practice. He's still bummed we aren't racing the Cascades with Tobias and Jonas later, but the idea of Spokane cheered him up.

With a freshly washed towel around my waist, I shave carefully.

My clean clothes are folded and sitting on the bed. Thank the powers that be for the staff who does our laundry.

Amira's underwear rests on the top of the pile, a pink scrap of lacy fabric against lots of black. I stick it in the dresser next to mine and put the rest of the clothes away. I'll give it back later.

Nothing's going wrong tonight. It's going to be perfect.

Options, options... I get dressed in dark jeans, a black Henley, and my leather riding jacket. Can't look like I'm trying too hard.

I pull out the purse from under the bed, looking it over. *Water dragon skin...* Fuck, maybe I should just toss it in the trash. No, that's wasteful. I'll let Amira decide if she wants it or not. I lock my door behind me and cross through the first-year common room, burnt orange purse in hand. I'm a little early, but I head straight down the girls' hall to Amira's door and knock lightly.

"Come in," Amira's voice calls.

I enter, surprised to see Carina on the bed. She rises and gives Amira a half hug. "Have fun tonight, babe." She exits with a small wave.

Amira smiles from the rug in front of her giant mirror. She called it a leaner when I helped her drag the heavy thing up the stairs on move-in day. I'll be dragging it up the stairs again in a couple of weeks when we move to the second floor. A bunch of makeup litters the floor around her. It's like the bag on her desk exploded.

"I just need a minute. Carina was showing me a new trick." She turns back to her dazzling reflection and adjusts her black shirt. Her phone lights up and vibrates with a new message in her group chat. "Ugh, Honoka's driving me nuts." She ignores her phone in favor of her makeup. "Could you please hand me the concealer?"

"Sure." I step over to the bag, and over a dozen little containers stare back at me. I didn't have siblings or a steady girlfriend to prepare me for this challenge. I have no idea what's what.

"Which one is it?" I ask.

"The umber Fenty tube with the white cap." She's tracing her eye with a dark pencil that matches her dark jeans, leaving me to paw through the bag containing six different tubes that fit the ask. "Oh, and the skin tint, please. The fancy glass bottle."

Giving up, I lift the makeup bag and set it next to her. "Seemed more efficient."

"Probably." Her eyes light up, but she keeps her laugh to herself.

My mouth goes dry. "So... I have something for you, but I'm not sure if you'll like it."

Her eyes catch on the purse. They widen, and she smiles, showing off her dimples. "Is that a Yong?"

"You tell me." I hand it over and sit on her bed. It's soft and fluffy and covered in silk pillows with bold geometric patterns.

She opens the bag and eagerly looks over the Dancheong-patterned silk. "It is! Thank you. I adore the color." Her response is a relief. "Is this why you skipped the library?"

"No. The commandant sent me to Portland on a mission last night to look into some stolen cargo, and I had to report back. Part of my mission to keep Loki. We snuck the bag out of the crate for you. From the crates of stolen cargo, by the way. Full disclosure." Not fucking that up again.

She cocks her head to the side as she studies the bag. "Well, it certainly has an interesting origin story." She sets it down and goes back to her makeup, dabbing some liquid stuff over the adorable tan line from her flight goggles. "What assholes, stealing a Yong. Did you know they're one of the only companies that sustainably source water dragons?"

"Tell me about it." I love her tangents.

"The water dragons are all pole-and-line caught." She runs a giant, fuzzy brush over her high cheekbones. "Yong found a way to use every bit of the body. The meat for food, of course. It's a delicacy in Korea, equivalent to shark."

She unscrews the cap of her lipstick and runs the color along her lips. Like she wasn't kissable enough without it. I readjust on the bed and picture falling thousands of feet from Loki's back.

Once the cap is screwed back onto the tube, she continues. "The skin gets used for leather goods, and the ground-up bones are used for fine china. The rest of the body can be made into medicines and toiletries, and Yong continues to invest in product research." She packs up the makeup bag and puts it back on the desk. "Ready."

I hold out my arms. "Come help me up."

She grabs my arms, and I pull her into my lap, flipping her onto the bed. Her delicious vanilla scent takes over my senses.

"Oops." I kiss her cheek and nuzzle into her neck, resisting the urge to explore the rest of her. "You look gorgeous, by the way."

She laughs, and the sound is precious music to my ears. "We should go, or we'll be late. I made a reservation."

I stand and pull her up with me.

"Loki's ecstatic, by the way." Minus wanting to race.

"Really?"

"Of course! He loves you."

"Right." She grins. "How could I forget?" She grabs her jacket and my hand.

As we meander across the courtyard, she tells me all about a woman who might win a Nobel Prize in chemistry for developing a new method of genome editing within dragonology.

We enter Loki's stall, and he jumps up immediately. *"Amira!"*

She snuggles against his cheek. "Hi, Loki. I missed you, too."

Loki nudges me with his tail. *"Don't be jealous. I'm just lovable."*

"Thanks, bud." I smirk at him and shake my head as he continues to distract Amira.

Once Loki's saddle is secure, we head to the exit of the cave. I mount and offer Amira a hand up. Once I'm buckled in, she settles in behind me. I strap her to me with an extra safety belt and pull it tight, enjoying her arms around my waist.

The only falling she should be doing is falling for me.

Loki takes off into the cloudless sky, aiming for the Summit House. It's only about twenty miles as the dragon flies. The warm summer air wraps around us as he keeps a lower altitude. The Cascade mountains in the distance appear extra blue today. Evergreens cover the slopes and Mount Rainier's snowy top glitters in the sun. Pretty great view for a first date.

Loki catches a gust of wind and glides higher. *"We can still make the race."*

My limbs feel heavy as my mind is thrown back to Mamba in his stall at the Den. I scratch Loki's neck and glance back at Amira. "I know you don't race, but have you heard of the Dragon Wars?"

"Of course. Tobias lives for them. I went with him last year, just to watch."

"Would a certain adrenaline junkie have fun?"

"Absolutely." Amira laughs. "Loki would love it. If you go, I'll come along as well. Just to cheer him on, of course. Tiger doesn't like racing."

Loki perks up, and a sharp spike of excitement rushes through our bond.

"Hear that, bud? You'll even have a cheering squad."

Our picnic table on the deck of the Summit House has a front-row view of Mount Rainier. Red and white flowers line the tops of the railing surrounding the dining area. The building itself is half wood, half stone, all old-cabin charm. The sunset lit the sky on fire, so now oranges and reds fill the sky. Loki naps in the grass next to the porch, the sunset casting a colorful hue across his gray-spotted white scales.

But none of it is even half as stunning as Amira.

She's been in fine form all evening, and I haven't had this much fun in a long time.

"I'm now mandating all your meals be eaten with me, Obi."

"Oh, really?" She raises her eyebrows, but her eyes light up.

"Yep. Your brother and his gang, they can't have you anymore. I'm not sharing." I cross my arms and throw on a pout to really drive the joke home.

Her eyes crinkle with laughter. "Tobes would laugh at you for calling them a gang. They're a team."

I relax and lean forward, elbows on the table. "How did it start?"

She takes a sip of her water. "It's kind of a long story."

"I've got all the time in the world. Are you going somewhere?"

"You haven't scared me away yet." She chuckles. "Well, Jonas grew up in the apartment next door to us. He was always over at our place, just hanging out with Tobias. He ate dinner with us every other night, and I got a bonus big brother."

No wonder he's so protective of Amira. He feels a lot less like competition, now that I know that tidbit. I gesture for her to go on.

"Tobias met Carina on their first day at Dragild. They've been together ever since. And Theo... well, a month into school, some assholes were tearing him down because he's gay. Tobias stood up for him. Since then, they've stuck together like glue."

"That story wasn't long at all."

"I suppose not." She takes my hand and squeezes lightly. "Thank you. For making an effort with my brother."

The cold air hits the moment she lets go. I want her hand back.

"Anything for you." I smile and take a sip of water.

"Speaking of... I thought maybe you could come to dinner with my family tomorrow night?"

Meeting her dad?

"Why are we panicking?" Loki asks, his tone alert.

I choke on my water, and my face heats a million degrees. "Sorry. Spoiler, don't breathe liquids."

"Noted." Her face betrays her concern. "Are you okay?"

"Of course." I clear my throat. "Sure, dinner tomorrow sounds great."

And utterly terrifying, but it's fine. It'll be fine.

"It's just dinner." Amira smiles, and it melts my insides.

We rise from the table and wander back to Loki. Beneath the stars, he nuzzles Amira. The light from the restaurant casts a faint white glow across the grass.

"Spokane?" Loki holds still for once, watching me with bated breath.

I lean against him. "I haven't asked her yet, but I bet it's a yes."

"Asked me what?" Amira wraps her arms around my waist, distracting me with her soulful eyes.

Loki nudges me with his tail.

"Do you want to get dessert in Spokane? Loki used to race there and back with his last rider."

Her expression goes soft. "Of course. That sounds great."

A jolt of excitement hits me through the bond. I mount Loki, buckle in, and help Amira up, strapping her safely to me. "Let me know if you feel cold, okay? Or if Loki goes too fast."

"Not possible." Loki's body shakes with laughter.

"And you"—I shoot him a look—"stay low. We aren't in full flight leathers."

"Nothing to do with your fear of heights?"

I give Loki the side-eye. Goldwings aren't afraid of heights. We simply respect the fact that a fall from a dragon would result in immediate death.

Katie flashes through my mind. I tighten the straps, double-checking them one more time.

Amira puts on her riding gloves and flight goggles. "I'll be fine. Don't worry so much."

"See?" Loki launches into the air, not giving me a chance to respond.

The energy rushing through our bond is pure freedom. The wind rushes past, making conversation difficult, but Amira clinging to me the entire way is pretty fucking great.

Loki navigates the one-hundred-ninety-mile flight in about an hour and a half. The flat, dark expanse of Washington state stretches out below us.

As we approach Spokane, the lights glitter along the mountainous terrain. We fly along the Spokane River and turn left at a bridge. The buildings are all older, mostly brick, and one or two stories tall. Loki touches down in a parking lot next to a small café.

"No wonder Tobias said you pimped him when you raced two nights ago." Amira laughs as she slides down to the ground.

"Lies and slander. I did no such thing." I jump down after her. "What are you in the mood for?"

"A hot chocolate." She tucks her freezing hands against my body, and I'm torn between wanting to pull the rest of her against me and wanting to rip her ice-cold hands away. It's fine, I can take the ice against my chest if it means warming her up faster. Probably.

"You"—I kiss her nose—"were supposed to tell me if you felt cold. We could have slowed down or turned around."

"I'm fine. It was fun. Loki was having fun."

Loki nuzzles her and blows warm air at us. *"I fixed it."*

My dragon's the best.

"Let's warm you up. Loki, chill on the roof, okay? No naps. Stay alert."

He perches along the ridgeline while Amira and I enter the café.

Couches, lounge chairs, and modern art fill the welcoming space. The smell of coffee blends with the sound of jazz music. It's devoid of people, other than a barista cleaning behind a green counter. We approach the bar and order. A few minutes later, armed with two hot chocolates, we settle onto the couch along the back wall.

"I've been sharing most of the stories tonight." Amira clings to the warm cup with both hands. "Tell me something new. Something you've never shared."

I shrug. "You know everything there is to know about me. You always see right through me."

She scoots closer. "Not everything. What made you want to be a dragon rider?"

I hook my arm around her shoulders. "It started with my dad. Every night when he put me to bed, he told me stories about Goldwings and their dragons. He read them from history books or newspapers. Sometimes he came up with stuff on the fly."

"Tell me your favorite." She nestles into my side.

"The attack on Fort Bragg." I don't even have to think about it. "Enemy forces were swarming, and four suicide planes were on their way to take out the entire military base. Young Captain Paveith"—her mouth forms an *O*, and she's clearly impressed that I know my history—"mounted his Black, took off at full speed, and took out all four planes in the air, saving thousands of lives. No backup, no support, just determination to protect his country." I settle back into the couch, let the tension drop from my shoulders, and take a deep breath. "That was the day I decided I was going to break a Black."

"I can totally picture baby Markus with those wide blue eyes, completely enraptured." Amira giggles. "Clutching a stuffed dragon beneath a dragon-print bedspread?"

"You know it. All Blacks, of course."

My mind wanders back to Mamba, unbroken and trapped underneath the Den with no hope of escape. No sunshine, no blue skies, no freedom. That scene definitely wasn't what I pictured as a kid. Loki would hate it if we couldn't race anymore, and it sounded like Mamba and Amira's mom raced all the time. How does Mamba feel, stuck down there?

"Markus?" Amira gazes up at me, face etched with concern.

"Sorry, what?" I blink away the thought and focus on her.

"I said I had a good time today. Thank you."

"I did, too."

Her lips part, and I lean in. She sets down her drink, places her hands at the nape of my neck, and closes the gap between us. Her kiss is soft, and she tastes like the hot chocolate she's been sipping.

I want to get lost in this amazing woman forever.

My hands hold onto her hips and pull her against me, right where I want her. I deepen our kiss. Our tongues collide, and she lets out a small groan.

Someone clears their throat. Twice. Shit.

I give Amira one last peck.

The barista grimaces and goes back to cleaning the counter.

"Sorry," I mumble to him, cheeks warm.

Amira picks up her hot chocolate and hides behind her mug.

"Not sorry," I whisper into her ear. "Not sorry at all. Ready?"

"Yeah, let's get out of here." She finishes the last sip and licks her lips, immediately shooting warmth to my—

We're out in public. Think unhappy thoughts. Falling from ten thousand feet.

I follow her out the door. We make it ten steps before I back her against the brick wall and kiss her neck, nudging her chin away for better access.

Her breathy little moan is my new favorite sound. The rapid flutter of her pulse beneath my lips drives me wild. She grabs a fistful of my shirt and yanks me closer. I press my lips to hers, and she whimpers as our tongues collide. Throaty noises betray her needs, and I want to meet every last one. The taste of Amira's lips torments my senses, and all I want is *more*. My cock stiffens, and I press it against her. She groans so deeply it echoes in my bones.

"Let's get back, yeah?" I trace my hands along her sides. I want her writhing beneath me as I explore every last inch of her body.

She blinks, takes a deep breath, and nods.

"Hey Loki," I shout.

"Kind of distracted up here."

Bloody hell, he felt all of that. "Sorry, bud. Ready to race?"

He jumps straight down. *"As soon as we get back, I'm going to sleep."*

"Fair enough." I climb up, buckle in, and secure Amira behind me. She clings tightly. I keep my smile to myself. "You okay?"

Amira gulps. "Mhmm."

I pat Loki and grip the saddle. "Go as fast as you want, bud."

He has us back at Dragild an hour and a half later. Back in his stall, I remove his saddle and quickly check over his scales. "All good?"

"I'm fine." Loki curls up in his usual corner. *"Don't wake me up any time soon."*

I suppress a chuckle and close the door. Amira is leaning against the wall, waiting patiently. As I place my hands on her hips, her breathing hitches.

"Amira..." I move my kisses to her neck. "Do you want to come back with me?"

She bites her lip before she gives a single nod. I scoop her up bridal-style and start a quick pace back to the dorms.

She laughs and wiggles in my arms. "Markus, I am perfectly capable of walking."

"You won't be when I'm done with you," I whisper into her ear. My husky tone warms her cheeks. I carefully set her down.

She grabs my hand and hurries me along, her pace faster than mine. We make it to the front of the school in record time.

"Hold on." I swing open the painting guarding the door of my favorite secret passage.

Amira's eyes widen. "What's this?"

"A shortcut. I'm trusting you with my secret."

"How did you find it?"

"I accidentally kicked a soccer ball through a painting."

She shakes her head and steps through. I close the door behind us and grab her hand, pulling her along the staircase.

The moment we enter my room, I kick off my shoes and throw my jacket on the desk.

She guides me toward the bed. Her vanilla scent sucks me into her orbit, exactly where I want to be.

I sit against the headboard, and she straddles me, trapping me with her legs. She presses a soft kiss to my lips as I pull her closer, desperate for more. A shiver runs through my spine as she grinds slowly against me. The friction drives my need higher and has me moaning beneath her. It's pure torture, but I let her set our pace as my cock throbs.

My breath is ragged as I look into her eyes. "If you don't want to go further, that's okay. Now would be a good time to let me know."

Amira leans back, blinking.

I shift awkwardly beneath her.

Please don't run away again.

Her lips crash into mine as she knocks me back into the headboard. I groan beneath her as the desperation to please her ratchets higher. She peels off her jacket and grabs the hem of my shirt, tearing it over my head. I kiss her again before rolling her onto her back.

Her braids splay out against the white pillow. She looks up at me through long, dark lashes, her eyes darkening with desire. I didn't realize it was possible to get even harder.

Kicking off my pants, I toss them on the floor. I remove her black shirt the way I've wanted to for the last two hours. Underneath is a lacy cheetah-print bra, white with gray spots.

"I match Loki," she says with a shy smile. Hints of dark skin peek through, and my breath hitches.

"I love it." I kiss Amira's delicious lips as I strip her down to her lacy underwear. I can't wait to rip them off and bury myself inside her exquisite body.

I shed the rest of my clothes and carefully climb over her, kneeling between her legs in supplication to this powerful body laid out before me. I'm about to worship every inch of her.

She licks her lips as she notices my straining erection. Her puckered nipples beneath her lacy bra practically beg for my mouth. I lick and suck them through the fabric she picked just for me. She was thinking about me, and she wanted this.

Wants this.

She wants me.

She arches her back with anticipation, pressing into my erection, and lets out a breathy moan. "Please, Markus."

The sound of her. The taste of her. Knowing I'm about to dive in. *Every piece of me is hers.*

I unsnap her bra, pulling it off and tossing it to the floor, then slide her underwear down her legs. Gods, the muscles she's built are a force to be reckoned with. She shivers beneath my touch while I trace the lines of her tattoos. I want to memorize every last one of the inked dragons flying along her body and decorating this brilliant woman.

Her skin feels like silk as I lay against her, skin to skin, kissing her neck. I suck and nip at the sensitive spot below her ear until she lets out a throaty gasp. The intoxicating sound sends a shock of pure electricity through me. My body presses into her as my cock throbs, seeking relief.

Reaching my hand between her legs, I stroke her slippery wetness. With coated fingers, I massage her clit in slow circles. She writhes beneath me, her whimpers begging for more.

I swallow. "You're sure?"

"Yes. Please." Her voice is breathy. She grinds her hips into me, seeking relief of her own.

I grab a condom from my nightstand and roll it on quickly. I lean in close to her ear, kissing her softly, nipping at her sensitive skin. "I want you to scream my name when you come."

"Earn it," she rasps.

"Challenge accepted."

Possessive desire envelops me. This woman is all I want, and I fully intend to make sure she knows it.

I line up my cock with her entrance and push, sinking inside her with one deep thrust. My eyes close and my breath hitches as her tight body surrounds me.

She shifts her hips impatiently, silently demanding I move. I hold myself above her as I glide slowly in and out, and the tight friction has me soaring.

My tongue meets hers again as our lips crash together. She is so deliciously Amira. I could never have enough.

Amira lets out a little gasp as I increase the speed. Her breasts bounce with each thrust. She claws at my back, whimpering with pleasure. She's so fucking beautiful. I hold myself back, desperate for my name on her lips.

I pull her leg up and angle deeper into her, driving harder and faster. She moans, breathless and throaty.

Her hands grip my arms as she closes her eyes. Her muscles clench around my shaft and pulse around me as an orgasm takes over her body. I keep pounding into her as she falls apart, clawing the sheets while she comes all over my cock.

"Markus," she whispers.

"Oh, no, you don't. We had a deal." That scream is mine.

I slide out of her and shift onto my knees. She gasps as I reach underneath her, grab her glorious ass, and tilt her hips up, pushing back into her with a thrust. I go hard, fast, and deep as her body clenches around me again. It only takes a minute before another orgasm pulls her under, her muscles pulsing around me a second time. She glistens with sweat, her legs shaking.

"Markus!" Her scream reverberates off the walls.

My cock strains as pure pleasure races through me. My body goes weak as I climax, my cock jerking inside her.

I nuzzle into Amira's neck as I let my body come back down from the high. "That was better."

Amira reaches around me and smacks my ass. Her eyes are hooded, and she looks sleepy and sated. Yeah, I did that.

"Want to wash up, Obi?" I kiss her collarbone.

She snuggles into me. "In a minute."

I kiss her forehead and climb over her, tossing the condom in the trash on the way to the bathroom. As I step back into my room, Amira's pulling on her shirt.

"I like it better when you're naked."

"Walking through the hallways, though?" She raises her eyebrows.

Wait, what? "Where are you going?"

"Back to my room."

I tuck her half-naked body against me. "Or you could stay. Here. With me. If you wanted."

"But you just..." She bites her lip as she gazes at me. "You don't do sleepovers. With anyone."

"You're not anyone. You're Amira Obi." I run my hand along her spine. "Stay."

She hesitates. "I don't have my pillow, and your pillowcases are cotton."

"I'll get it for you. Where are your keys?"

"In my jacket." She stares at me like I'm a goddamn alien.

I grab sweatpants, a t-shirt, and her clean underwear from the dresser. "Here, you can sleep in these if you want. Or naked. Naked is good, too. You can get cleaned up. There's girly shit for you under the sink." I kiss away her scowl before grabbing another pair of sweatpants and her keys. "I'll be back soon."

The first-year common room is empty as I wander across it toward the girls' hall. Most of us would rather hang out in our rooms, considering the beat-up furniture and persistently empty snack bar. Only fifteen more days until graduation, and then we'll be moving up to the second floor. The second-year common room doesn't compare to the third-year lounge, but it's better than this.

Amira's room smells just like her vanilla lotion. A photo of her with her family sits on her nightstand. I pick up the frame and look at her dad, who I'll be meeting tomorrow night. He's taller than the sixteen-year-old Tobias in the photo, with the same amber eyes and face shape. Tobias wears his signature scowl. Her mom... The teenage Amira hugging her waist, dedicated to her family, would have never let go if she knew what was coming. Their smiles are radiant. The pair are carbon copies of each other. I set the frame down, my chest tight.

I grab her silk-covered pillow and hurry back, slipping through my door.

"What took so long?" Amira asks.

I tuck the pillow behind her and kiss the top of her head. "Just snooping."

She narrows her eyes. "Find anything interesting?"

"No. The most interesting part of your room happens to be in my room right now."

She laughs as I shut off the light and slide into bed next to her, into the tiny twin meant for one.

Tonight was perfect.

"Get over here, Obi." I wrap my arms around her and tug her close, then pull the covers over us. The mattress springs adjust as she shifts her weight, taking her role as the little spoon seriously.

"I like it when you call me Obi," Amira whispers into our shared silence.

I kiss her cheek and settle back in. "Yeah?"

"In Igbo, one of the languages spoken in Southeastern Nigeria, it means *heart*."

Appropriate, since this girl stole mine.

10

The driver swerved out of the flames' path and scrambled for his phone, putting it on speaker.

"Chief Paveith," a voice answered.

"There are two of them!" he screamed.

Fire ripped across the night sky toward the central Oregon highway, and the semi-truck's engine exploded. As it burned, three dragons landed nearby.

A loud knock on the door yanks me from my sleep. The clock reads ten past four. The only person who should be waking me up right now is Amira asking for another round, like she did two hours ago.

Amira starts against me as the knocking continues. "Markus?" she whispers sleepily.

"Don't move, Obi," I whisper back. I jump out of bed, pull on sweats, and crack open the door.

Well, fuck.

Commandant Eirikssen wears his signature scowl, a tumbler of coffee in his hand. "There was—"

I step into the hall and close the door behind me.

He raises his eyebrows. "Another attack last night. We're infiltrating the Jonjung warehouse at sunrise, and you're coming along to help us locate the evidence. We meet the chief in an hour. Get dressed."

Ice rushes through my veins, shoving out the morning grogginess. Well, that's one way to wake up.

"Got it." I slip back into my room and turn on the bathroom light, casting a faint glow across the bedroom.

"What's going on?" Amira leans up on her elbow, her adorable scratchy morning voice making it hard to focus on anything else.

"The commandant is pulling me in for a bust."

She sits up straighter. "The stolen handbags?"

"Yep." Among other things. "But once it's over, Loki's officially mine." I sit on the bed and kiss her nose. "Take good notes for me today."

She snuggles back into bed, looking warm and inviting. I'm glad she's not worried.

"You're lucky you're cute," she says through a yawn. "Dinner tonight?"

Shit, dinner with her dad. Well, we're busting the Jonjungs in two hours, and I'll already be in Portland if we run late. "Definitely. What time?"

"Seven."

"Sounds good, Obi." I kiss her soft lips, wishing I could stay.

Later. I'll get back to this later.

I dress quickly in full riding leathers. They're freezing cold compared to Amira's body snuggled against mine. After digging the dragon-scaled armor out of the back of the closet, I tug it on. The commandant already knows I didn't break my dragon, and everyone else is sleeping, so my secret will be safe. Finally, I pull out my balaclava and tuck it into my pocket. It's cold outside.

I hustle to Loki's stall, grabbing a thermos of coffee on the way. "Good morning, sleepyhead."

"It's too early for this." He doesn't even open his eyes. I don't blame him.

"Sorry, bud." My throat tightens. "The commandant needs us to help bust Ren. We're going to Portland."

He finally opens his eyes and stretches out like a cat. *"Fine, but I want an extra sheep."*

"You can have two. Come on." I get the saddle mounted and we exit the cave, passing by the sheep pen on the way.

Loki snaps up three sheep in quick succession, and his eyes glitter with delight at his bonus breakfast. *"Stop fidgeting. You're so jumpy."*

I probably should have grabbed a protein bar instead of coffee.

The commandant waits at the mouth of the dragon cave with Professor Schloss, who's already strapped into his Black's saddle.

As the most stoic Goldwing on Dragild's faculty, I'd be shocked if Schlossy said much today. Though he'd yell at me if I called him *Schlossy* to his face...

"Let's go," Commandant Eirikssen says, mounting Mars.

I climb up and buckle in, double-checking the straps with shaky hands. My stomach flutters, but I shove away the nerves. I pull down my balaclava and settle the goggles over it.

We take off in tight formation, the commandant in the lead. The stars twinkle, the world otherwise bathed in shadows. All the bedroom windows in the dorms are dark, including mine, so hopefully Amira's fallen back asleep. I appreciate her confidence in me.

Mars's giant frame cuts down our wind resistance as Loki and I follow in the airstream. With a wingspan of at least sixty feet, Mars is one of the largest dragons I've ever seen. Aries, Professor Schloss's dragon, is only fifty feet across, but he's faster. Younger, too. None of his facial scales are turning gray yet. I guess the third-years won't have military training today since he's here for the bust.

Professor Hauk isn't here, so the second-years will still have flight practice at sunrise, and Amira will have flight practice with the rest of the first-years this afternoon. Definitely wish I was still tucked in next to her. No Professor Rhettford either, but ethics is Amira's favorite class, and she'll be happy to tell me all about the lecture when I see her tonight.

Maybe I'll have time to take a nap before dinner.

We hit the outskirts of Portland, and the Columbia River rages below us. Moonlight dances over the white caps. Streetlights pierce the darkness along the dock, now empty of motorcycles. Dim light shines through the windows of Ren's warehouse.

Our trio touches down on Government Island, wrapped in the shadows of the pine trees.

A dozen Goldwings congregate around a cardboard coffee box from a chain donut shop, a small lantern providing a low-powered glow. They've all got armor, guns, and confident postures that come from years of experience I don't have. Dragons create a circle around the group, standing at attention and keeping the riders warm with their radiating heat.

I straighten, take a deep breath, and dismount. My mouth is dry, but more coffee would make my shaking hands worse. I shove them into my pockets.

Loki curls up and tucks in his tail. *"Wake me up when something happens."* He falls asleep immediately. I wish I could do that.

"Chief Paveith," Commandant Eirikssen says. "Any movement?"

"Nothing." The chief's frown deepens as we join the circle, although no one looks my way. "The warehouse has been silent since we got here. The dragon stable, too."

"Are we waiting on anyone else?"

"No. Our undercover agent went off the grid two nights ago."

The chief looks around the circle. "No cops today. No other military units either. We're keeping this one in-house."

Professor Schloss nods, grunting approval. A few other Gold-wings chime in, supporting the choice.

"Rizzo and Newton, guard the stable." The chief narrows his gaze at the pair. "Heat scanners indicate three sleeping dragons, so your job should be easy. Don't fuck this up." His gaze wanders over the rest of the group. "Core four, one door each. I want two at each warehouse door, so pick a partner. One ground, one roof. Heat scanners saw four bodies inside. If anyone tries to take off, kill by fire. The remaining five, head into the basement—including Markus."

I blink off the surprise, stand taller, and give a quick nod. Chief Paveith basically just declared my presence critical. My idol just declared me a necessary asset to complete our mission.

"Eirikssen, stick with the kid. Schloss, you're cracking the safe. We're going in, and we're taking them down." The chief slams his fist into his hand and mumbles something under his breath. I make out the words *those fuckers* and *office*.

Loki wakes as I pet his neck. He shakes off his cat nap. *"Not long enough."*

It never is. I mount up and strap in safely before adjusting my armor and my goggles over the balaclava.

The first rays of sunlight peek out over the horizon, cutting into the darkness. Once the chief is mounted on Zeus, all fifteen dragons rise into the air. The flapping wings interrupt the sound of the waves.

Our flight surrounds the warehouse, and everyone gets into position. The only sound left is my heartbeat pounding in my ears while adrenaline floods my system.

"Move in!" the chief shouts. "Eirikssen, fire!"

Zeus and Mars shoot their raging blue fire directly at the aluminum door and melt it into a puddle with ease, revealing the empty warehouse.

Oh! Not empty anymore!

Three semi-trucks are parked inside.

Hell yeah! Nailed them! I give a small fist pump. This is justice for Loki's last rider and Loki's torn wing.

"Get moving!" The chief pushes forward on Zeus, and we all rush into the warehouse.

A guy in jeans, a Portland State T-shirt, and an Oregon Ducks baseball cap is sitting in one of those awkward foldable fabric chairs near the first truck, his eyes wide and his face white. He raises his arms over his head. Ren's second-in-command is sitting next to him, thermos in hand. Ren steps out from the back of one of the semi-trucks, followed by the fourth man wearing jeans. Ren's face betrays pure rage, and the cords in his neck pulse.

Roars rage from the stable next door. Loki jolts backward. My hands slip on the pommel, now coated in sweat. We're safe from their dragons, though.

Zeus rushes to the truck, snaps Ren up with her jaws, and dangles him precariously from her full height. Luckily for Ren, his dragon armor can't be pierced by her sharp fangs, although her jaws can still crush him. Gods, I would not want to be him right now.

The other Goldwings dismount their dragons and apprehend the remaining three accomplices. Zip ties bind their wrists together behind their backs, their guns are confiscated, and the men are lined up along the wall. Ren remains angrily dangling above them, trapped in Zeus's jaws.

I take a deep breath, settling into the saddle as my heart rate comes down.

"The fuck is this, Paveith?" Ren screams.

"The fuck you doing with the cargo?" the chief shouts back.

"Selling it!"

Loki tilts his head. *That was probably a bad answer.*

He's not wrong. Considering Ren just admitted to the crime, I guess our work here is done. Go us! Our spy skills are officially top-notch, and there's no denying it now.

The Goldwings surround Ren, guns pointed, as Zeus sets him down. They pin his hands behind his back and bind his wrists. The vein on Ren's neck is ready to explode, and he glares at every face in the room in turn, memorizing them. A shiver runs down my spine. I'm glad I wore my balaclava and armor. Ren can't recognize me.

Loki shrinks back. *I'm glad this was quick.*

Way easier than last time, when we set the tree on fire. Not my brightest idea.

One of our Goldwings climbs into the back of the semi-truck. His footsteps echo through the cargo hold.

The chief dismounts and walks over to the lineup. "Your illegal operation ends today."

"Illegal?" Ren says, tone spiteful. "Now it's illegal to have a side job that doesn't revolve around your goddamn bid for a political office?"

"It is when you're tarnishing my campaign by stealing from the goddamn government!"

The chief has spent the last thirty years building a career. Ren's not going to get off easy. I cross my arms in solidarity.

Ren's eyes narrow. "The fuck are you talking about, Paveith?"

Cracking wood sounds from the back of the truck. Loki lays down, and I dismount and peer into the cargo hold. Four crate lids sit on the floor. The Goldwing cracks open the fifth while the commandant dismounts and joins me.

"Zimmer, what did you find?" the chief calls.

"Leather purses," he calls back. "The crate is full." He pulls out a bag and studies it. It's another Yong, just like the one I grabbed for Amira.

"And where did it come from?" the chief asks.

"From Korea," Ren snaps, "where my family manufactures them."

With their sustainable water dragon operation Amira raved about.

Fuck. I didn't steal stolen goods. I stole from Ren.

"I don't like what you're implying, Paveith." Ren spits out the chief's name like venom. "Even if my operation was illegal, who gives a damn? Are you pissed that the donations for your campaign stopped when I took over from my father? Is that what this is?"

The commandant frowns. "Where is the basement?" he whispers to me.

I lift my chin toward the back door. "Through there. The safe with the collars is in a back room."

He walks over to the chief. They hold a conversation, too low for any of us to hear. I shift my weight from one leg to the other.

"You're coming with us," the chief tells Ren.

Zimmer, the chief, the commandant, Ren, Professor Schloss, and I all walk toward the back wall, our footsteps a stampede. The chief nods to Zimmer, who presses the button to open the garage. It remains just as quiet as it was the last time I was here. We descend into the darkness, Zimmer in front with his rifle. In the dimly lit bunker, we pass by the crates. Ren mumbles curses aimed at the chief.

We don't stop until we're in front of the safe, where bloodstains still coat the cement floor. My stomach lurches at the sight. The memory of the gunshot two nights ago sends a chill down my spine. I shove down the feelings and take a deep breath. With Ren tied up, there's no risk of being shot this time. Especially not with the chief and the commandant here.

"Open it," the chief demands.

Professor Schloss steps forward and does the same trick Jonas used to crack it. Those old Cary Co. safes really are useless. As he swings it open, Ren glares from behind him.

Eight obsidian collars glitter in the dim light. Beside them, four dust-free spaces stare back at me. I picture the collar hiding under my bed.

We've nailed Ren and the Jonjungs. You can't fight the evidence.

"Where did all this obsidian come from?" the chief asks, tone accusing.

Ren knows exactly what he did. His Adam's apple bobs as he swallows. "This is about the hijacking." He takes a deep breath, but his nostrils flare. "It wasn't me. These collars have been in my family for generations."

Wait, what? Ren has to be lying.

"You expect me to believe that?" The chief crosses his arms. "The collars are supposed to be turned in when a dragon dies."

"And we did turn them in." He pinches his lips. "At least, the ones from our own necks. We retired these collars after the dragons died, to honor them," Ren spits out. "Not that you know anything about honor."

The chief stares him down.

"You really think I'm behind the hijacking?" Ren lets out a

hysterical laugh. "Pavvy, Pavvy, Pavvy," he says, shaking his head. "If I were behind the heists, I sure as hell wouldn't be hiding the obsidian in this old clunker of a safe."

He has a point.

I swallow. I didn't steal stolen goods; I stole a collar worth hundreds of thousands that's been in Ren's family for generations.

Fuck.

I study the eight collars left. The intricate Dancheong pattern would have taken months to create. Even working around the clock, they couldn't have made twelve collars when the first batch of obsidian was only stolen a month ago.

I avert my eyes as my stomach flips. Can I bring the collar back?

The chief studies him critically before he glares at me. My face heats beneath my balaclava. He nods to Zimmer, who releases Ren's ties.

"Get the hell out of here, and take your dirty politics with you," Ren says.

We all head back up to the warehouse.

"Clear out!" the chief yells.

Our Goldwings release the apprehended victims. The guy in jeans lets out a sigh of relief as the other two glare at us.

"That was... unfortunate." Loki nudges me.

I quietly mount, buckle into my saddle, and follow the commandant back to Government Island. Professor Schloss flies close behind. The sun sits just above the horizon.

Once we land, I remove the sweaty balaclava and breathe in the fresh air. My relief is short-lived.

The commandant studies me from the top of his Black. "Amira was in your room this morning, wasn't she?"

I nod once, locking my gaze on his.

"I said from the start, it's the Ejo clan. Were you holding out to protect her family?" he asks. "If so, that was really fucking stupid."

That's exactly what it looks like. I shake my head, throat choked.

"Then you've been lying to yourself, for a goddamn girl. And you've embarrassed all of us."

He's right. I was so fixated on nailing the Jonjungs that I ignored the obvious signs Ren's clan was innocent. They may as well have been written in neon lights. The dust on the collars in the safe, the twelve finished collars with elaborate designs... And what a dick move on my part, assuming the stuff in the bunker was stolen.

But Tobias broke in to steal two of the collars, even though Derkomai already has a second collar. And that second collar had to have come from somewhere. Maybe it *was* his clan hijacking the trucks and stealing the obsidian.

Chief Paveith lands nearby. "We just found *nothing*." The chief seethes, glaring my way. Zeus blows smoke, mirroring the chief's rage. "This mistake is *unacceptable*. Is this the kind of intelligence I can expect from your career?"

I stand straighter and bite my tongue. It's a rhetorical question. *Don't answer, Markus.*

"It's probably the damn Ejo leader himself." He looks at me with disgust. "Your tenure as a Goldwing is *over*, kid."

Loki's body heaves. I've failed, and he's going to be reassigned. This is my fault. Lowering my gaze, I swallow, pushing my slumped shoulders back.

"Eirikssen, if this gets out to the public, it's going to spread like wildfire. Get your shit together, and get eyes on Obi and the Ejo clan. Next time they hit, I'm going to blow those *two fuckers* out of the sky." The chief takes off, leaving us in silence.

Professor Schloss remains stoic. "Let's get back."

Our trio rises in tight formation, aiming for Dragild. The only sound is the beat of our dragons' wings.

I... I'm so goddamn empty, but my limbs are heavy as stone.

Stupid stolen collar. Stupid decisions. Stupid...

How could I have been so blind? Not only did I embarrass myself, but I embarrassed the commandant and the chief. I embarrassed everyone in the formation back there. This is a mess I can't put back together.

Loki and I have come so far, and for it all to dissolve here... I'm about to lose him. I'm about to lose our bond. The best dragon I could hope to ride, who never asked for any of this but went along with all of it...

The hollow cavity inside my chest aches. This can't be it. This can't be the end.

But it is.

They're about to reassign him to someone who has their god-damn shit together. And what can I even do? Chief Paveith just claimed my career is over. For the Goldwings, his word is law.

I'm not just losing Loki. I'm losing Amira, who slept tucked against me last night, her body soft and warm. She won't want to be with someone who got kicked out of school. And now, here I am. A man who couldn't even break his own dragon; who failed at his mission; who has nothing.

Amira... She deserves everything.

There's no enjoying our last flight, but I scratch Loki's neck and settle in. I don't want my sadness to bring him down—not that I can really control it. I force my feelings away, but melancholy washes over me through the bond. So Loki feels it too...

Back at Dragild, we land at the mouth of the dragon cave.

The commandant dismounts first. "Get Loki inside. I'll be there shortly."

I nod. Words fail me. My throat is still choked up anyway.

Loki and I head back to his stall, each step heavier than the last. With his saddle off, Loki settles into his favorite corner and lays his head down.

Loss washes over me just like it did a month ago, when I first put on the collar. Not quite as intense, but still heavy. I sit down next to him, leaning against the wall.

He'll be bounced to a new rider. Probably the one who lost their dragon in the last attack. What if Loki doesn't like them?

What if they don't give him extra sheep?

What if they don't let him race?

I'm not sure what to say to fill the silence.

An image of Mamba, tired and broken, takes over my thoughts. He never had the chance to get out. But Loki could.

"Loki..." I keep my voice low. My chest is tight. "I never asked you... do you want to be free? We can get you out."

He shakes his head. *"I like sleeping, but not enough to be stuck in a volcano all year. I'd rather race."*

"Okay." That tracks. Of course, my favorite adrenaline junkie wouldn't want to be trapped in Mount Rainier until the summer solstice. "New rider, it is."

He nuzzles me. *"Maybe my next rider won't be afraid of heights."*

"Ha, ha, bud. Very funny." I place my hand on his nose, leaning forehead to forehead. "I'm really sorry I failed."

Loki's forehead is wet. He closes his eyes. *"We both did."*

I scratch his neck, rise, and brush off the dust from my leathers. "Okay, tough guy." I force a smile. "You're the best."

I study Loki. His long, serpentine neck; his white scales; the gray spots all along his back; his tail that looks like it was dipped in gray paint...

"Quit leaking." He curls his tail around his body and lays his head down, blinking up at me. *"And don't do anything stupid. I won't be around to watch."*

"Thanks, bud." I wipe my eyes. "For everything."

I exit Loki's stall and close the door, locking it securely for the last time.

The commandant clears his throat and holds out his hand. "The collar."

I unclasp the collar from my neck, holding it in my shaking hands. Without it, my head feels strangely light. There's more space to think, more space to exist, and more space to simply be. The burden is lighter, though my grief still runs deep.

My feet are rooted to the floor. I can't take that first step toward the commandant.

But I have to.

Except I can't. I physically can't move.

He lowers his hand. "The collar's effects are wearing off. Give it a minute. It'll pass."

I swallow and take a breath. My hands won't stop trembling, but the rest of my body is frozen. "The hijacking last night. Did the driver make it?"

He shakes his head.

That makes five dead. I was supposed to help stop this. The driver's blood is on my hands. My pathetic, shaking hands, clasped tight around the collar I didn't forge, connected to a dragon I didn't break. I was so determined to pin the hijacking on Ren that I failed to see the evidence right there in front of me.

The chief was so sure the Ejo clan was responsible. Tobias has to know something. He *has* to. I just...

I'm kicked out. It's someone else's problem.

"Who are you going to tap for the mission?" And will they get Loki? Can I still see him sometimes?

Commandant Eirikssen raises his eyebrows.

Of course. Privileged information. "Right. Well, Tobias was in the Cascades last night, but—"

"How do you know that?" The commandant narrows his eyes.

I shift my weight, feet still glued to the floor. "He invited me and Loki to race."

His eyes widen. "Why didn't you say that? What happened?"

"Oh..." I swallow. Lying has gotten me nowhere. "I didn't go."

The commandant's jaw drops. "You *didn't go*? When your *mission* was to *get close to him*?"

"I..." I had a really important date. But I don't want to say that. I value my life too much to say that. Silence is better than *that*.

"Are you kidding me right now? What else haven't you shared?"

"Dragon Wars is tomorrow, and he'll be racing. And..." I swallow. "I was supposed to have dinner with Amira and Tobias tonight. At their dad's." Except there's no way Amira will want a dragonless screw up. So I guess that's not happening, ever. Goddamnit.

"Markus..." Commandant Eirikssen drags his hand down his face and sighs deeply. "I can't believe I'm saying this considering you've been fucking up for weeks, but there's no way I can get someone else that close this quickly. I'd be an idiot not to send you in. You have until midnight tomorrow to crack Tobias and pin the culprit."

He turns on his heel and leaves me standing, collar in hand.

Holy shit.

My head spins. I don't deserve this. But I'm not screwing this up. I can't. We can't. Because this is my last chance to remain a Goldwing.

I snap the collar back on, and heaviness washes over me through the bond. But Loki doesn't need to feel heavy anymore. I zip back into the stall, and Loki's eyes look up at me as I close the door behind me.

He tilts his head. *What's going on?*

"We're getting another shot!" My excitement crashes through the bond and hits him hard. He rises and dances in a circle, and I dance along with him. "We have thirty-six hours to—" I stop, dead in my tracks. "Pin someone in the Ejo clan for the hijacking."

Oh, fuck.

Good feeling, gone.

The chief said we're keeping this in-house. If it's Amira's father behind the hijacking, the chief could sentence him to the firing squad, no questions asked.

I lean my forehead against the cave wall and take a deep breath.

The clock is ticking.

11

O bsidian was the key, and they had an entire crate of it, hard-fought and sorely won. The muscle of the operation walked in with a crowbar. He pried the crate open, cracking the wood as he went. Once it was unlatched, he threw the top to the floor.

The trio gazed into the stone-filled crate. White marble stared back at them.

The mastermind scowled. "They played us."

And nobody played a mastermind for a fool.

T he obsidian collar I stole from Ren hangs from my shoulder. Smoke billows out as I open the door to Dragild's workshop. A wave of heat hits me from the furnaces as the burning smell of wood overwhelms my senses, just like it did every day for three months earlier this year, when I crafted my first collar.

"Hey, Tobias?" I call out. I missed his note earlier today, not that it came particularly early. With Professor Schloss helping bust the Jonjungs, their class was canceled. Apparently, Tobias slept in.

"We're in the back." His voice is distant and slightly muffled.

I try to wave away the smoke, but it's useless. The drab cement floors and walls are concealed behind the plumes. The last thing I need is to crash into the metal tables or equipment, which are sure to leave more nasty bruises. Why didn't they turn on the ventilator? Running my hands along the wall, I hit the ventilator switch, and the room slowly clears of smoke.

"Thanks," Theo says. "I forgot where the damn switch was."

Closets span the entire left wall. I head to the first door and pull out dragonskin gloves. Ovens line the back wall. Jonas is throwing wood into the blazing fire while Tobias and Theo supervise. They acknowledge me with a nod as I cross the room.

Tobias's brow furrows. "Get your collar in. It needs to heat up slowly, and the oven's already warming."

"Right." My chest tightens. The Dancheong pattern carved into it is too pretty to destroy, the story behind it too special. But I need to, if I want to stick with Tobias and keep my place at Dragild. I crack open the door and carefully place the collar next to the other three.

"What took so long?" he asks. "You were almost too late."

I'm not about to share the failed bust. "Busy morning."

Theo laughs. "Amira could barely keep her eyes open when I saw her in the food hall."

Tobias's jaw goes slack, and he holds his hand up in a stop gesture. "I don't want to know."

I don't feel too bad, considering she's the one who woke me up in the middle of the night. As if I'd ever deny her anything.

Jonas scowls at him but continues to throw wood on the fire.

Tobias blinks, locks his jaw, and turns to Theo. "Give us the game plan. We only have a couple of hours before I head to the Den."

"For family dinner?" I ask. "Amira invited me. We're leaving at five."

Jonas glares at me. It's not like I'm trying to rub it in.

Theo rolls his eyes at all of us and pulls a detailed schematic of a collar from his bag, laying it on the table. "Come on, guys. Focus. We're going to heat the collars and grind off the top layer, erasing the pattern. Then we'll wet sand and acid polish, just to clean it up."

"What about diamond paste?" Tobias asks. "You said we might be able to fill the pattern instead."

"I found some studies that showed the paste interfered with magnetizing the obsidian, although I suppose it wouldn't have mattered for the second collars since we aren't connecting them. But it's unlikely to fully hide the pattern, and it's a lot harder to grind off if it doesn't work. It's not worth the risk, all things considered."

Tobias nods once. "What's the chance of the obsidian cracking?"

That would suck. I have no desire to break into the Jonjung

warehouse again to steal another. And I doubt we'd be able to, after the raid this morning.

"Lower than if we wet sanded the whole layer," Theo says, "but we're still better off taking the temperature higher and giving it a longer cooldown before the polish."

"No, we need them for tomorrow. Damn new student open house, cockblocking us from the shop yesterday." Tobias gazes out the window toward the courtyard. "Ren is going down at the Wars."

Theo points to some math scribbled in pencil along the edge of the schematic. "This is the cooling quotient. We should have a half hour to grind."

"Looks good to me."

"You aren't even looking at it." Theo pinches his lips into a thin line.

Tobias turns to him with a smirk. "You're part of my team. Am I not supposed to trust you?"

"Right." Theo blushes and digs out his tablet from his bag.

We lay out dragonskin cloths on four tables, turn on the table warmers, and retrieve the grinders and equipment from the closets.

Theo taps my arm with a pair of safety glasses. "Protect those pretty baby blues."

"Thanks." I put them on along with a respirator before pulling my collar out of the oven.

The buzzing makes conversation impossible. Slow and steady, I grind carefully clockwise, just like I did when I made my first collar. Guilt weighs me down as I erase the collar's culture. I'm the last person who will ever see the pattern, handcrafted by Ren's family however many years ago.

"Back into the oven," Theo says once I've ground down the pattern. "Warm it for ten minutes and then take the sander to it."

I set the collar into the oven and lean against the table. "Is this what you research all day?"

"I've started looking into obsidian implants, actually."

"How would that work?"

"Okay, so... follow along. I'm only gonna say it once. Amira goes too easy on you." He smirks. "The collars are cut from the same rock and magnetized together, and that forms the bond, right?"

I nod.

"But look at where we put them. They're on the neck near the spinal cord, with all that tissue to get through, and with a huge risk of breaking or being damaged. Obviously, we can't implant an entire collar's worth of obsidian into a body, but we don't need to. We can get an implant much closer to our nerves. You follow?"

I nod again.

His eyes light up. "I read this study on bioactive glass implants. And obsidian is, at its core, a glass. So what if we take the smallest amount of obsidian to keep the connection, coat both pieces in the bioactive glass, and implant directly against the cervical nerves in the spine?"

"That's really cool." At least, if the dragon wants it.

"Yeah, for sure. We'd still have to use a collar for the initial break-ing. It's not like we can surgically implant obsidian as a dragon flies off, right? But consider the savings in time and resources once we got the dragons back to the cave. The practical applications, too."

I guess there would be a lot of them. "How would you test it?"

"Oh, pythons. The same way they tested the obsidian collars. Granted, it's a lot harder to keep a collar on a snake than a dragon."

My thoughts drift back to Mamba. He wouldn't have been able to escape the implant, not like how he broke the collar off. But would he be happier, still paired with a human he didn't choose once they moved the implant to another rider?

Theo pulls his collar out of the oven and smiles. "Perfect."

We smooth away the last of the grooves and let the glass cool in the temperature-controlled cabinet. After an acid bath, we polish the collars until they shine with a mirror finish.

Culture officially erased.

But I'm forging ahead into Tobias's inner circle, and that's the part I need to focus on.

Tobias studies my work. "Looking good. Perfect for the Wars tomorrow."

My throat thickens. "Thanks."

Theo hoses down the entire back half of the shop, washing the black dust down the drain. "Like we were never here. Once it dries, anyway."

I look at the clock. "It's four-thirty. I need a shower. Are you flying down with us?"

Tobias shakes his head. "Heading to Carina's room. We like to give Tiger a head start. She's a slow poke, and Amira lets her get away with it."

No wonder Tiger hates racing.

I grin. "We'll see you at the Den."

Get over here, Obi." I wrap my hands around Amira's thighs and lift her up, putting her back against the wall of the dragon cave, exactly where I want her. She places her hands on the nape of my neck. I kiss her deeply, losing myself in her delicious scent.

My chest tightens as I consider what I have to do to keep her, Loki, and my place at Dragild. I need to nail down whoever is stealing the obsidian and report back to the commandant, and he's convinced it's someone from the Ejo clan. Considering Amira's dad runs it, he must know something. And I'm about to eat dinner with him.

"You okay?" she asks, keeping her voice low.

I swallow, setting her down gently, and readjust Loki's new collar around my shoulder.

She hooks her finger through the collar and pulls me toward her.

"Where's this from?" she asks.

"I took it when I grabbed the purse. Theo helped me prep it for Loki after I got back from the bust."

"At least Theo's using his powers for good."

"Right." I smile, but I'm pretty sure it comes off as a grimace. I place my hand on the small of her back, and we walk down the cave. I glance at her neck. "Obi, why did you craft your collars thin? Why risk a weak connection?"

"Theo helped me calculate the exact amount of obsidian to make it strong enough. It's fine."

"But you fell, during the breaking. I..." My cheeks heat as we stop walking. "I watched you."

Her soulful eyes stare deep into mine. "I told Tiger I wouldn't force her to do anything. She knocked me off to prove a point, but as I fell to the ground, I was fully prepared to die. She realized I wasn't kidding, and she chose to save me."

I hug her tight, my throat choked up. This girl...

"So how was class?" I ask as we continue through the cave.

Amira's expression brightens. "You missed a great lecture. Professor Rhettford was on fire today. We discussed whether or not the Goldwings' actions during the last war were ethical. Which, obviously, they weren't, although half the class disagreed." She rolls her eyes.

I don't remember anything about it. "Remind me?"

"Two dragons were forced directly into enemy territory on a

suicide mission, and of course, they died horribly tragic deaths as they brought down the enemy's tower." Her frown deepens. "They were used as a means to achieve the Goldwings' end, and not as an end in themselves. It was exploitative and cruel, and it resulted in mass protests across the entire country. Coachella even shut down for a day."

I rack my brain but can't remember ever hearing about the protests.

Amira opens the door to Tiger's stall, and the dragon immediately bounds over. Amira caresses Tiger's nose. "Ready for our flight to Portland? We have company today."

Tiger nudges me affectionately, and I scratch her chin. "Loki's coming, too."

She narrows her golden eyes, but I have no idea why she's... upset? Annoyed? Suspicious?

Amira laughs. "Don't worry. No racing for us. Loki and Derko-mai will inevitably race each other later, though, and we can laugh as they try to show off."

"Loki would take offense to that." Even though it's true.

"Well, it's a good thing he isn't here to hear me. I wouldn't want to discourage him before Dragon Wars." Her smile is infectious. She turns to Tiger. "We're going along tomorrow to cheer them on, but we'll stick to the sidelines."

I head for Loki's stall and get him saddled up. I put his new second collar around his neck. It falls against the first with a clang.

"What do you think? How do you feel?"

Loki blinks. *"Not really any different. Let's test it."*

Of course, my favorite adrenaline junkie can't wait. "We're flying with Tiger and Amira. Maybe we can try it out later tonight against Derkomai. Sound good?"

A ping of excitement hits me through our bond.

"Fine," he huffs. *"I'll wait until the Dragon Wars tomorrow for a real challenge."*

We leisurely fly the hundred miles in a bit over an hour, sticking close to Tiger and Amira. Clear blue skies and a light breeze accompany us the whole way, a fitting contrast to the terror raging inside me. We land in front of the garage door to the Den, and it opens immediately.

"Amira!" The guard greets her enthusiastically. His formerly dark eyes are bright, and he's no longer the harsh bodyguard who gruffly waved me on.

"Ray! How are the babies?" She slides down from Tiger's back.

His expression softens. "Jay and I can barely keep up with them. He says hello, by the way. Thanks for the baby blankets."

"Of course." She gestures to me. "Ray, this is Markus."

Loki nudges her.

"And Loki, of course." She rubs his nose affectionately. "We're heading up for dinner. Dad upstairs?"

He nods. "Hasn't gone out this week."

"We'll keep trying." She begins the walk toward the ramp.

Loki and I follow behind, but Ray grabs my arm, pulling me back. He keeps his voice low. "Don't mess with our girl." He narrows his eyes. "I'm watching."

I gulp, nodding once. If Amira's dad is this protective, it's going to be a rough night.

He smiles and lets go, waving us on.

Loki glances back. *"He was kinda scary."*

Yeah, probably why he's the bouncer.

We follow Amira and Tiger down the ramp, across the parking lot, and through the not-so-secret charred-wall door. I fully expect the automatic lights when they blind me. The smell of sulfur fills my nose.

"Hey, Amira." The crotchety old guard stands up and hugs her, a big smile plastered across his face. "How are you, kiddo?"

"Survival of the fittest, as always." She grabs my hand and pulls me forward. "George, this is Markus and his dragon, Loki."

Happiness fills our bond as Loki revels in his introduction. *"You should be more like Amira. She listens."*

George holds out his hand and greets me warmly. "The stories I could tell you about this kid—"

"Not today, hopefully not ever." She bites her lip. "I'd like Markus to stick around."

Laughing, George checks his watch. "Get up there, girl. I'm sure your dad's missing you. Tobias got here fifteen minutes ago."

We pass through the cavern and the amphitheater, and Amira

places her hand on the scanner. The door of the family stable slides open, and she opens the first stall. "Okay, Tiger. In you go."

Tiger disappears, and we get Loki settled into the stall next to hers. *"Do I get dinner too?"*

I raise my eyebrows. "Hey Amira, Loki would like to know if he could please have another bonus sheep on top of the two bonus sheep he already ate this morning. Apparently, we don't care to follow Kristoffer's healthy dragon diet plan."

"Sure, Loki. I won't tell." She laughs, the sound light and airy, before bringing him his fourth sheep of the day. "Before we go up, I want to check on my dad's dragon."

"Sounds good." I force a smile. After meeting Mamba, I'm not looking forward to this.

Amira laces her fingers through mine and pulls me into the final stall. "Hey, Mami."

The Black blinks awake and lifts her head to full height, gaze directed toward us. Her head tilts to the side, and she watches me with curiosity. Her blue-tipped black scales glitter under the bioluminescent orbs. While smaller than Mamba in stature, strong muscles ripple beneath her scales. It looks like she's ridden regularly, and she's definitely strong enough to hijack a semi-truck.

First bit of evidence: acquired.

My stomach drops. The commandant and the chief are convinced it's someone in the Ejo clan, and it looks like the leader himself is a suspect.

Amira drops my hand, crosses the floor, and rubs the edge of Mami's wing. A soft purr fills the air. She gestures for me to join her. "She won't bite. Hard." My eyes widen as Amira smiles. "Just kidding. Come over here."

I approach slowly. Mami lowers her head to my height, and her golden eyes stare straight into my soul. I hold out my hand. She places her nose against it before refocusing on Amira, who hasn't stopped stroking her wing.

"See?" Amira gloats. "She's great."

"At least she isn't out to kill me."

Her eyebrows rise, eyes dancing in amusement. "Who would possibly be out to kill you?"

Ren and the Jonjungs, Tobias, Amira if she figures out I'm... fuck. "Mamba might. Tobias introduced me two nights ago." Has he moved since we left him? Or is he still in the corner?

Amira frowns and bites her lip, the glimmer in her eyes gone. "He's had it rough. Don't blame him for it." She sighs. "He won't let anyone near him. Not even me. I think... I'm pretty sure I just remind him of my mom. She used to bring Tobias along for races, but... well, I don't really want to talk about it. Not right now."

"You don't have to."

I take her hand and softly kiss the back of it. I get it, after the things Tobias shared. I'm glad she wasn't there to see it.

Amira hugs Mami's neck. "We'll see you on the way out."

We exit the stall.

She cracks the next stall's window to check on Mamba and gazes at him, her expression one of defeat.

In the elevator, I rest my hand on her lower back. She snuggles into me and places her hands on the nape of my neck. The door closes, and the metal box lurches before it begins its ascent. There are only two buttons on the wall: *stable* and *penthouse*.

"Still feeling nervous about meeting my dad?" she asks.

I swallow, ignoring the growing distance between us and the ground. "Maybe a little."

She kisses my cheek. "Don't worry too much. He's harmless."

"Anything I need to know before I enter the dragon's den?"

"Not really. If you can handle Tobias, my dad's a cakewalk."

Considering how difficult it was to win Tobias over, that's not making me feel better.

"Also..." She bites her lip again. "You're the first boy I've ever brought home—and I didn't tell him you're coming—but no pressure." She speaks so fast it sounds like one word.

Now you tell me?

The elevator pings, and the doors slide open to reveal a white foyer with a marble floor. I've run out of time to worry about it.

We step out beneath a crystal chandelier. No evidence of obsidian is visible in the otherwise sparse space.

"You're late, Mia." Tobias comes around the corner, followed closely by Carina.

"By five minutes." Amira raises her eyebrows. "You're on time."

"Ignore him, babe." Carina hugs Amira, glancing back at Tobias with a smirk.

He hugs Amira. "Dad's his usual," he says in a low tone.

She nods and laces her fingers through mine. "Come on."

The four of us enter the living room, quiet except for the sound of our footsteps. White walls, white furniture, floor-to-ceiling windows, and an amazing view of Portland greet us. Everything is bathed in the orange of the sunset. A giant canvas covered with black scales hangs from the back wall. A large, painted version of the family photo I found on Amira's nightstand hangs over a marble fireplace.

No hints of stolen obsidian or Amira's dad.

We pass through, entering the dining room. Six white leather chairs surround a rectangular glass table. Irises perch in a vase in the middle of four place settings. Hidden in the corner, Amira's dad stares out the window, his eyes dazed. His hair is grayer than it is in the photo, and Tobias is taller than him now. Does he even have enough muscle to ride his dragon? His black shirt hangs loosely on his frame. A collar glitters around his neck, carved with a geometric design similar to Amira's.

Our footsteps don't faze him. Tobias and Carina take their places at the table. Amira lets go of my hand and walks over to him.

"Dad," she says happily.

He seems to wake up at the sound of her voice, exiting his trance. I'm familiar with the effect.

"Hey, baby girl," he says, wrapping her in a hug.

"This is Markus." She waves me over.

He blinks, looking confused for a moment, before he smiles wide, his eyes crinkling in the corners. "Markus. I'm Mr. Obi. Welcome."

I shake his hand. "Thanks for having me."

"Of course!" He glances at his watch. "Dinner will be out soon. Sit down, please."

Tobias and Amira exchange a look as she and I take our seats across from him. Did I do something wrong? I shake some of the tension out of my hands.

The door opens, and a gray-haired woman enters with an extra place setting. "I made your favorite tonight," she says to Amira. "It's a good thing I made extra. Who's this?"

"This is Markus. Markus, Fatima. She's the best."

Fatima blushes and exits to the kitchen.

"Stay on her good side," Carina says in a low voice. "That's your ticket to extra dessert."

Tobias grins and kisses her temple.

Mr. Obi sits at the head of the table, opposite the last empty chair. "So, Markus, I assume you're at Dragild, too?"

"Yes. I'm a first-year with Amira. She mentioned you graduated from Dragild."

"I did. So did Sade, my wife. That's where we met. But that was back when Professor Fortid had black hair. I hear it's gray now."

"What's left of it," I say.

The whole table chuckles. Amira scoots her chair closer to me and rests her hand on my thigh. Finally, I'm doing something right.

Fatima comes out with a giant metal bowl and sets it on the table, filling the room with a delicious, smoky aroma. "Jollof rice with chicken, heavy on the tomatoes." We pass the bowl around the table.

"Markus, what type of dragon do you ride?" Mr. Obi asks.

He rides a Black, and he's disappointed Tobias rides a Ruby. Will he judge me for my dragon?

My mouth goes dry. "A Graytail. His name is Loki."

"Ah, good choice," he says, and the tension drops from my shoulders. "They're extremely docile, and their genes are perfect."

Amira tilts her head. "Really?"

"I..." Mr. Obi's expression darkens, just for a moment. "Never mind, baby girl."

Second piece of evidence: acquired. He's obviously got some secrets. The butterflies in my chest remind me that I still need to figure them out.

Tobias and Amira exchange another look. She frowns this time.

We direct the conversation back to dragons, Dragild, and the upcoming graduation ceremony, enjoying the meal. Mr. Obi remains animated, Amira grows happier as the night wears on, Carina's wit shines throughout, and Tobias... is Tobias.

Guilt and rice churn in my stomach. I've eaten two servings of the delicious meal, and now it's time to find some clues. "Which way to the bathroom?"

"I'll walk you." Amira rises, and I follow.

Guess I'm actually going to the bathroom.

We cross through the living room and head down the opposite hall, turning a corner and wandering all the way to the end. She opens the door to a very pink bedroom.

"Obi, what is this?" I place my hands at her waist and pull her toward me. "It's like bubblegum exploded on the walls."

"It was a choice I made with my heart, not my head." She leans up on her tiptoes and kisses me softly. "I'm so glad you came tonight. My dad hasn't been this... well, *him* since my mom died."

"Really?" I rub her back slowly.

"We've been really worried, but he refuses to talk to anyone. He's basically shut himself into the penthouse, and he never leaves."

But Mami clearly flies regularly. Her muscles haven't atrophied like Mamba's. Something's going on.

"Anyway," she says, biting her lip. "Bathroom through there. And hurry up. We aren't waiting for you to start dessert."

"I'm pretty sure you're over here distracting me. But I'd never ask you to make that big of a sacrifice." I kiss her forehead. "Fortunately, I'm not in the mood for the edible sort of dessert." My stomach is already in knots.

"Lucky me." She happily wanders out the door.

When her footsteps fade, I cross the hallway and silently enter the master bedroom. If anyone catches me snooping, I'm toast. I wipe my sweaty palms on my pants.

Nothing under the bed.

Nothing in the dresser, other than clothes.

Nothing in the first closet, other than more clothes.

Absolutely nothing in the second closet. Shit, this must have been Mrs. Obi's. They probably emptied it when she died.

My chest tightens with guilt. Amira would definitely not approve if she caught me right now.

I quickly poke my head into the other rooms, but nothing jumps out. At this point, if I don't go back to the dining room, it's going to look really bad. With thirty floors in this building, the evidence I need could be anywhere, but it's apparently not lying around the penthouse.

Well, that was a bust.

Amira's almost through a bowl of vanilla ice cream as I sit next to her.

"Excited for the Wars tomorrow?" Tobias asks me.

"Loki's ecstatic." Not a lie. "I swear, that dragon was born to race."

Mr. Obi chuckles and takes a sip of coffee. Something about him isn't adding up. No evidence of the hijacking, a lack of riding muscles on his frame, a dragon that flies regularly, and a knowledge of Graytail genetics...

"We should grab the steel tent while we're here," Amira says.

"Okay. We can grab it before we leave," Tobias says. "We'll fly out at eleven. The hundred-mile snowtop starts at sunset, but it's a party all day."

"There are also sprints in the afternoon," Carina says. "Goose and I usually do some of those. You're welcome to join us."

"Thanks," I say. "Loki will love that."

Amira finishes her last bite. "Carina, do you want to fly back with me so Loki can race Derkomai home?"

Carina grins. "Of course, babe! I want to hear all about last night."

My cheeks heat. I really hope Mr. Obi doesn't know what she means by that...

Tobias shakes his head. "Derkomai's gotta rest up before tomorrow. We're taking Ren down. Priorities, little sister."

I guess Loki won't get to try out the new collar tonight. Maybe we can race to Government Island and back before... No, that didn't go well last time.

"How's Ren doing?" Mr. Obi asks.

"He's as frustrating as ever," Tobias says.

Mr. Obi's chin lowers as he studies the table. "It wasn't his fault, Tobias. He changed things after he took over."

Amira narrows her eyes, silently trying to murder her brother with just her gaze. That look definitely runs in the family. "Yong is continuing to climb in popularity. His company's quickly taking over the luxury goods space. It would've been a great investment."

So the deal that fell apart...

"Carina, let's get back." Tobias stands and pushes in his chair. "Thanks for dinner, Dad. We'll see you next week."

Carina rises, clasping his hand. "Thanks for dinner, Mr. Obi."

Amira follows the pair out, but I stay put. Tobias is about to hear an earful. I know better than to be around for that. Besides, this is my opportunity to go fishing. Will Mr. Obi bite?

"Any tips for the Wars tomorrow?" I ask.

Mr. Obi blinks and looks up at me. "Fly fast." A hint of a smile crosses his face. "My wife was the racer. She'd have a list of course tips ready for you, off the top of her head."

Not the most helpful. I need evidence. "What about a boost?"

His eyes narrow slightly. "Are you talking about obsidian?"

Bingo. "Loki has a second collar for tomorrow. We haven't tried it out yet, though."

He shakes his head. "I've never used one, but Graytails were born to race."

Well, there goes that theory. But Mami...

"Right. With his perfect genes." I chuckle. "Like Loki's ego isn't big enough already."

"Sade was never wrong." He winks. "Did Amira mention she studied genetics in the research branch?"

"She doesn't really like talking about her mom."

He nods sadly. "It hit her hard. She's a carbon copy of her, though."

Amira's footsteps stop me from responding. She rests her hands on my shoulders. "What did I miss?"

"Nothing, baby girl." Mr. Obi stands. "Heading out?"

"Yeah, we should get back."

"Don't forget leftovers," Fatima says, coming out of the kitchen with a giant bag. "You need your strength. There's some for you, too, Markus."

"You mean I have to share?" Amira hugs Fatima and takes the bag.

"The fastest way to a man's heart is his stomach," Fatima whispers. I pretend not to hear. Food might help Amira burrow deeper, but she's already there.

Amira laughs. "Good looking out." She turns to her father and hugs him. "Goodnight, Dad. We'll see you next week."

At least, Amira will. The jury's still out on... Well, what does getting my shit together even look like at this point? I didn't find any evidence, although there are twenty-nine other floors, plus the Den below.

After goodbyes, I follow Amira into the private elevator, plastic bag in hand. "Since I'm carrying the food, does that mean I get to help eat it?"

Amira snatches it from me. "Nope."

I take it back and put it carefully on the floor. "That's fine, I've got something better."

Cupping her jaw, I tilt her chin up and kiss her. She moves

against me and deepens our kiss, meeting my tongue with hers. Desire floods through me, along with her delicious vanilla scent and the taste of vanilla ice cream. A small moan escapes from her lips.

The elevator door slides open behind me. She takes a step back and grabs the bag from the floor. "I don't trust you with it anymore."

"Fair. It was delicious."

She glances at her watch. "Do you want to let Loki race before we head back?"

"Just against himself?"

"Against Mami. Don't tell Tobias, but I always take her out to fly before I head home. I'm sure she'd love to race."

Just like that, all my evidence is shot to hell. There's no way her dad has anything to do with the stolen obsidian. All I feel is relief. I hug Amira tight, accidentally knocking the food bag to the ground.

"So, that's a yes?" she rasps.

I'm squeezing too hard. I loosen my arms. "Sorry. Yeah. Yeah, he'd love that." I enter Loki's stall. "Let's race, bud. You've got Mami tonight."

A jolt of excitement flows through our bond as I put on his saddle and get him ready. Amira has her dad's dragon ready to go before we're done. Only she could be so emotionally in tune with a dragon that the collars are moot.

The four of us race beneath the stars. Loki zigs, Mami zags, and both of them zoom happily around the Portland skyline. It definitely beats evading Ren and the cops.

After an hour of playtime, Amira gestures that we should wrap up. We head straight to the cavern.

"I'm just going to take Mami to her stall and grab Tiger. I'll be right back." She kisses my cheek, and off they go.

"So, Loki, did you have fun?"

"Mami is way faster than Derkomai."

That's a yes.

We wait by the bottom of the ramp, watching the gamblers play and the bartenders serve at the center of the cavern.

Theo enters the cavern from the amphitheater and walks our way. "Hey, Markus. What are you doing here?"

"Obi family dinner. Amira will be back in a minute."

"That's right. You mentioned this morning." His cheek has a smear of dust on it.

"You've got something right..." I point to the black mark.

He rubs it with his hand and looks at the dust on his palm. "Shit, it's obsidian. I thought I washed it all off." He rubs it on his pants.

"Hey, Theo!" Amira walks up with Tiger. "Going back to Drag-ild? We were just leaving."

"Yep." He calls for Baldur, who flies down and lands next to us.

The three of us exit, hightailing it home on the backs of our dragons.

Back on campus, we get the dragons settled in their stalls for the night.

Amira and I head directly to my room. She playfully straddles me on the bed. I flip her over and crawl on top, desperate to please her, desperate to taste every inch of her.

Afterward, we settle into my bed for the second night in a row. Her warm body nestles against me, and her breathing evens out. I bask in Amira's glow as my brain tries to make sense of the day.

I've got twenty-four hours left to figure out who's stealing the obsidian, but at least it's not her dad.

Adrenaline floods my system. I open my eyes to the pitch-black darkness.

Amira stretches out beside me. "You okay?" she croaks in her sleepy voice.

I swallow. "Never better. Just a bad dream." I kiss her head. "Go back to sleep."

She snuggles into my side. I caress the length of her back, letting her warmth thaw the ice in my veins.

Derkomai already had two collars before we broke into Ren's warehouse, and Tobias had to get that obsidian from somewhere. With Jonas's muscle and Theo's brain...

Fuck. I'm blind as a bat.

12

The mastermind set down his phone. "They're delivering the motherlode tomorrow. Thirty collars' worth is headed to Dragild for next year's new students."

He grinned. "We're taking all of it."

And burning Chief Paveith's reputation to the ground.

Amira's voice flutters through the dragon kaleidoscope of my dreams. "Wake up, Markus."

She's right. I need to wake up and face reality. Her brother has to be behind the hijacking. Either I'm turning him in and losing her, or I'm getting kicked out of school and losing her. But the evidence has been around Derkomai's neck the whole time.

"Markus."

Gods, her voice. Her affection. Her brilliance. All of her.

"Markus! It's ten thirty-five."

I open my eyes, yawn, and stretch out, uneasily entering the land of the living. "Hey. Hi. Good morning."

I'm running on... three hours of sleep?

"Morning's almost over," she says. Fully dressed and ready for the day, she straddles my waist and stares down at me, trapping me on the bed. "I brought you back a coffee."

"You..." I glance at the thermos on the nightstand. What an awesome way to wake up. "You are a goddess." I pull her down and kiss her as though I'll never get to kiss her again, taking my time to savor the taste of coffee on her lips, her warmth, and the calming thumps of her heartbeat.

She breaks away and climbs off the bed. "Okay, seriously, get up."

It's a rush to get ready for Dragon Wars. At five minutes to eleven, we scramble out to the dragon cave and find the gang waiting for us. Carina dances beside Goose, her speaker blaring an energetic song about the eye of the tiger. Tobias leans against Derkomai, Jonas juggles a soccer ball next to Poseidon, and Theo plays with his tablet from Baldur's back. Each dragon wears a second collar.

Poseidon and Baldur have ropes around their bodies that are tied to a giant crate between the two of them with a collapsed white tent and a cooler inside of it. Dragon transportation at its finest. And probably how they carry the crates of obsidian. More evidence.

Tobias gives us his signature scowl. "You're late, Mia. Second day in a row."

"Don't even start with me, Tobes." Amira rolls her eyes. "You know how many times I've waited hours for you to get your shit together?"

"Not for Dragon Wars! Get moving, or we're leaving you behind. Chop, chop."

At least he isn't threatening to throw me in with Mamba.

We hustle down the cave, and Amira darts into Tiger's stall as I head straight to Loki's.

He's up and about, standing next to his saddle. *"Hurry up!"*

"Everyone's a critic today."

"It's racing day, Markus. Come on!" He lays on the floor and nudges the saddle with his nose, begging me to speed up. Once his second collar and saddle are situated, I buckle up and let him run for the exit.

Our six dragons take to the cloudy July sky, and their shadows cross the courtyard below us as we fly leisurely southeast. Dragild shrinks into the distance, nestled among the mountains. The Cascades spread out in all directions, the tops of the ridges tipped with snow.

Chatter flows through my earpiece. Carina and Amira want to visit a new shop in Portland next weekend, Theo might even join them if they're willing to stop at a tech shop, Tobias still can't aim his shots for shit, and Jonas can't wait to try out the new collar. It's all very normal. Me exploding the group is so far below the radar it might as well be buried six feet under.

They won't see it coming. This totally sucks.

"We've got all day to figure it out," Loki says.

I take a deep breath, and his excitement rushes back through the bond.

We fly the one hundred miles to Mount Hood in under an hour. A flat expanse at the mountain's base is covered in white. We close in, and I realize it's a sea of large canopy tents like ours. At least fifty are spread across the abandoned airfield. Everyone's decked out in black, so they're all riders. Dragons perch on the steel frames or sleep in the grass.

I close my mouth, completely speechless.

"Welcome to the Dragon Wars, kid," Tobias shouts from Derkomai's back. "It's basically a historical institution."

We touch down in a clear space. The crate hits the ground with a thud as Poseidon and Baldur land. Jonas is the first off his dragon. He unclasps the sides of the crate and moves the ropes from the box to the steel frame of the tent itself. As he walks Poseidon one way, Theo walks Baldur the opposite, and the heavy-duty tent with a thick center pole opens outward and springs up. I help them disconnect the ropes from the dragons and put up the canvas sides. Tobias and Amira arrange the cooler and a couple of chairs. Carina sets up the speakers. Just like that, we have a dragon tailgate.

"I've got this one, you get the next," Amira says, handing me a beer as Tobias wanders off. I should probably follow him, but maybe that would be weird.

"Thanks, Obi," I say. "Cool tent."

"It's an old two-dragon model. Two dragons to assemble, and two can perch on the frame." Amira takes a sip of her beer. "My mom used her whole first paycheck to buy it after she and my dad graduated. She was tired of baking in the sun all afternoon during the races."

I look around. "It's in good shape, considering it's older than we are."

"We don't use it enough. But that changes, starting today." She smiles and kisses my cheek as my chest tightens. "The sprints won't start for another hour. Come on. I want to introduce you to one of my friends."

She laces her fingers through mine, and we walk across the field together, leaving Tiger and Loki to guard the cooler from the top of the tent.

A few tents over, a short girl with long black hair that's tied back in a ponytail waves us down. The dark purple scales on her vest have an ethereal shimmer, which I've never seen before. "Amira!"

"Honoka!" Amira drops my hand and rushes to hug her. "I thought you were staying at Dorogan Dojo this time, what with your teaching schedule?"

"I decided to fly commercial at the last minute. No Yagi and no racing, but I wasn't going to miss seeing you and Imani." Honoka turns around. "Imani! Get over here!"

Imani sees Amira, and her face brightens immediately. She speeds over and wraps her in a giant hug. She's an inch taller than Amira and has similar tattoos snaking down her arms. Makes sense, since they're legacies who grew up together.

Amira's smile is just as wide. "Look at those muscles! How's Kilimanjaro? And Shule ya Joka?"

"We're all counting down to the summer solstice. Only five more months." Imani straightens, chest out. "I'll be ready."

"I don't doubt it." Amira steps back and laces her arm through mine. "Markus, meet Honoka and Imani."

"So, you're Markus." Imani's eyebrows rise. "We've heard all about you in our group chat."

"Only good things, I hope," I say.

"Don't worry. We only talk about great... big... *things*." She wiggles her eyebrows.

Honoka laughs as Amira buries her face in my shoulder. "Maria wouldn't embarrass me like this," she mumbles, letting me go and crossing her arms. "Stupid Popocatépetl decided to erupt the day she was going to depart. You'll meet her soon, though."

"Ugh, poor Maria," Imani says. "And we were supposed to celebrate her graduation."

"Where's Tobias?" Honoka asks.

Where *did* he go?

"With Carina," Amira responds pointedly. Does she actually know that? He wandered off alone.

Honoka smiles, but her expression is pinched.

Oh, there's more to this story.

"I want to meet Tiger," Imani says. "Are you racing, Amira?"

"No. Tiger doesn't want to." The pair nods, just a simple acknowledgment. "Markus is, though. Loki can't wait for the snowtop." Amira turns to me. "You should take him to the sprints. We'll come and cheer him on from the sidelines."

"After another beer or two," Honoka says. The three girls laugh together.

I kiss the top of Amira's head before making my escape.

Enough distractions. I need to find Tobias. Back at the tent, there's no sign of him. Jonas and Theo are enjoying beers in the shade, their conversation centered on the latest soccer match.

I call Loki down. "Let's go race. Did you see Tobias?"

"Nope. But Carina and Goose were here a minute ago."

'With them' is a logical place for him to be.

We find Carina standing next to Goose at the edge of the old runway. Weeds grow through the cracked cement, so planes won't be landing here any time soon. Fortunately, a dragon can land just about anywhere. Riders are lined up along the sides of the tarmac, cheering and drinking as they watch the sprints, the mountains serving as the backdrop.

"Markus," Carina says, nodding at me. "No Amira?"

"She's catching up with Imani and Honoka. They'll join us in a bit."

She shifts her weight, forcing a smile. "Was Tobias with them?"

"Nope. Just the three of them."

Her shoulders relax. "Those Obis will steal your heart when you're not looking. Trust me, they never let go. We have to stick together, kid."

She drops the serious expression and ruffles my hair playfully.

"No way." I ruffle her hair back in retaliation. She squeals and ducks.

"Why are we just standing around?" Loki eyes us impatiently.

A man approaches us from behind Carina. His orange hair matches his orange dragon-scaled armor. "Hey there, gorgeous."

She's standing right next to me. What am I, old roadkill?

"Still not interested." She ignores him, her loyalty to Tobias clear.

Taking her lead, I cross my arms and follow suit.

"Come on," he says. "Don't you want to cheer me on?"

I glare at him. I'm standing *right here.*

"How about we race instead?" Carina smirks. "Two grand, quick sprint, right now."

He ogles her. "Feisty, aren't we?"

"Fucking misogynist, aren't we?" she snaps back. "Put your money where your mouth is."

"Done." He strides back to his dragon, the same way Tobias does.

Loki nudges me. *"Can we race, too?"*

"Carina deserves to be the one to tear that asshole down," I whisper back. "We're gonna cheer her on. Next one, okay?"

"Okay."

We turn our attention to the pair. Goose's second collar glitters as Carina mounts and straps in safely.

"Talk to me, Goose." She hums and sighs, listening to her dragon speak to her through their bond. "Agreed. He's going down." She turns toward me. "Come kick off the race."

I swallow. "You want me to do it?"

"Gods, Markus. Sticking together, remember? I swear we just talked about this." She rolls her eyes. "Hold the cash and make sure he doesn't cheat."

"On it!"

I head to the starting line at the edge of the half-mile tarmac. Loki waits at the side as I stand in the middle of the two racing dragons. Goose snaps at the Orange, who lets out a puff of steam.

"Cash, please." I hold out my hand.

Carina hands a roll over, and she and I stare at the asshole until he hands me a roll, mumbling under his breath the whole time. With four grand in my pocket, I raise my arms the way Carina did four nights ago.

"Three, two—" I catch the man's dragon step over the line. There's no way I'm letting him get a head start. "Back up," I say. He glares at me, but I wait until his dragon steps back in line. "Okay, let's try that again. Three, two, one, *go!*"

The dragons take off at full speed. I whip my body around to watch.

They're flying at over a hundred miles per hour in less than three seconds.

I blink, and they're halfway down the course.

My heart pounds as Carina and Goose give the sprint their all.

She raises her arms in triumph, and Goose shoots flames into the sky.

"Victory!" I cheer as loudly as I can.

The man flies off, but Carina and Goose fly back to me, and she jumps down to the ground.

"Good race." I hold out the cash.

"Thanks." She only takes half. "I just wanted to kick his ass. Keep it as your buy-in for the mountaintop."

I hadn't even thought of that. "Really?"

"Yeah. Derkomai only won the rooftop race with a boost. Loki was amazing."

Shit. Derkomai. Tobias. Where the hell is Tobias?

"Thanks, Carina." I tuck it back in my pocket. "Appreciate it."

"Okay, me next." Loki pads over to me.

"Sure, bud. You next."

"I want to race Goose. Where's my cheering section?"

"She said she'd only be a minute..." I scan the sidelines of the airstrip. Where is Amira? "I think we should go find them."

He chuffs. *"You take the* race *out of dragon racing."*

I laugh. "I'm sorry, bud. We can find her after if you want to race first?"

"No, let's find her. But tell her she better cheer extra loud."

We leave Carina at the airstrip and cross over to the Ejo clan tent. As we approach the entrance, Amira's voice stops me dead in my tracks. "—but Tobes, you can't go tonight."

"I'm doing it for us," Tobias responds.

"Don't even play that," she says. "You're doing it for revenge."

On Ren? Is this about the race?

Whatever it is, Amira knows exactly what Tobias is doing.

"It's not worth it," she says. "Why can't you just let it go? Play the long game? This won't end well."

"This isn't a discussion," he says. "I'm going."

Footsteps start from inside, and I loudly step the rest of the way to the tent. Tobias lifts the door flap and walks right past me, not even saying hi.

I step inside as Loki perches on top. Amira's red-rimmed eyes find mine. I put on a brave face and pull her against me. How can I make the tears stop? I try to wipe them away, but they keep coming. The mission is futile. I give up and hold her.

"What was that about?" I ask.

"Nothing." She takes a breath and wipes away her tears.

"It didn't seem like nothing, Obi. Do you want to talk about it?"

"Stupid sibling shit." She snuggles into me.

If she was asking him to skip the race, she'd tell me or ask me not to race either.

Fuck. The evidence is solid.

To keep Loki, I'll have to find the commandant and let him know Tobias is going to hijack another semi-truck tonight.

But Amira will be implicated, too.

The sun sinks behind Mount Hood as a dozen of us gather on the airstrip, waiting on top of our dragons. Loki and I stick with Tobias, just like we did all afternoon. Jonas and Poseidon stick close, too. Sweatband Man made it to the party, though his Brown seems pretty tired already. I'm glad he escaped the bust at the Den, even if he was a dick. Two Yellows, three Oranges, and two Whites join us, but I don't recognize them or their riders.

An older rider with long salt-and-pepper hair shouts for attention. "The hundred-mile snowtop is a race to the peak of Mount Jefferson and back. First to the halfway point, signal with fire. Two grand buy-in, unlimited entries, and first place takes the whole kitty."

We all cheer as she wanders around and collects our cash. That's a huge payday, enough to... well, definitely not enough to take care of a dragon. They're way more expensive. I hand my roll to her. She nods and tucks it into a small bag at her side before continuing on.

"The other racers will be eating our dust." Loki continues to scope out the competition. *"Except maybe Yongwang. She looks ready to go."*

Ren watches patiently from Yongwang's back. She's in fine form today, her black scales polished to a shine. Seeing him now, I'm glad I wore a balaclava at the warehouse. That would not be a fun conversation.

"You've definitely got this, bud." I pat Loki's neck and shove down my feelings, and his excitement instantly takes over. "And if you win, you can have an extra sheep when we get back."

"With that sort of payday, I want more than one."

"Kristoffer is going to wonder where all the sheep went. He's started keeping count this week after so many have gone missing."

"Meh. I'm worth it."

"It's true. You are." I chuckle. "Two sheep then."

Loki narrows his eyes before facing forward. *"Four."*

We're going to get caught breaking Loki's diet. I double-check the straps of my saddle, buying time. "Three sheep. Final offer."

"Deal. I'll be eating like a champion tonight." He straightens his shoulders and puffs out his chest.

Amira practically bounces up to us. "Ready to go? You've got a tight competition."

Loki chuffs and nudges her shoulder. With a laugh, she wraps her arms around his neck, giving him a quick hug.

"Don't be jealous," Loki says to me, nudging her again.

She walks to his side and reaches for my hand. I pull her onto my lap, and she settles in front of me, side-saddle. "Are *you* ready?"

"Of course, Obi." Just eleven experienced racers and me.

She grins, places her hands on the nape of my neck, and kisses me. A couple of assholes throw out some wolf-whistles. Fuck them. I pull her closer, deepen our kiss, and lose myself in the scent of her vanilla lotion and the taste of the beer and pretzels, desperate to hold onto her.

"Get a room," Carina shouts from Goose's back, and Amira pulls away, glancing her way. "But later. Come on, Amira. Get in the air."

Loki leans down and Amira slides to the ground. "Good luck. We'll be cheering you on from the sidelines." She mounts Tiger and helps Imani up. They take off.

"Line up!" the salt-and-pepper-haired rider shouts once she finishes collecting the money. Considering the twenty-four grand in her bag, one of us will be going home extremely happy. Hopefully, it's me. If I'm kicked out of Dragild, the money would... I just need to focus. I can't let my feelings screw us up.

The twelve dragons stand at the edge of the airstrip, barely far enough apart to spread their wings. Fortunately, our spot is near the end of the row, so we have a bit more room. The overwhelming smell of sulfur fills my nose.

"Loki," I whisper. He brings his head back. "Instead of taking off right away, let's run two dragon-lengths first and fly low for a minute. If we go fast, we can cut up in front of everyone while they're trying to take off from the start line. It's going to be a cluster."

Loki nods. *"Good idea."*

"Keep an easier pace until the halfway point, and we'll up it in the second half." I observe the dragons in the line. "Yongwang, Derkomai, and Poseidon all have second collars. We better watch for them, especially near the finish line. If we can keep in the lead, we can beat them."

He looks over the competition again. *"We're going to win."*

"Absolutely." As long as I can keep my head focused.

The salt-and-pepper-haired rider holds up her arms, a checkered flag in each hand. "Riders, at the ready!"

All twelve of our dragons shift, fully alert. A couple shuffle into the line. Loki tenses beneath me, aiming forward.

"Three, two, one, *go!*" She swings the flags down and waves them excitedly.

Loki darts forward at full speed as the dragons behind us spread their wings and beat hard, creating a windstorm none of them can escape.

"Prepare for liftoff!" Loki jumps, wings spread wide, and lifts us fifty feet in seconds.

The sky is full of spectators on their dragons. To our right, Tiger lights up the sky with fire, and Amira and Imani wave from her back. Carina and Goose hover near them, and Theo and Baldur watch from the other side.

"There's your cheering squad, bud!"

Pure energy flows through our bond.

"Go, Loki, go!" I tuck my body against him, cutting wind resistance as much as I can. Glancing back, I spot a couple of dragons still fighting to escape the pack. It's exactly the cluster I predicted, and we've got a major advantage. "We kicked ass with that start. In five more miles, settle into your pace. We've got ninety-five miles left."

We're cruising along at a decent pace and climbing higher above the mountains. The other dragons are following suit, conserving their energy for the second leg. Forty miles in, a White and two Oranges speed up. Yongwang drops from the sky, level with us.

I pat Loki's shoulder. "We're almost halfway through. How are you feeling?"

"Like I'm gonna win."

That's my dragon. "You've got four dragons flanking you. We're about four minutes from the turn. Stick with it."

Derkomai drops down a few dragon-lengths behind Yongwang, and both speed up, overtaking us. Panic rushes through our bond.

"Let them." I force calm feelings back to Loki, despite our ridiculous speed at this ridiculous height. "We don't need to light the halfway fire. That's not our race. We'll get them in the second leg."

Yongwang hits the midpoint first, filling the sky with blue fire that sends waves of heat back. Loki lifts up, protecting me from the intense heat. It costs us precious seconds, but at least I won't have a heat rash.

"Solid maneuvering. Thanks, bud."

"Hold on!" Loki hits the midpoint and quickly flips the opposite way, turning me upside down.

Oh gods, it's a long way to the ground.

I cling tightly to him as he rolls his body back up, thanking the powers that be for my saddle and extra safety straps. Talk about turning on a dime. "Awesome. Speed up to keep pace with them. They'll be finishing strong with their boosts, so we've gotta keep up and try to get ahead."

The only response is the beat of his wings as he pushes harder.

Derkomai and Yongwang fight it out for first place, but it's still early. And while they're busy fucking around, we're going to win.

A Yellow crashes into an Orange, and they trip each other up, but we stay out of it. We pass Sweatband Man and his Brown, still going in the opposite direction.

"See, Loki? This is why Kristoffer has all of the dragons on controlled diets."

He ignores me.

I glance behind us. A couple of dragons have fallen away, and some are farther back. Loki's still going strong, but Derkomai and Yongwang have pulled ahead slightly. With the pair of them in front, we're at a major disadvantage.

"Increase the pace, bud. The river's below us, so twenty miles left."

If we go above them, we lose the precious seconds needed to lift.

If we go below, we gain speed but risk them coming down on us. I swallow, debating the options. Those two are so focused on each other, they probably won't notice us anyway.

"We're fifteen miles out. Let's pass underneath them."

"Sounds good." Loki speeds up, darting down.

Loki's powerful strokes close the gap. We've almost caught up.

"Okay, bud. This is it. The last ten. What have you got in you?"

He pushes harder, and we're below them within a minute.

"Five miles left. That's like two minutes of flying—not even. You've totally got this."

Derkomai jolts left, knocking into Yongwang's wing directly above us. We can't stay below them. "Speed up, Loki!"

Panic roars through the bond, and I can't calm myself. We're about to be torpedoed out of the sky.

Yongwang shakes it off and steadies. With movements so quick I barely catch them, she flies into Derkomai's side, knocking him downward.

"Bank left!"

Loki banks, costing us precious seconds as Derkomai drops. We evade, barely. My hands slip on the pommel as my heart races.

"Only a mile left." Deep breaths.

Flying back up, Derkomai roars and knocks into Yongwang's side. She falls into Loki's wing, throwing us off balance. I cling to the saddle as Loki pulls in his wing and dives, tumbling downward and sending my stomach churning.

We straighten out a dragon-length above the ground and glide toward the finish line.

Derkomai pulls across and lands moments before us.

Loki lands behind him. He stands with his chest puffed out, but disappointment washes over our bond. *"We lost."*

"I'm sorry, bud." I pat his neck as the adrenaline comes down, shoving aside my own disappointment. "You did so great. That wasn't your fault."

Tiger lands directly behind us and Amira jumps to the ground. She rushes over. "Are you okay?"

I slide down, and her arms wrap around me immediately, knocking the air out of me.

"Yep," I rasp. "I'm fine, Obi."

Loki flutters his wings and tucks them in again.

"You did so good, Loki." Amira strokes his wing.

"Not good enough."

Goose and Baldur land, and Carina and Theo jump down to join our group.

Yongwang touches down a dragon-length away, and Ren hits the ground a moment later. "What the hell, Tobias?"

"You started it," Tobias responds, the bag of winnings in hand.

"The takeoff was a goddamn clusterfuck! We didn't start anything," Ren says.

Amira releases me and storms over to stand between them, hands at her waist. "Both of you, stop it."

My heart rate spikes. I want her out of there.

"You don't have anything to do with this, Mia." Tobias stands his ground, staring Ren down. "Move."

Poseidon lands a dragon-length away. Jonas quickly dismounts and runs to Tobias's side.

I reach for Amira and she comes back to me, safely out of the line of fire. I hold on to her tightly.

A couple of Ren's people join the circle, evening out the numbers. All of us watch Ren and Tobias face off.

Ren looks around the group, and his nostrils flare. "Really, Tobias? I started it? Your gang shows up with four brand-new, freshly polished collars, and you think I won't realize where they came from?"

"We aren't in your half of Portland right now, Ren." Tobias turns his back on him and takes a step.

"Tobias!" Ren shouts.

Tobias stops in his tracks, but he doesn't turn around.

"Pavvy blasted his way into my warehouse." Ren's nostrils flare as he curls his fists, just like he did at the docks. "He disrespected my entire operation because some asshole passed him bad information."

I cringe. I don't want to relive that bust.

Tobias's frown deepens. He crosses his arms and remains silent, but his gaze locks onto me.

He knows.

Oh, fuck. I'm going to live in a balaclava now. I'm going on the lam. I really could have used that twenty-four grand...

"And who else could that narc be," Ren says, walking toward him, "except the asshole who stole four of my family's heirlooms? Your mother would be ashamed of you."

Tobias's expression ices over. Derkomai lets out a roar.

Turning around, Tobias throws a punch at Ren and tackles him. Ren grunts as he hits the ground.

"I never narced on you!" Tobias throws another punch, and another, knocking Ren's head against the ground.

Ren pushes Tobias back and rolls out of the way of Tobias's fist. Ren's second-in-command jumps in, taking aim at Tobias.

Jonas grabs Tobias's waist, but he isn't strong enough to pull him back. Theo clutches Tobias's arm, almost earning a punch to the jaw, but he can't hold on either.

This is a shitshow.

Amira fights in my arms, but there's no way she's going into that brawl. Tiger lets out a burst of fire, throwing waves of heat. Derkomai roars again, and Yongwang responds in kind.

Ren's second-in-command jumps Jonas, and all bets are off. I release Amira and launch toward the second. Smashing my shoulder into his stomach, I tackle him to the ground.

His hands wrap around my neck, choking the air out of me. I elbow his nose, flip him over, and push my knee into his back, pinning him down.

Finally free, Jonas regains his grip on Tobias.

Ren doesn't move. No one moves. The crowd is silent, except for the ruffling of dragon wings.

I let Ren's second go, and he lifts Ren from the ground, helping him stand. Jonas lets go of a seething Tobias.

Tobias takes a deep breath and mounts Derkomai without a word. Jonas, Theo, and Carina follow, and the four of them take off. The rest of the crowd scatters.

"Your neck is starting to bruise." Amira runs her hand across my eyebrow, and it comes away bloody. "Let's get you patched up. I have skin glue in my bag."

Will glue fix our relationship after I launch a missile at it? Tobias knows I gave the chief bad intel. There's no way I can hide it from Amira.

We walk back to the tent, unable to avoid the stares of the crowd. Loki and Tiger perch on top as we enter and close the flap behind us.

"Sit down." She digs around in her giant bag, which seems to hold every manner of first aid possible. "You'd think I've been through this before," she says sarcastically, her shoulders slumped. "I'm sorry you were roped into that."

"Don't be. It wasn't your fault."

She closes her eyes for a moment, then continues digging through her bag.

"Obi."

"We're gonna clean it first, and then a little glue, and you'll heal okay. It might scar a bit, but you don't need stitches."

"Amira," I say, this time with more force.

She stops rummaging and looks at me.

"I'm okay. This isn't your fault."

She remains quiet.

I take her hand and kiss the back of it. "Will you still think I'm pretty, even with my scar?"

An amused smile cracks her stony expression. "It'll look sexy. Very mysterious, in a don't-mess-with-me sort of way."

"See? It's an upgrade."

She smiles softly as she cleans and glues my eyebrow, taking care to put me back together. Every touch conveys her affection.

"When will the others be back?" I ask.

"We'll see them back at school."

Bloody hell, I thought they were coming back to our camp. "Amira, are they heading back to Dragild right now?"

She blinks at me, expression neutral.

"Are they?" I ask again.

She swallows, and her expression falters slightly. She schools it in an instant, becoming a guarded stone fortress.

Her brother's planning to hijack another truck of obsidian and kill another innocent driver. The chief said he'd blow the hijackers out of the sky.

Tobias will be dead before dawn.

I have to do something. I have to tell her.

"Amira. My mission yesterday was busting the Jonjungs for hijacking semi-trucks full of obsidian."

"But they're—" Her eyes widen and her jaw drops. "They put a first-year—*you*—on the hijacking mission?"

Talk about a blow to the ego.

The blood drains from my face. "I gave the bad information to the commandant. He needed me to infiltrate your brother's inner circle and find evidence of the hijacking."

"Your mission to keep Loki? You..." Her expression hardens. She takes a step back, and it's worse than a punch to the gut. Tiger lets out a roar above us. "You fucking used me?"

"No." I step toward her, but she steps back again. "I mean, okay, yes, but not on purpose. Everything between us, Obi. It's real. I've—"

"Stop. Just... stop." She runs her hand down her face. "What the fuck, Markus?"

Anything I say will sound like an excuse. My hands shake. "You can be as angry as you want, but this isn't about us right now. This is about your brother. Is he on his way to hijack another truck?"

She shakes her head and starts packing the bag, done with the conversation.

"Obi, please."

Her eyes flutter rapidly, beating away moisture. "I would prefer Amira."

She just stabbed me with a knife and twisted. But I deserved it.

I desperately clutch her arm. "Amira, you have to talk to me if Tobias is going to come out of this alive."

Her gaze meets mine, eyes laced with worry. "What are you talking about?"

"After the last attack, the chief said he'd shoot the hijackers out of the sky. Your brother could be killed. Carina, Theo, and Jonas, too."

Her stony expression falters. I'm getting through to her. Please, let me get through to her.

"If you don't want anything to happen to them, you have to help me."

As her beautiful brain processes my words, she studies my face.

"You're the only one who can help stop them." I swallow. "Please."

She nods once, but her expression turns ice cold.

And it rips my chest in two.

13

The Central Oregon Highway stretched out in the darkness around them.

"Tobias, look at me." Carina gripped his shoulders, her hands shaking. "Amira begged you not to do this. I'm begging you not to do it. This isn't worth it."

She'd never understand. She couldn't.

Tobias pushed her away. "I've been waiting three years for this moment. That asshole murdered my mother, and everything he cares about is going up in flames tonight."

Chief Paveith would pay for his unanswered crimes.

His career. His reputation. All of it would burn.

Theo and Jonas stood nearby. Four dragons lay in the grass next to the road, each a shadow in the moonlight, napping off their flight across the state.

Tobias mounted Derkomai, waking him.

"Already?" Derkomai asked through their bond, rising slowly.

"Yep. Up you go," Tobias said. "Theo, keep tabs on the tracker."

"Roger." Theo climbed onto Baldur's back. "The truck's only about ten miles out. No Goldwings with them."

Good. They wouldn't have to take down another rider.

"Jonas, mount up," Tobias said.

Jonas loaded his long-range rifle before settling in on Poseidon's back. Always at the ready, he was the best right hand a man could ask for.

Carina climbed onto Goose's back and strapped in safely, protected from the fray. She'd be fine. They'd be home in a couple of hours, celebrating hard and fast, just the way she liked it. Considering the twenty-four grand in his pocket, maybe they'd stop for something fun along the way.

Theo's eyes remained glued to his screen. He zoomed in and out of the map, monitoring the truck's location and the Goldwing operatives in the area. "They're light tonight. Sort of surprising, actually."

"Nah," Tobias said. "They probably want us to think it's a second decoy."

Six and a half minutes later, headlights appeared in the distance, right on schedule.

"Time for liftoff," Tobias shouted. "You know the drill. Jonas and Theo, flank the sides near the ground. Carina, hang tight, love."

Three dragons rose into the air, moving east. The whoosh of their beating wings drowned out the sound of the late-night breeze. Their routine was flawless, now that they'd done it four times.

The crack of Jonas's gun sliced through the sky, but the bullet bounced off the windshield. Bulletproof glass. Time for plan B.

"Fire!" Tobias shouted.

A wall of bright orange flames cut through the night sky as the three dragons advanced on the semi-truck.

It swerved off the road, crashing into a dragon with a bone-crushing force.

Poseidon shrieked on impact. He landed with a heavy thud three dragon-lengths away, in a giant cloud of dust.

The truck's engine exploded.

"Jonas!" Tobias's heart pounded in his throat.

He raced toward Poseidon, tailed closely by Theo. There was no rise or fall of Poseidon's chest, his wings akimbo. Blood continued to pool around him.

Tobias dismounted Derkomai. He rushed to Jonas's side, unstrapped him, and lowered him carefully to the ground. Cuts and blood marred the exposed skin. Jonas wasn't moving. He wouldn't be able to, with his connection to his dragon severed.

Tobias placed his fingers on Jonas's neck. A feeble pulse beat beneath his fingertips. He choked back a sob of relief.

Shaking, Jonas moaned. He opened one eye, the other covered in blood. "Poseidon?"

Tobias shook his head. He pressed his hand against Jonas's forehead, staunching the blood. "We need to get you to the hospital."

A shrill whistle filled the air.

"Missiles!" Theo screamed.

Tobias ducked behind Poseidon's body, covering Jonas.

An explosion rocked the ground.

Ringing filled Tobias's ears. The stench of charred flesh assaulted his nose. He rose shakily, taking in Goose's carcass and Carina's bloody body, their limbs blasted apart.

Carina, his better half, who would have followed him to the ends of the earth, who would—

"The Goldwings are moving!" Theo yelled from the back of his dragon. "We have to go! Baldur, grab Jonas." The Brown swooped down, lifted the limp body with his claws, and flew north, quickly disappearing over the horizon.

Whistling filled the air again. Another missile was coming, and only his dragon remained.

"Go, Derkomai!" Tobias shouted from Poseidon's side. He pushed the urgency through their bond, willing him to fly.

The dragon lifted into the air and darted westward at top speed.

The missile hit Derkomai with a burst of fire, and he crashed to the earth, limbs scattering.

Tobias fell to his knees.

His body froze, their dragon bond shattered.

There!" I shout from Loki's back. What's left of the hijacked semi-truck burns in the middle of the highway, flames licking at the sky. Heat radiates from the fire as we close in.

Shit. We're too late.

If we'd just been faster, we could have...

Overwhelming disappointment fills me, and I'm not sure if it's mine or Loki's. It's probably coming from both of us.

Loki and Tiger land a safe distance from the wreck. The smell of charred flesh churns my stomach.

I dismount quickly and catch Amira as she slides down Tiger's back. She shakes in my arms, taking in the blood and limbs that litter the ground.

Two downed dragons. A Green is blown apart, and a Blue lies a couple dragon-lengths away.

I want to protect Amira from it all. Shield her.

But I don't know if my presence is a comfort or a crime.

"Poor Goose," Loki says sadly. He plods behind us. *"We never got to race."*

Where's Carina? Jonas? Theo? Baldur? Derkomai and Tobias?

We slowly make our way to the Green, and Amira lets out a choked sob as she takes in the limbs still strapped into the saddle. "Carina!"

I can't look. The beer I drank will be on the ground if I don't hold it together.

"Mia!" Tobias calls.

Fuck, he came out of nowhere. Thank the gods he's still alive. Amira would shatter if it was his body blasted to shreds.

"Tobes!" She runs over and launches herself at him, almost knocking him to the ground. "Are you okay?"

"Yes. Maybe," he rasps, ripping the collar from his neck. The menacing glow of the fire highlights the blood on his hands.

I approach slowly. "What happened?"

"Dragon-seeking missiles." His eyes reflect only loss. He glances behind him. "One of them blasted Derkomai."

"He's across the field," Loki says.

Three dead dragons. Damn.

Amira sags against Tobias. "They're going to know you were a part of this. Derkomai's body is hard evidence."

A siren cuts through the night, shooting my heart rate sky-high.

Tobias blinks back to life. "The Goldwings are on their way. We have to go."

Amira's face is covered in tears. She steps back. "Tiger won't be able to outfly them."

I run my hand through my hair. If they flee, I can race after them, bust Tobias, and keep Loki. I'd be given top honors and put on the chief's Top Squad when I graduate. I'd make my father proud. Loki would get the justice he and his last rider deserve.

But the woman I love is breaking down in front of me, and her brother will be put to justice by Chief Paveith. Zeus will burn Tobias's body here on the field, right in front of Amira, with no trial and no questions asked.

"Do you want to race with Tobias?" I ask Loki, keeping my voice low. It's his choice.

Loki blinks.

And blinks.

And blinks again.

"Yeah." He stands up, at the ready.

I unsnap the collar from my neck, wincing when my knuckles hit the bruises from the fight, and push it into Tobias's hands before my body realizes it can't move anymore.

"Take it. *Go.*"

14

I don't always know the line between Markus's feelings and mine—and it's a thousand times harder when he won't admit his feelings to himself—but I do know Amira being forced to watch her brother die would devastate her. I can't let that happen.

"Hurry up, Tobias." He's supposed to be fast, but he has nothing on a Graytail. Granted, I was born to race.

Tobias hugs Amira quickly before he climbs on, a bit shaky, and buckles in. "Okay, Loki. Ready."

I paw the ground. My nose has been all messed up since we landed, and I can't wait to get in the air. I'm not sure how to tell Tobias he needs to shed the last piece of Derkomai. "I can't smell right, and—"

"Fuck, sorry." Tobias shrugs off Derkomai's scales and tosses the armor to Amira. Sadness and shame flow through our bond.

"You've got this, bud." Markus's eyes are leaking again.

He can't hear me anymore, but I nuzzle him anyway, the same way I nuzzled Benny in the infirmary when I had to let him go.

Benny, with his penchant for high speeds. Messing with everyone, calling me 'Stallion.' We were supposed to infiltrate the chief's Top Squad as soon as he graduated.

I miss him.

What would Benny think if he saw me? Jonas's rifle shot us out of the sky. Should I tell Tobias? He thinks Benny and I are both dead, but here I am. And it's his fault Benny isn't...

I can't worry about it right now. I have to focus. We need to get out of here. Three dragons are dead, and I don't want to be next.

I wasn't fast enough to save Benny.

I wasn't fast enough to save Katie.

But I'm fast enough to save Tobias.

Markus believes in me. He knows I've got this.

We take flight, and this is the moment. This is the start of the most important race I've ever flown.

And in the moments we race, nothing else matters.

At this moment, we are free.

L oki's powerful wings carry Tobias north into the night sky. Within moments, they disappear.

He'll be okay. He has to be.

That was probably the last time I'd ever see Loki. Even after only a month together, I'm an empty shell, missing the coolest piece of myself. My dreams of being a dragon rider are shot to hell. Goldwings don't get second chances, and this would be... well, my fourth.

The sirens intensify, mixing with the crackling of the fire and the engines in the distance.

Amira has her hand on Tiger's saddle as a flight of dragons approaches from the west. She's pushing herself away from me.

"We can't leave," I say, and she stops moving. "If we do, we'll look like we were a part of this. We have to stay."

Her eyes are red-rimmed and swollen. "What do we tell them? This is exactly as bad as it looks."

Good question.

My body is still half-frozen, but the effects of the collar are wearing off. "Amira, please." I hold my arms open. She keeps my secrets, and I keep hers. "Will you trust me?"

I won't let her out of my sight.

"If they try to take Tiger, unclasp her collar immediately." She steps into my arms, and Tiger moves close to us. Dragons descend, slamming into the ground.

"Got it," I whisper.

The Goldwings swarm the site, plunging it into chaos. A woman in riding leathers places a blanket over what's left of Carina's body. A fire engine parks by the semi-truck and pulls out the hose.

A Black descends into the madness, barely a shadow against the night sky. I hold Amira tightly against me as Zeus lands and Chief Paveith jumps to the ground.

"Markus," he says, striding over to us. He focuses on Amira, tucked against me. "What are you doing here?"

Chief Paveith doesn't know I got another chance from the commandant. He doesn't know Loki is supposed to be here with me, so he has no reason to believe Tobias and Loki are racing north right now.

Don't fuck this up, Markus. The best lies are rooted in the truth.

"I tagged along to the Dragon Wars today and heard Tobias would be pulling a heist tonight. I begged Amira to help me stop him. We raced out on her dragon, but we were too late."

Amira gasps, but with her face buried in my shoulder, I hope it sounds like a choked sob.

Chief Paveith ignores it. His dark eyes rake across the scene, taking it in. "And where is he?"

"We don't know. We arrived to find…" I nod toward the dead dragons.

An obnoxious beeping signals a dump truck backing up. Two men in blue jumpsuits exit the cab and tie chains around Derkomai's body. They push a button, and the dragon's carcass is unceremoniously pulled into the bed of the truck. Poseidon and Goose will be loaded the same way, and their bodies will be taken to the landfill.

Goldwings continue to scramble around us. Stress grips my chest like a vise. I glance back toward what's left of Carina. A lab tech is carefully packing the pieces of her body into a body bag. Considering what little is left, they'll probably cremate her remains.

Paveith takes in the scene and steps closer to us. "Do you really expect me to believe his sister was entirely uninvolved?"

A tremor runs through Amira's body.

"Yes," I say. "She's been sleeping in my bed. Call the commandant. He caught us two nights ago, during the last hijacking." I swallow, feigning the confidence I don't have. "Your campaign is safe. I guarantee Tobias is done since his dragon and his girlfriend are both dead." Cold, crass, but true. I hope my bark advertises a nasty bite.

Amira sags against me, face buried in my shoulder, and heat radiates from Tiger. I rub my hand along her back, my gaze locked in a staring contest with the chief.

"Miss Obi." Chief Paveith sneers as she turns to look at him. "Make sure you don't follow in the footsteps of your mother. Although, I suppose, with a dragonless boyfriend, you're already diverging."

She pinches her lips, remaining silent. Tears well in her eyes.

"If you're done asking questions, there's no reason for us to stick around," I say.

"Dismissed," the chief says with a wave of his hand. He walks toward a group of Goldwings hanging around a cardboard coffee box.

The obsidian is being moved to a new truck now that the fire has been extinguished. *Of course* that's the priority. It's millions of dollars' worth of *rocks*.

"Come on, Amira." I pull her to Tiger. Anger and exhaustion coat her features.

We mount Tiger quickly, strapping in. We're in the air a minute later, heading back to Dragild. I breathe easier once we've put some distance between us and the carnage.

Sunlight peeks over the horizon as we fly over the Cascades. Our pace is slow, which I don't mind. It means more time to cling to her before I have to let go. I memorize every last bit of her, taking it all in. Her polished box braids running down her back, her adorable ears with tiny points at the tips, her long graceful neck with her thin collar...

"Amira..." I start, but I'm not sure how to ask the right question.

She doesn't turn around. "I don't want to talk about us, Markus. Not right now."

"No, I get it. I... I was wondering what the chief meant about your mom?"

She looks over her shoulder at me. Indecision wages war in her eyes.

I swallow. "Tobias told me how she died in the fighting arena at the Den. I'm really sorry."

She closes her eyes. "Zeus's fire burned her alive. Chief Paveith was the rider on the opposite platform."

My stomach lurches, and my head feels light. "You didn't think I should know that?"

"About your idol? Who you gushed over during our date?" She

massages her temples. "He's been defining his own brand of justice for years, Markus. And the Goldwings? They all allow it to go on."

Well, shit. "I didn't know."

"Ignorance isn't an excuse."

She's not wrong. My throat is thick. I couldn't speak right now, even if I had something worth saying.

Tiger speeds up, and Dragild comes into view in the distance. We land at the mouth of the dragon cave.

The commandant is waiting next to the giant stone archway. He puts his phone back in his pocket. "Markus, join me."

We silently dismount, and I follow him to his office. He gestures to my usual seat and sits behind his desk, currently covered with ads for palm scanners like the ones at the Den.

"I heard the details from the chief," he says. "Where's Loki?"

Don't fuck this up, Markus. Also, don't get arrested.

"Tobias wrestled my collar off, and they rode south."

He eyes my neck, where the bruises from the fight have probably surfaced by now. "Why didn't you share that with the chief?"

"He didn't know you gave me another chance, and I didn't think I should tell him." That's legit, right? Please don't question that.

He nods once, stony eyes locked on me. "Well, Markus, I'm impressed you managed to figure things out."

"Thanks." I think...

"Unfortunately, without a dragon, you can't remain a student." He glances down at his desk. "I need to finish lining up the installation of the new security system for the stalls. Come back this afternoon so we can process your discharge papers."

"Right." With slumped shoulders, I exit his office and head back to my room. I'm not sure where to go now.

I dig through the back of my closet and pull out the duffel bag I came here with eleven months ago. It's not like I have a ton to pack. My old clothes broke the rules because they weren't black, so I passed those on a while ago... I'll keep the jeans and some of the rest, but I really don't need all the leather. Well, maybe the leather jacket.

"Knock knock," Theo says from the doorway. He looks fine, but tired. We all are.

"Hey, man. You made it."

He enters and closes the door behind him, keeping his voice low. "I got Jonas to the hospital over in Spokane. Left him near the door and watched from the lot. He had his fake ID on him, so he's fine. Well, I mean..." He leaves it unspoken. Jonas isn't really fine, and he definitely won't be coming back here. Poseidon's body is probably in the landfill by now. "He just messaged."

Can't someone monitor the messages? Who am I kidding; Theo probably has special channels. He's hacked into government servers for his research, so covering up texts should be a no-brainer.

"I'm glad he's okay."

"So..." Theo bites his lip. "Have you seen Amira? She's not in her room."

Did she go back out? No, Tiger was exhausted. "She's probably still in the dragon cave. I'm sure she'll be back soon." I gesture to the bed and sit in my desk chair. Ten minutes later, he has a full brief, minus the part about my undercover mission to infiltrate the gang.

"What a night," he says.

I nod, letting the craziness of the day percolate.

"So, where to next?" Theo asks.

"No idea." All I know is I'm not going back to Portland. "I need to go back to the commandant's office later. Discharge papers."

"He couldn't fill them out earlier?"

"No. He's busy getting new locks installed on the stalls, or at least trying to. Looked like the same kind as the ones at the Den."

"Damn, they track activity with timestamps." His eyebrows furrow, and then he relaxes. "No worries, I can wipe the records."

Of course he can. "What about you?"

"Twelve more days until graduation. I'm hoping they'll put me at the Portland Research Center. If they do, I'm getting an apartment above the Den. You're welcome to be my new roommate."

Damn. That actually would be a good idea. "I'll think about it."

He rises from the bed. "I'm going to see if Amira's back. Safe travels, Markus. Wherever you're heading."

I nod, and Theo leaves me to finish packing my duffel bag. An old book of dragon fairytales, my beat-up stuffed black dragon, a photo album from my dad... he'd be so disappointed.

Now what? If only this little toy had the answers...

Light footsteps race down the hall, and my favorite human appears in the doorway. "Markus."

"Amira." I shove the dragon into my bag. That's embarrassing.

"You're leaving?" She glances at my bag.

Bloody hell, the dragon fell on the floor. My cheeks heat. She grins, biting back a laugh. I'm never living this down.

Her expression falls. "I can understand why you kept secrets, but it hurts because they were *your* secrets to tell. You could have shared, if you trusted me."

"I get it." I swallow. "I never meant to..."

"I know. And I know it goes both ways." She sighs. "I just need some time to process how I feel."

We'd all like some of that. "You don't really have any, Amira. Being a student at Dragild is predicated on breaking your own dragon and, well, having a dragon, neither of which apply. So, uh... This afternoon, I won't be a student at Dragild anymore."

She chuckles. "I get you're averse to technology, but phones *are* a thing."

I guess I'll have to get one. Maybe Theo can hook me up.

"Amira..." I can't connect the dots. She lets Tiger call the shots, and she purposely made her collar as thin as possible, but she's a Goldwing at the top of the class. "If you don't believe in the system, why participate? Why stay here?"

She hesitates, her gaze locked on mine. Her hands fidget. She steps into the room and closes the door behind her. "You can't dismantle a system from the outside."

My jaw drops.

I force it closed, swallow, and nod. "And you're..." Words are failing for the millionth time today.

She stands perfectly still, jaw set. Her amber eyes are like a blazing fire. "I'm going to smash it to pieces."

Fuck, that's hot. That's not supposed to be hot. That's not supposed to be what I'm thinking about right now. Fuck. No, don't fuck. *Focus, Markus.*

"You're seriously getting hard right now?" she chokes out through a laugh.

"It's not..." My cheeks heat again, a thousand fucking degrees. "Have you seen yourself? Maybe in that giant leaner I dragged up the stairs for you?"

For a moment, it feels okay. For a moment, I can forget the mess I've gotten myself into.

She smiles softly. "You always say that."

I grin. "And you never ask me to stop."

"So..." She studies me. "We can talk in a couple of weeks, maybe?"

I can live with that. "Of course. But don't you want a..." Why would she want a Goldwing? She just said she wants to dismantle the system from the inside.

"No, I don't want a Goldwing. I never did." Her eyes stare deep into my soul. "Prove that's not you. Break the world with me, Markus."

"I'd love to, but... I don't have a dragon."

"We might be able to fix that."

I swing open the door of Mamba's stall. The smell of sulfur and decay hits hard. Mamba glares at me, his golden eyes piercing straight into my soul the same way Amira's do. He huffs back, ready to burn me to ashes.

"Hi, Mamba. I'm Markus. I know you've been stuck here for three years." I swallow, my stomach in knots. I hold out my empty, shaking hands. "I want to get you out."

Mamba narrows his golden eyes, but he doesn't incinerate me. That seems somewhat promising.

If Loki were here, he'd nudge me forward. He'd believe in me. *I can do this.*

My body shakes. "I'm letting you choose." I slowly sit down on the floor in front of him, in the middle of the track marks he's carved into the floor with his pacing. "There are a lot of things going on that shouldn't be, and I want to help Amira stop them. But I need a dragon to do that."

I take a deep breath and point to the collars on the floor, resting beneath the outline of the last guy who tried to break him. "I'd like to put that collar on you to get you out of here. You can choose if you want to stick with me. If you want to fly back to the nest instead, that's okay, too. I can take the collar off when we get outside."

He lowers his head toward me, watching me closely.

And he nods, just once.

Okay. Great. I'm not a pile of ashes.

Taking another deep breath, I stand up and walk slowly to the collars. I snap the human-sized collar around my neck. It's heavy compared to my other collar. I don't like it, but maybe I can shave them down if we're sticking together. I'll have to ask Theo.

I glance back at Mamba, who simply watches.

Okay, still not barbecued. This is good.

I pick up the dragon-sized collar and face him.

He doesn't move. His atrophied muscles need rehab, but Kristoffer could help him. I know we can help him return to full strength, the same way we helped Loki. At least, if he wants our help. Otherwise, the magic of the nest could surely heal him.

I walk slowly toward his towering form, my heart pounding in my ears. Stopping two feet away, I stare up at him.

He blinks at me, not quite like Loki used to. Then he lowers his neck. I carefully place the collar on him, taking care not to ruffle any of his scales. Just like that, I've got it snapped into place.

A rush of overwhelming emotion floods my body.

Rage, hatred, deep-seated pain...

"My code name is Apep, the god of chaos." His deep voice cuts through me. *"I have every intention of burning this world to the ground."*

I gulp.

Holy shit.

I, Markus Fredriksen, the First of His Name, Certified Badass Top-Secret Undercover Double Agent, officially ride a Black Clubtail.

ACKNOWLEDGEMENTS

I'm grateful for April 9, 2023, the day I realized writing about horse-racing but with dragons wasn't actually fun—and my husband dutifully chimed in, "What about drag racing?"

So thank you to my husband. If you weren't around, my story would be far more boring. *You were right.*

To my family and friends who supported me along the way, I appreciate each of you. Your encouragement keeps me going.

Huge gratitude and the sincerest thanks to my beta readers and my amazing critique circle, who read every chapter and considered every last detail of the story many times over. This book wouldn't be half of what it is without each of you.

A special thanks to the amazing team of people who helped bring this book to life and gave it that final polish.

Booksellers, librarians, and the fabulous individuals who help connect people with books: thank you for all you do to make the world a better place.

Most importantly, thank you to each reader who has given this book a chance. I hope you enjoyed the ride.

Writing Playlist

"Fallin' (Adrenaline)" – Why Don't We

"Ferrari" – James Hype ft. Miggy Dela Rosa

"Five More Hours" – Deorro ft. Chris Brown

"Flames" – Mod Sun ft. Avril Lavigne

"Heaven" – Niall Horan

"I Can See You (Taylor's Version) (From the Vault)" – Taylor Swift

"Last Night" – Morgan Wallen

"A Little Party Never Killed Nobody" – Fergie

"Runaway (U & I)" – Galantis

"She Wolf (Falling To Pieces)" – David Guetta ft. Sia

"Sweat (David Guetta Remix)" – Snoop Dogg

"Unholy" – Sam Smith ft. Kim Petras

"Wild Ones" – Flo Rida ft. Sia

"You're Gonna Go Far, Kid" – The Offspring

"5 O'Clock" – T. Pain ft. Wiz Khalifa & Lily Allen

"10:35" – Tiësto ft. Tate McRae

Markus's Theme Song

"Make Your Own Kind of Music" – Mama Cass Elliot

ABOUT THE AUTHOR

Kriss Dean is a hopeless romantic and an obsessive reader. By daylight, she puts her BA in Mathematics to use in the financial services industry. Come nightfall, she can be found writing books in the dark corners of coffee shops. She lives in Florida with her husband and their two golden retrievers.

Made in the USA
Monee, IL
18 July 2024

62145074R10171